25. 12. 98.

Graham

BORROWED SWORDS

In Memory of

Captain Nigel Marshall, Royal Marines
Captain Michael Shipley, Royal Anglian Regiment
Captain Nigel Loring, Light Infantry

Killed in Action
Dhofar 1975

JOHN BOOTH

Borrowed Swords

Shemagh Productions
1998

Published by Shemagh Productions
7 Little Penny Rope
Pershore
Worcs WR10 1QN

ISBN 0 9532657 0 6

Cover by Peter Blagojevic, Artwork Plus, Worcester

A catalogue record for this book is available from the British Library

Typeset in Palatino 11/12pt by Scriptmate Editions
from the author's disk
Manufacture coordinated in UK by Book-in-Hand Ltd,
20 Shepherds Hill, London N6 5AH

CHAPTER ONE

The dog fox lifted his delicately pointed snout and sniffed the cool, pre-dawn air. It had been a lean night for hunting, his only catch being a hard-shelled centipede. The night air was still and damp in the wadi bottom. The old male shook his thin frame to raise the fine hairs of his pelt and then padded between the smooth boulders of the dry river bed. Here and there he caught the smell of a skink but the scent was old and besides it was too early, too cold, for the wily lizard to be about.

Raising his head towards the head of the wadi, where once ancient torrents cascaded down, he spotted movement. Breaking into a trot he climbed the steep slopes in short, traversing bounds and was soon in the shadow of thorn bushes and dwarf acacia trees. After climbing another hundred feet or so he caught sight of the source of the movement; blackbirds. As agile as he was, he knew that his chances of catching a healthy bird on the ground were minimal so he contented himself to some desultory digging at the roots of the acacias.

The eastern sky was showing the first pale streaks of dawn. The old dog knew that the Arabian sun's first rays would bring the lizards out to bask on the bare rocks on the plateau above. Off he trotted, weaving in and out of the thorn bushes until he gained the rim of the plateau. Once on top he bounded forward and then stopped, frozen in mid-stride, ears cocked, snout probing the still air. He turned his head towards the yellowing sky. It was only the faintest vibration but it was alien to the natural order of the jebel. The blackbirds took off in a ragged formation and swirled over the plateau. The fox trotted back towards the lip overlooking the wadi. The faint vibration was becoming a throbbing hum. He turned abruptly away and bounded over the rim and zig-zagging down through the bushes and trees gained the safety of the wadi bed. In his comparatively long life the little predator had experienced the throbbing sound before and knew that it meant the arrival of man, metal and death.

The young blond Englishman in the helicopter's rear compartment twisted round on the canvas bench to gaze between the white-domed heads of the pilot and co-pilot. The grey-brown landscape moved with agonising slowness in the perspex panels between the pilot's feet. His eyes scanned the barren peaks and dark, twisting gullies for movement but the ground that panned beneath him was as still and as dead as the surface of the moon. The dawn-facing slopes were turning pink then a yellow ochre while to westwards all remained in blue-grey shadow.

'Ten minutes, Matey,' the pilot's voice burst in over the earphones. James Faulkner nodded then, realising that the speaker could not see him, fumbled for the intercom switch.

'Roger,' he answered hurriedly and then grinned nervously at the other occupants of the cabin. He turned back with difficulty from his cramped position and wedged himself back onto his seat between the helmeted crewman and one of his soldiers. He picked out Mahmood Ali, amongst the jumble of green-clad arms and legs. Leaning forward he tapped the section commander on the ankle and then held up his right hand, flexing the fingers and thumb to signify the figures ten. The areef nodded as if he had been waiting for the signal all his life and then began to relay the information by jabbing the other soldiers with his fingers and yelling inaudibly at their startled faces.

Faulkner watched as the cabin gradually erupted into a fit of fumbling, fidgeting soldiers as each one tried to prepare himself for the landing. He half turned his head back to see if the pilot had noticed the increased turbulence from inside. Normally, a forty minute helicopter flight was enough to send most of the soldiers to sleep but not this morning. There was fear in the air; fear of the unknown, fear of the known. For some it came from memories of past actions, for others it was the uncertainty in their own future performance. The cloying smell of kerosene and the constant throb of the rotors were beginning to make Faulkner feel sick and now he just longed to burst free of the hot, cramped cabin, whatever was waiting at the landing site. He leaned forward and rested his cheek against the barrel of his Armalite assault rifle. The coolness of the metal against his sweating skin gave him comfort for a moment. Looking out of the starboard door he mused on the sight of the other Agusta Bell 205s gently bobbing alongside like so many dragon flies on an English summer's eve.

In the leading helicopter of the wave of ten the company commander had also been watching the jebels and wadis pass slowly below. Major Peter White turned a well-creased air photograph on his knee, trying to identify a cluster of razor-edged ridges in the distance. The 205 started to turn back in a wide arc towards the glimmer of the fast approaching dawn.

'Lining up for a run in from the south west, Peter,' boomed his pilot's voice through the intercom, anticipating any enquiry. White glanced back to look over his shoulder and saw a maze of peaks and gullies swirl past the forward perspex as the craft banked round to begin a left hand orbit. The other nine Hueys followed round in echelon. The pilot chipped in again. 'Just waiting for Strikeys as usual. Thought I'd put you out of your misery, knowing your map reading an' all.'

'Cheers, Harry,' answered Peter through his throat mike, 'Where you going to put us?'

'On the flattest bit, of course,' retorted the squadron commander.

About three kilometres away he made out a broad plateau rising out of the surrounding egg-box of ridges and wadis. The plateau rose in the west to a jutting bow-shaped peak. In the east it broadened out to form a broad back with prominent humps along the spine. The feature looked superficially like a reclining animal, the peak forming its head. It was obviously named: Jebel Assaad, Mountain of the Lion.

The small formation of Hueys cautiously spiralled down from the operational cruising height to within range of whatever small-arms ground fire may be waiting for them. White checked his watch for the third time in less than a minute. The Huey suddenly bobbed and the familiar shape of a BAC Strikemaster flashed over the canopy as if prompted by the cue. Another followed immediately in its wake.

'Buggers,' cursed the pilot. 'Bloody kids everyone of them.' The chocolate and sand camouflage pattern on the small fighter-bombers upper surfaces blended briefly with the mottled patterns of the landscape before they climbed again against the blue-grey hills to the north.

White heard the pilot switch from intercom to one of his tactical frequencies then, after a pause, switch back.

'Mac says it looks all clear. Do you want him to blast it, just in case?' White fumbled for the pressor-switch.

'No thanks, no sense in waking the entire northern zone.'

'Okay, then,' replied Clayton, 'last chance to back out,' he added facetiously.

'Take us down,' Peter replied. He let the switch go and forced a smile at Clayton and his co-pilot, hoping that it would mask the tightness he now felt in his throat and the queasiness in his stomach. He heard Clayton start to brief the squadron on the landing details in the same flat, matter of fact tone all aviators seemed to use. The routine sound of it comforted him a little. He looked around the cramped rear compartment at the wide-eyed, brown faces of his headquarters jundis and forced another smile for them.

Faulkner in the lead craft of the second flight, found himself mesmerised by the procession of the helicopters gently drifting across the starboard perspex as the squadron broke up into its landing formation. It was then that he noticed the monotonous landscape developing into recognisable features: dark green blobs became thorn bushes, dark-coloured creases became wadis with boulder choked stream beds and acacia-clad slopes. It was hotter too. Reaching into the adapted bandoleer strung across his chest, he withdrew a fully-charged magazine, the top round a red-tipped tracer.

Holding the magazine aloft he shouted, 'Ya'hammil.' He waited till all the jundis were fumbling in their equipment pouches before sliding the magazine into the housing of his Armalite. He pressed the base till he heard the re-assuring click. Looking down he noted with satisfaction and not a little surprise that his hands were rock steady.

At about three hundred feet the squadron was in its tactical formation for a hot landing. All doors were slid back; the crewmen crouching menacingly behind their belt-fed machine-guns. The jundis knelt in the doorways, their eyes straining for any movement. The leading flight dropped down to skim over the ridge immediately south west of Jebel Assaad, then they were over the broad sand-filled wadi, the plateau loomed before them. In an instant the Hueys were over the crest and fanning out to land, noses pulled up simultaneously. Dust rose up to meet the rotors. The plateau was transformed into a melee of stooped figures, roaring machines and swirling, stinging dust. No sooner had the disgorged soldiers scrambled clear than the 205s lifted off and, dipping their noses as if in a reluctant farewell, charged off into the sky towards the rising sun.

Lying prone with his headcloth pulled across his eyes and nose Faulkner felt that sudden pang of loneliness. From the days when he was kissed, waved at and left in the prep school's dorm, the sound of receding transport always made him feel abandoned and not a little frightened. He was soon shaken from these melancholy thoughts by the sound of his company commander. He looked up to see Peter White standing up holding his rifle high in his hand.

'Y'alla, Y'alla,' he was shouting at all within earshot. Little knots of green-clad soldiers started to rise and burdened by their assorted arms and equipment, trundle out towards the edges of the plateau.

Getting up onto one knee, Faulkner drew his fingers across his eyes to clear the dust and grit. He remembered his goggles and his hand dropped to find them safely stored away in his shirt pocket now they were no longer needed.

'Damn,' he cursed himself. 'Get a grip of yourself.' He then became aware of his own small party who were sitting around patiently waiting for his command.

'Y'alla, Areef,' he called, not being able to recognise the cloth-swathed, begoggled faces.

'Sah'b.' Areef Mahmood Ali, stood up raising his goggles over his head cloth.

Faulkner directed the little corporal over to a small hillock of loose rocks some fifty yards away. He watched as the areef marshalled his small team of signallers and other HQ wallas and led them off in the appointed direction. Having gained some time for thought, Faulkner got his bearings and moved off away from the enviable efficiency of his leader to check on the dispositions of the rear platoons.

The helicopters were now high in the sky and almost lost in the blinding glare of the morning sun. James felt the gentle night breeze fade and give way to the unrelenting oven-heat of the Arabian day. The first platoon, he realised, were atop the long low hill which rose up on the south west corner of the main feature and then dropped away through a number of steep spurs to the wadi below. The platoon were arranged along the crest in groups of six or seven. The jundis had been lying still, silently scanning the distant ridges when he breasted the rise. They must have taken his casual approach for a signal to relax as they started to sit up and chatter as soon as he reached them. James picked out Fawzi Hussein, the senior lieutenant and strode over and squatted down between him and his platoon sergeant, a tall Mechran Baluch.

'Fawzi, Kull she zayn?' he enquired. Fawzi braced up where he sat.

'Everything is good,' replied Fawzi in halting English, placing his right palm across his chest.

'Al Hamdu'Lillah,' intoned James.

'Indeed, we have gained surprise,' Fawzi continued earnestly.

'Nam.' James grinned at the little bearded officer. It seemed to be the current favourite of the local officers to reply in English whenever a Brit spoke Arabic or vice versa. After a few perfunctory comments about the disposition of machine-gunners and arcs of fire, James stood up and moved off to look over the platoons. Already the soldiers were starting to scratch away at loose rocks in the surface and worm themselves into the ground.

'Tell them not to dig too deep, Fawzi,' James warned. 'We'll be moving again.'

'Nam, Sidi,' snapped the ever smiling Fawzi. James started down the crest back towards the landing site.

Peter White stopped on the rock-littered slope and looked back over the plateau. He felt like death. He had only climbed about two hundred feet and still had another hundred to go. Waving the platoon commander on he sat down and took out his binoculars as a visual excuse for stopping. The wiry, lithe jundis of the rear sections passed with light brisk steps; their Belgium automatic rifles balanced on their shoulders. White could not see anything through the glasses for the sweat stinging his eyes and filling the eyepieces. He let them drop on their neck cord and waited for his chest to stop heaving. His mouth was dusty dry, the sides of his throat appeared to be stuck together.

'Come on, White. Get your act together,' his mind admonished. Thus spurred he wiped his eyes with the corner of his shemagh and after cleaning the binoculars, scanned the scene below. He spotted his second in command striding along between the rear platoons. White dug his transceiver out of one of his pouches, extended the aerial and croaked into the microphone.

'James, How's it going?' He waited, watching Faulkner fumble for his set through the glasses.

'No problems, over.'

'Join me up here when you're through then,' invited White.

'Wilco, out.' White smiled at the young Guards officer's persistence with British Army radio procedures. Using his rifle as a crutch, he heaved himself up and looked up the hill. The jundis were now out of sight. Slinging the heavy FN and resolving to get hold of the lighter Armalite as Faulkner had done, White recommenced his trudge to the top of the hill.

After finishing the rounds of the rear platoons Faulkner felt more confident and strode out towards his company commander's position on the hill which formed the northern part of the feature. The soldiers were plainly relieved at their unopposed landing and were now content to watch over the empty hills whilst the remainder of the battalion flew in. Faulkner was content too. Though he had been in the Emirate for six months, this was his first real operation. His main concern in the helicopter had not been whether he would have the courage but whether he would have the competence. Perhaps now he would have a more gradual baptism of fire.

He stopped briefly at the landing site to talk to the Company Sergeant-Major, a tall Omani, who was busy haranguing the helicopter marshallers, porters and guides. Having satisfied himself that the odds against chaos were no more than fifty percent, he continued on his way. Faulkner had adopted a more personal philosophy concerning the Arab way of soldiering. This was simply that when things went wrong the soldiers first looked for the nearest Brit but if they could not find one they would probably solve the problem themselves; God willing. To this end, Faulkner was quite happy to plan, advise and give instruction on any given task but studiously avoided being present at the execution. As Mike Clayton and his pilots never took any notice of the ground marshaller, brown or white, Faulkner was content in the knowledge that any mistakes would not be fatal. He continued at a steady lope up towards his older co-patriot.

Peter White leaned back and contemplated his situation.

'There was no reason,' he reflected, 'that there should have been any opposition. Even if every last beggar in the suq knew that an operation was on, there was no reason to suppose the adoo should have the where-with-all to respond. No, it was just the Old Man laying it on a bit treacly to make us take it seriously. Still it's not too bad. A couple of weeks in the field would do him good; getting soft in camp.'

He spotted his second in command coming up the hill in long, easy strides. He watched him for a moment, envying the young Guards' officer his graceful build, his youth, his carefree attitude to it all. Faulkner was strictly a short service man; filling the awkward years between coming down from Oxford and junior partnership in the city.

'God knows why he volunteered for loan service,' thought White, mutely shaking his head. Peter White was career infantry. Once a genial, stocky youth from a good county family in the North West he was now a genial if stockier thirty-four year old major in a northern county regiment. Though he had passed Camberley by dint of good hard graft, married well and had been promoted early, Peter felt that he was losing the race to half-colonelcy. Graduates were the apple of the Adjutant-General's eye now; good 'A' levels from a good school were just not good enough. Besides he had missed out on Northern Ireland having gone straight into a grade two staff job from staff college. He had persuaded Alison, to let him second to the Emirate. After all he would not see any more of her and the kids if he were on a two year stint in Ulster. So she had reluctantly agreed and he was on active service at last, well, of sorts.'

Faulkner flopped down and unwound his brown and white head cloth. He mopped his face and neck then rubbed his lank blond hair.

'Everything's fine below,' he said confidently.

'Are the boys happy?' asked White.

'Waagid,' replied Faulkner stifling a yawn. 'When is the next wave due?'

'In about thirty minutes.'

'How long do you think we'll be here?' Faulkner asked.

'Lost interest already?'

'No. The boys keep asking me.'

White leaned back and blew out his cheeks.

'All of three weeks, I suppose. I'm not really sure what the aim is. If we do manage to block any of the supply routes, the adoo will just go a bit further around.' White thought again. 'Maybe, sniping, a few mortar rounds perhaps. The adoo prefer something soft usually, the oil companies or the Development people. Still, we'll see won't we?'

Faulkner nodded his silent agreement and then turned around to squint at the now shimmering blue hills to the north.

CHAPTER TWO

Seventy miles from the Lion Jebel, at the same time as White and Faulkner were leaving the landing site, a silent group of Britons waited beneath a white canvas awning. Some sat, some stood but all were listening intently to the steady static babble coming from a small loudspeaker screwed down to a bare wooden table. Being only a few miles from the coast of the Arabian Gulf, the air was noticeably more chill than further inland. The occasional, involuntary shiver spread through the little group; partly from the cold morning air, partly through nervous apprehension of what was expected.

The officers were packed inside a tiny command post constructed Lego-fashion from sand-filled ammunition boxes, surmounted with a canvas roof. The command post sat between a small camp, a mixture of tents and corrugated iron shanties, and an oil-soaked strip of sand which served as an airstrip. The camp was set on the long dip slope of an escarpment which gave way to a narrow coastal strip and then the immobile sapphire blue of the Gulf. On the perimeter of the strip, in rows and clusters, sat or squatted some three hundred green-clad soldiers. Some dozed, their shemaghs pulled over their faces, others chatted or sat staring at the sea. All kept an ear tuned for the throbbing note of returning Hueys.

Lt Col Alastair Wilson had played second row for the Army but his once powerful chest and muscular stomach now combined into a blunt, rounded bow. His shoulders, well padded with fat, sagged forward as he listened intently to the static warbling of the high-frequency receiver. Cocking his head back, he drew deeply on the cigarillo held between his sausage-thick fingers. Though his face now supported a developing jowl and his cheeks and nose were becoming permanently red with broken veins, it still retained the vestiges of rugged handsomeness which attracted many a laird's daughter in the messes in Edinburgh and Aberdeen. His once thick, dark hair was now greying fashionably at the temples and getting, not so fashionably, thin on top. He let smoke tumble from his mouth; his eyes, curiously soft and moist for one of his profession, contemplating the canvas ceiling.

'Looks like another nice day,' cut in a Geordie voice. The Colonel's eyes dropped to fix upon the utterer of such a crass and worthless observation who had dared to break the officers' accepted silence. QMS Thompson ran his hand over his crew-cut, sniffed loudly and turned away to busy himself with his webbing equipment. Some of the other officers around the table turned briefly to add disdainful stares at the artillery warrant officer's back as he rummaged through one of the canvas pouches on his belt-order. He extracted a packet of biscuits. Starting to open them he abruptly stopped, picked up his rifle and sidled out into the morning glare.

The Sergeant-Major's facetious comments were such a regular feature at the officer-laden gatherings that they now raised no comment; just withering looks. The exception was from the incongruous being seated at the table. A small wiry man, wearing shorts, thong sandals, a faded cotton bush hat and a regimental shemagh, worn like a shawl. The hat was decorated with various utilitarian items such as a bottle opener, can opener, pencil stubs, erasers and even a teaspoon.

'The old 'major there cracks me up,' he chuckled, tapping out short tattoos on the pad in from of him.

Captain Mike Cook, late of the Royal Australian Regiment, welcomed any relief from the tedium of operations room watch-keeping. He was about to make further comments about his brother officers' lack of humour when the static from the loudspeaker cut out.

'Zeero theese eer wan,' an Arabic voice drawled from out of the ether.

'Zeero o-kay ober,' answered the voice of the command net signaller, unseen in the tent next door. There was a pause.

'One, okay. Tadpole, I say again Tadpole, over,' White's voice boomed out from the black box.

'Tadpole,' repeated the Colonel as if it were a verbal talisman.

'Zero, roger out,' replied Cook into a stem microphone in front of him and then to the assembly. 'Okay, boys, looks like the front doors open, nobody at home.'

Colonel Wilson looked relieved. He picked up his canvas map case and assumed what he considered to be an attitude of authority and assertive leadership. Glancing around at the remaining company commanders and their seconds-in-command, he addressed them solemnly.

'Well, Gentlemen, that is phase one. I shall be over to site your guns as soon as your companies are in position. Remember I want all fire positions completed by first light tomorrow, so keep the jundis at it. Any questions?' He paused looking round aggressively. 'Right then, go to it.' With that he stalked out to survey his troops. He was followed out by the other two rifle company commanders, Denby-Smith and Ross. The little party wound its way between the knots of soldiers until the company commanders diverged away to their respective sub-units. Wilson was left in front of group of Arab and Baluchi junior officers, non-commissioned officers and soldiers that made up his personal headquarters. They began to rise respectfully until he waved them down. One or two others from nearby groups edged closer to listen.

'One Company has landed, no enemy ... helicopters come back here soon for you ... us,' he explained in his faltering Arabic. Most of the audience nodded and smiled, others turned and repeated the announcement to others who were not as used to the Colonel's Egyptian-tutored grammar. Two or three even started to clap. The news then started to spread to other squatting groups in turn. The Colonel stood for a moment smiling benignly and sheepishly. He felt uncomfortable in the company of his men.

Not having to speak or listen to Arabic all day, every day, as did the company officers, the Colonel found the mental translation between the local dialect and his standard Arabic a great strain. The Arabs and Baluchis promptly returned to their idle chatter and contemplation. The brief flame of martial spirit within him died as he looked about at his men. His eyes passed from one to the other and seemed to focus in each case on their various forms of personal adornment. The henna-varnished finger nails, ears pierced with holes large enough to take a pencil, eyes seductively black-rimmed with kohl. All prepared for Paradise.

'Like a bunch of tarts,' he silently scolded. He found himself fondly remembering the rough hewn features and rougher ways of his regiment's Midlothian jocks. He had pondered too long for one or two of the younger jundis had started to giggle and whisper. Men of Alastair's girth were rare in the Emirate and his most popular name among the jundis was 'Father of Bellys.' Alastair felt conspicuous and awkward. As he looked about eagerly for an excuse to leave, he spotted the battalion second-in-command weaving slowly between the squatting, chattering groups.

'Harry,' he called, raising a finger. His audience parted to allow him access to Major Harry Shaw. One of the longest serving of the Emir's contract officers and a founder member of the Thaalith or Third Battalion.

'Harry,' the Colonel repeated to give himself time to think of some point to discuss. 'The move of Headquarters company and support troop?'

'Yes Colonel?' said Harry his head lolling on his right shoulder as was his habit.

'You're quite happy about moving up tomorrow? I mean it's rather soon after the companies have got in.' Wilson went on feeling as indecisive as he sounded. Harry did not seem to respond or even understand. The flustered Colonel tried again.

'I mean, I don't expect positions to be ... er complete by dusk tomorrow. You know how slow the boys are?'

'We'll be fine, Colonel, just fine,' Harry eventually answered. He reached down and withdrew an old briar from the top of his knee length stockings. Harry was exceedingly thin and looked positively emaciated in the voluminous shorts and oversized bush shirt he always wore in camp. His leathery flesh seemed to hang free from his bony skull. Harry's hair was shorn away at the back and at the sides in the style rarely seen in the British Army since National Service days. A few thin strands were brushed over his pate, and an equally sparse moustache surmounted his top lip. Two sad, jaundiced eyes looked out wistfully on the world from hollow sockets.

Tapping the pipe into his palm Harry nodded lugubriously.

'Yes, we'll be fine,' he repeated: The mournful yellow eyes fixed by the Colonel's stare like a rabbit in front of a stoat.

'God, what a state?' exclaimed the Colonel's inner thoughts. He now felt more uncomfortable with Harry than he did with the Arabs. 'Good, we'll be off soon then. One company is in position, no contacts, got to check something with Mike, see you later, Harry.' Thus excused he threaded his way back to the ammunition box command post and his Australian adjutant.

Harry watched him go and turned to survey the groups of

brown faces looking up at him. Picking out a pair of veteran jundis he moved into a ring of soldiers. After the ritual compliments and shaking of hands. Harry hunkered down and launched effortlessly into a string of enquiries about families, crops, villages and livestock, in fact, the standard conversation which occurs daily throughout the Arab world. Each soldier answering as if he had been at home the day before though none had been allowed leave for months.

The babble of chatter from this and all the other groups quickly hushed as from out of the now shimmering northern hills the first stream of returning Hueys rose into view. The helicopters lazily dipped one by one into the re-fuelling bays on the far side of the strip. Lines of heavily burdened soldiers then wound out to meet them as they rose and clattered over bringing with them their own whirling storms of dust. As the Hueys landed each line of jundis was crammed into the main cabin like a disjointed green jack-in-the-box. When the sliding doors were forced shut, to prevent them from falling out, each 205 roared, dipped and scrambled into the air. They orbited the airstrip till the wave was complete, then flight by flight they streamed away towards the north.

In the lead helicopter, Colonel Wilson, squirmed and wriggled his bulk further back into the nylon web seat. With the combat crew of two pilots he was denied the privilege of the left hand co-pilot's seat. Wedged between his Baluchi RSM and his operations officer he seethed over the facts of loan service life he detested the most: the noise and smell of helicopters and the close proximity of so many Arabs.

CHAPTER THREE

'Second company and Tac have just landed, sir.' The Force Duty Officer turned away from his desk to await the reply of the Force Commander.

'No contacts?' asked the senior officer perfunctorily.

'No, sir,' answered the officer, then added, 'choppers now inbound for Harrow.' An image of the glaring dust covered airstrip was conjured into the Force Commander's mind and then jumbled with a second mental picture of green playing fields and overcast English skies.

'Who's puerile mind blessed all our airstrips with the names of public schools,' he murmured. A sharp voice penetrated his musing. 'Pardon?' he said.

'I said so far so good.'

Major General Welles sniffed and rose from the ornamental cane chair that was his special preserve in the operations room.

'Well, we didn't expect a battle on the first day.'

He took a fresh King Edward from the box on the table by the chair and walked over to the nearest window alcove. He turned and sat on the stone ledge at the base. For a few moments he just sat rolling the cigar between his fingers and staring at the stone flags between his feet.

'I still feel that we should have made the stop line further back. If anything goes wrong they're too far away for effective reinforcement or …' he hesitated. 'Withdrawal. I mean, Henson, any line between Harrow and the sands would stop infiltration. Why does it have to be Jebel Assaad?'

Henson half turned from his perch on the edge of one of the clerk's desks. He held up one finger of his right hand.

'Because, A, it will shorten the war and with the state of the Emirate's economics that is eminently desirable. B, it extends his Highness's rule to the furthermost reaches of his domain and, C, he decreed it, personally.'

'But he saw my appreciation and plans, surely,' the general interjected, ignoring Henson's smugness.

'Of course, I can testify that his Highness went over every

detail but he decided on the line at Jebel Assaad and, may I say, with good reason and with my fullest support.' Henson consulted his wristwatch. 'If you want to discuss it personally with him, I'm sure he would oblige. He will be here in two minutes.' With that, the Emir's Secretary for Defence straightened up, adjusted his tie and walked towards the door.

'I'll wait in the courtyard.' He turned and added, 'I shouldn't express any opinion, General. The Emir was really quite determined over the site. He likes the name for the op though; Saladin. One of his heroes, I believe.'

An Arab military police corporal opened the heavy wood doors and Henson strolled out.

Henson stepped out onto the veranda which led to the staircase. He was relieved to be away from General Welles and further cross-examination. Part of him sympathised with the Force Commander. It was never easy for an able and experienced soldier to "do" but not to "reason why". Still he had not lied to the General, he just had not told him everything he knew. As an ex-regular officer he felt a brief pang of uneasiness at having to use and manipulate people but his political sense restrained him from opening up. He paused halfway down the curved passage and looked over the parapet into the courtyard below.

Even at fifty eight and after thirty two years as a regular officer, Henson still felt intimidated by taller men. At a slim five foot seven, he was not noticeably short but he felt it, sometimes acutely. To compensate he had warded off any tendency to middle age spread and even in the wringing humidity of the capital donned immaculate, seemingly creaseless, suits and crisp white shirts. Sailing in the Gulf kept his tan a deep copper which in turn set off this eyes; pale blue in clear whites. His pale straw-coloured hair was thinning yet always carefully arranged over his smallish head.

The young Henson had never been popular with his military contemporaries; a bit of a "thruster", "military shit" or "too clever by half". He soon realised even as a sharp, young captain in the Rifle Brigade that great command was not to be his and so he sought glory by a different route. A gift for meticulous staff work and an unswerving adherence to the military-diplomatic cocktail circuit brought its reward in a string of diplomatic appointments. As he approached retiring age, Colonel Henson recognised a niche for himself in the wake of the final British withdrawal from

Empire and was now the de facto Minister for Defence to his Highness, The Emir, Suleman bin Adullah As Shahaam. True there was a minister and a secretary nominally above him but they were uncle and cousin to the Emir respectively. The Emirate's military power lay with Henson. He watched the Headquarters guard shuffling into two files either side of the entrance gate. Straightening his regimental tie, he strode off towards the steps which led down to the dusty square below.

General Welles was not an original thinker. In fact in the grand traditions of British cavalry officers he professed not to think at all. If his cerebral qualities might have been in doubt he had two other assets which more than balanced the deficiency. These were the ability to pick assistants who could think and the courage to back them. Watching him pace up and down the operations room, was probably one of the sharpest military minds that the post-war army had yet produced: Colonel Gilbert Dixon, the Force's Chief of Staff.

General Welles had been a stocky, powerfully-built cadet at Sandhurst. Years of playing polo and rugby had helped to keep him proportionally the same, even if he was a little more generous with his belt fastenings. Since the departure of Henson he had adopted his frustrated-by-civil-servants bulldog attitude. The object of this minor charade was to coax some counter plot or at least sympathy from his sole spectator, Gilbert Dixon.

Welles stopped finally, exasperated by Dixon's continued silence.

'Come on, Gilly. What do you think? What's Henson playing at?' he demanded at last.

Gilly pursed his lips and leaned back in his own cane chair.

'I don't know,' he said quietly, 'I've been thinking about it though.'

'Glad about that,' muttered Welles.

Ignoring the weak sarcasm, Dixon brought his fingers together to form a steeple beneath his chin as if about to beseech much higher authority.

'At first, I thought it was just Henson or the Emir being over ambitious. The line we picked was well within our battalion's capability: but, at Jebel Assaad, well?' He glanced at the large scale map to his right and flicked off a long forefinger towards it. 'I doubt whether they could honestly cover half the wadis between the escarpment and the sands.'

'So,' retorted Welles as if trying to coax answers from a dull student. 'Why did they pick Jebel Assaad?'

Dixon stared back unintimidated by his tone.

'I've got an idea but ... ?' he hesitated. 'I'll need a day or two to check it out.'

Unable to tease any more thoughts from his chief of staff the General changed his tack. He glanced up at the watchkeeper's clock.

'Nearly half-past, Solly will be here in a minute,' he said, using the expatriates' in-house name for His Highness. 'I'll go down and meet him.' Picking up his cap and regimental riding crop he strode out of the air-conditioned chill of the operations room into the still, furnace heat of mid morning.

Colonel Dixon rose, straightened his bush jacket and then made his way through a side door into the briefing room. A tall man with long features, he had the ambience of a bank manager or a public school master rather than an infantry officer. The product of good East of England yeoman stock and a sound, county regiment, he had been one of the first of his generation of soldiers to be a graduate. He had cheerfully excepted the jibes of his less academic contemporaries, seemingly content to be a thinking soldier in the rather less than deep thinking army of the shrinking Empire. Mountbatten's shake up of the service hierarchies in the early sixties had given the young Major Dixon a chance to shine. He was then one of the few officers in the new combined staffs that the Oxbridge men of the Civil Service were prepared to accept as an academic equal.

Always a gentle man at heart, Gilbert Dixon had doubted his own ability to take the really hard decisions and still less to bear the responsibility for the failures. So he gladly accepted his role of a latter day Machiavelli, thinking for and giving options and advice to a succession of martial princes; always painstakingly careful lest they fall. He entered the briefing room nodding to the two staff captains who had begun to rise. He looked around checking the seating layout. He wondered if Henson felt the same about his Prince.

CHAPTER FOUR

The headquarters of the Emirate's Defence Force resided in an old mud brick fort, once white washed and now bleached by the relentless sun of the Arabian Gulf. The fort was originally built by soldiers of the British East India Company a few years before the Indian mutiny. Its purpose was to deny the indigenous pirates use of the natural harbour nearby in what was now the capital. The capital itself was guarded by a magnificent ring of curtain walls and towers built by the Portuguese when at the height of their power some two hundred years before. To any student of military architecture the simple mud brick fort with its flat roofs and loop-holed walls contrasted poorly with the crenallated towers of grey limestone which the Portuguese had inlaid into the headlands around the harbour, but two centuries of neglect had probably been the deciding factor to the practically-minded sahibs from across the Gulf.

The fort had been expanded and improved upon by a succession of soldier-builders according to the waxing and waning of British interest in the area. The turn of the century had seen the construction of a sprawling cantonment of bungalows to accommodate a Baluchi infantry regiment of the British Indian Army. Stables and gardens appeared in the twenties with the raising of a squadron of mounted levies from the local tribes. The discovery of oil in the Emirate was followed by the building of a helicopter pad and a swimming pool in the officers' mess gardens. Now the little fort sat like a grand-father surrounded by tin-roofed children and concrete grand-children. The coast was served with abundant fresh water from an irrigation system hewed out of rock by blinded Persian miners two thousand years before. Unexploited by the wandering tribes of goat herdsmen, the water found a natural ally in the lineage of amateur horticulturists and landscape artists amongst the lonely ex-patriots. The once barren rock around the fort was now an oasis of trees, shrubs and lawns. Plant life from every corner of the Eastern empire marked the obsession of creative men with little else to do in the torpor of colonial barrack life.

The headquarters cantonment of Eyun'a' Rashid was linked to the capital by a glittering new tarmac road constructed with unerring precision by a firm of West German civil engineers. Along it now snaked a small convoy of white Range Rovers and Toyota pick-ups. Two police outriders in outsized white helmets and gauntlets waved oncoming taxis and dusty landrovers off the black top and onto the sand . The Emir's procession curved purposely off the ruler-straight black line at a seminal roundabout from which there were as yet only two exits; the first to the fort the second back the way they had come. Only tyre tracks in the sand marked the way beyond.

A column of dust flew into the air as the vehicles left the black top and roared through the outer wire mesh gates leaving a rigidly saluting jundi staring intently heavenwards whilst he received a light coating of dust. The outriders, the Toyota and two of the Range Rovers veered away at the gates to the fort to come to a sudden halt in an angry storm of dust. The remaining vehicle slowed and disappeared beneath the port-way. The Range Rover stopped, its engine gunning throatily in the small, enclosed square.

Twelve jundis stood ram-rod straight in two ranks, their Belgian semi-automatics proffered towards the vehicles in the present. The guard commander, a lath-like Arab captain stepped forward and saluted the green fatigue-uniformed driver of the Rover as he emerged from the air-conditioned chill of the interior. The driver cast an eye over the guard and then stepped forward, right hand extended to the guard commander. The captain's saluting hand dropped together with his position of attention as he took the Emir's hand and leant forward to receive the swift bobbing nose-kiss of his tribal chieftain. This brief ceremony complete, the Emir stepped briskly around the guard and on towards the steps which led to the upper storey. Two green-uniformed aides immediately leapt from the rear of the Rover and fell into step behind. At the bottom of the steps he received a clipped neck-bow from Henson and a dignified salute from Welles.

The Emir, a youthful and lithe thirty-seven year old bounded up the worn stone steps leaving the two older men behind. He stopped on the balcony and made the pretence of surveying the courtyard while they followed. Then, together, they strode along the balcony and into the briefing room. The Emir acknowledged

Colonel Dixon's salute with a wave, removed his beret and took the only cushioned, cane armchair in the centre of the front row. Henson and Welles settled onto plain chairs either side.

Colonel Dixon stepped back behind a wooden pedestal upon which his notes were balanced. Removing his cap, he picked up a pair of half rimmed spectacles and positioned them carefully on his nose. The two captains adopted positions either side of a rolled-down map hung against the wall like supporters to a coat-of-arms. Dixon looked down at his notes and then over the half moon rims at the small audience. This mannerism irritated Welles slightly as it reminded him of a long-buried English master at his school.

'Your Highness,' the chief of staff began. 'At zero six twenty hours today one company of the Third Battalion landed on Jebel Assaad.' A supporter flicked up a thin telescopic rod with a fluorescent tip to indicate the landing point. 'There was no contact made with the enemy nor any sign of recent occupation ...'

As Dixon continued, Welles cast his eyes to the right to observe the Emir's reactions. The ruler was leaning slightly forward, elbows on the arms of the chair, fingers and thumb of his right hand gently stroking the black beard on his chin. His soft brown eyes fixed intently on Dixon.

The General reflected for a moment on how lucky he was to have such an active and alert young man as his contractor. So many of the other tribal leaders fell into the downward spiral of over indulgence which spread like a decay through their governmental hierarchies. The young Sandhurst-trained Emir was different in many ways. Perhaps it was his lineage through the successive union of Arabian kings to Indian princesses that had produced, in him, such a physically robust and mentally alert example of Islamic nobility. More likely it was the precarious nature of existence that is experienced by all absolute rulers and especially in the vulnerable little states in such a politically turbulent region such as the Gulf.

Dixon was now well in to "future intentions". The heraldic supporters were busy unfolding strips of green plastic crosses across the map. Welles watched as his chief of staff suddenly came out from behind the defences of his lectern and crossed the room to start spreading his right finger span across the packed contour lines in the centre of the map whilst his left hand made probing jabs down from the top. All the time he explored the options of the enemy in all his likely configurations and what the Third Battalion would do in response. Then he stopped, removed the incongruous half rims and moved crab-wise back behind the lectern.

'Your Highness, if you have any questions?' he offered with supplicant nod of the head. The Emir leaned back and stared at the map, now covered in green and blue symbols neatly overlaid on plastic film.

'Well done, Gilly,' thought Welles, 'never seen you so animated.' He smiled inwardly. A slight movement in his lips gave it away and attracted a flicker of gratitude from his chief of staff.

'When do you expect contact to be made, Stewart?' asked the Emir in his slightly sing-song English, swinging round to his left. General Stewart leaned back clasping his big, paw-like hands in front of him as if holding back a polo pony.

'Difficult to say, Your Highness.' He paused, pursing his lips and then rubbing his palms together. 'Given that there is obviously no enemy presence on the jebel, I would say a week to recce and move up weapons and equipment. Then probing attacks, sniping perhaps in ... what ... eight to ten days. Less if we move out to look for them.'

'Look for them then,' rejoined the Emir, fixing his General with his gaze. 'This war has gone on long enough.'

'Very good, Your Highness,' Welles assented, a little taken aback by the Prince's sudden pointedness.

'Now then,' Suleman said, rising from his chair and satisfied that he had made his point. 'When would be a good time to visit?'

'The positions should be complete by Friday,' replied Dixon, who instantly regretted his choice of day as he remembered that Yaum a Jumma was the Islamic Sabbath.

'I shall be flying in on Saturday?' offered Welles, knowing that the Emir would have the sense to leave a respectable interval between their calls.

'Good, I shall have my staff arrange for a visit the following week,' the Emir concluded having received his cue.

'Ah, coffee and dates,' their attention was redirected to a khaadim attempting to push a cup and saucer laden trolley into the room without looking up from the floor. The Emir followed by

Henson and Welles moved to the back of the room. The Emir set the awe-struck boy at ease with a few words of dialect Arabic. The khaadim, thus restored to normal, set about serving coffee and offering fresh dates to all who were present. The Emir had served in the Jordanian army as a platoon commander and then as a regimental signals officer and so was familiar with the effects of Royal visits on any unit or headquarters. Though he was a frequent visitor to Eyun a' Rashid he never lingered and expected only the minimum of compliments. Accordingly, he finished his coffee and was soon on his way, taking Henson with him. After talking briefly to one or two of the signallers and clerks whom he passed on the balcony, the ruler and commander-in-chief sat behind the wheel of his Range Rover, the immaculate Henson beside him and roared off through the gate to surprise his escort who had been lounging beside their trucks and cycles.

Welles stood beside Dixon on the balcony and watched the convoy emerge from their dust cloud to race along the tarmac towards the roundabout.

'He seemed pleased,' observed Dixon. There was a pause between the two which neither seemed willing to break.

'Y'know,' began the General, 'I never used to hold any sympathy for that Yank at Anzio. What was his name?'

'Lucas.'

'Yes, Lucas,' Welles continued. 'I always considered the man wet, indecisive. Just sitting there, not taking advantage of the situation.' He turned slightly towards Dixon and leaned on his elbows and stared down over the parapet. 'We can all be great generals with the benefit of hindsight but, Christ, I know just how Lucas must have felt on the first day and I bet poor, old Alastair feels the same.'

'I know, I wish we'd sent Marcus Hunt now,' his chief of staff mused hazily, still following the progress of the white vehicles.

'Yes, Marcus, wouldn't have given it a second thought but Alastair? Oh, I can just see him now ...' Another silence prevailed for a minute or two.

'Where's young Rolls, the Gurkha?' asked Welles. Dixon turned round to give his eyes a rest from the glare.

'Umm. We sent him off with the Border Scouts Regiment six months ago, Two IC to old Buffy Hancock.' Welles straightened up and made slowly towards his office. He stopped and spoke to the door.

'Get him up here, will you. Tell Buffy anything you like.' He turned to show Dixon his concern. 'Make it waagid feesah, Gill, I want to see him as soon as you can get him here.' He turned and walked off to the end of the balcony.

Gilbert Dixon caught the inside of his cheek between his teeth and pondered but a second before turning towards the operations room and the nearest signals pad.

CHAPTER FIVE

The company and headquarters's elements of the Third Battalion had passed a quiet if anxious night crouched in their shell scrapes and half-built sangars. The pre-dawn chill made the expatriots grateful for the short process of the equatorial dawn.

By six o'clock the first flickerings of breakfast fires signalled stand down and the end of the night. The troops rose from their battle positions and regrouped into their platoons. A variety of blackened pots were filled with water for shai. Curried mutton was gouged from tins. Marble-sized pieces of dough became plate-sized chapattis and ready for the pan in the flying hands of the company bakers. Breakfast was always a semi-frenzied affair. Here and there the more devout soldiers were kneeling over their water bottles carrying out their ritual ablutions before giving acknowledgement and praise to Allah for the enlightenment of his Prophet Mohammed. Soon, all would be squatting round in the foundations of their sangars mopping up the mash of hot curried mutton and peas with pieces of the scorched, unleaven khubz.

Mid-morning found the jebel alive with activity. The dominating promontories, resembled marmot colonies with jundis bobbing up and down as they prised boulders and earth from their shelter pits or scurried back and forth with offerings of rocks and stones to be added to the surrounding walls. Each section of twelve or more constructed a large communal sangar with stone walls four feet thick and beam and sandbag roofs for overhead protection. Around each main sangar were numerous small two-man, open sangars to which they were supposed to disperse and fight should they come under direct assault.

Ideally the sections were to be sited to cover not only all the approaches to the position but to give fire support to each other; the rear sections able to fire onto the flanks and rear of the forward positions. The undulating plateau and slopes of the jebel were not always so accommodating to such ideals in defensive theory. Consequently the company commanders had to compromise between the evils of isolating sections or leaving intolerable gaps in their allotted sectors.

The headquarters elements of each company were sited in the centre of their sub-units. Living quarters varied according to the personal tastes of the commander. Some shared sangars with their little entourage of HQ wallahs, others preferred isolation or the company of their co-patriot second in command. Some had bunker-like command posts constructed from which to orchestrate their units, others preferred to take their chances in the open sangars alongside their men. Peter White was one of the latter and this second morning on the jebel found him in the machine gun sangar of his left forward section. White was sitting alongside the sentry, methodically scanning the sea of ridges and gullies in front of him. On his knee was a large scale map inside a plastic cover. White would look down at the swirling contour lines and then stare through his binoculars to follow the unremitting landscape out to hazy blue oblivion. The map was merely a large scale transposition from air photographs and so ultimately dependent on the state of the light at the time. What appeared to be long snaking ridges to a hard-pressed military cartographer, occasionally manifested themselves to be dry river beds on the ground. Peter White was deliberating over such a dilemma when the sentry intruded on his thoughts.

'Pardon?' he said absent-mindedly, then in Arabic, 'marrathanee?'

'Marshay adoo, sah'b,' beamed the jundi pointing to White's binoculars. White smiled, partly in relief.

'Al Hamdu lillah, Assif, marshay adoo.'

He turned back to the map and then gazed out towards the shimmering blue haze. 'No enemy,' he thought, 'no, not one we can see.' He reflected a moment on the adoo. The Colonel's opening statement about this operation came to mind.

'Establish the authority of the Emir where it had not existed for thirty years … Heartland of the enemy …'

He thought too about the transcripts of the Radio Sofia news broadcasts circulated by Mike Cook as part of intelligence brief … "The People's War was entering its final, victorious phase. The Gulf People's Liberation Front would receive the support of all freedom-loving Socialist States … British mercenary jackals etc." He wiped the sweat from the eye-pieces of the binoculars, pondering on the image of the enemy; his enemy. The GPLF, a highly motivated army of freedom-fighters dedicated to throwing off the feudal yoke of centuries or just another fractious tribe of nomads carrying on the traditions of their fore-fathers. Born in 1967, that must put them in the same stable as the NLF and FLOSY in the days when British Toms patrolled Aden in knee-length shorts. All had been to the same schools too ... Patrice Lumumba School of Terror in Moscow, a spell with the comrades in Havana or Tripoli with a month or two's practical weapon training courtesy of the Chinese in the Hadramut. Harry Shaw said that when the first cadres arrived in the Emirate they were just laughed at and stoned from village to village. The goat-herders of the Hawaafi Kabeer did not need any of the "Godless ones" to teach them how to revolt. They had been fighting the "Pirate Emirs" and their "slave" soldiers since the first glorious victories of Islam.

It was a curious fact, first learned by the colonial powers in Asia and Africa, that those wild-eyed fanatics who had endured the tedium of Communist enlightenment in such places as the Lumumba College were notoriously hard to put off. So with a little on the spot tuition in terror from experts, on loan from the Chinese Peoples Liberation Army and latterly Al Fatah, the GPLF became a popular movement. But who were they? He had never seen one; alive or dead. The odd fuzzy pictures of fierce-eyed, turbaned tribesmen clutching Kalashniknovs, "squaddies snaps", that was all.

'Sah'b, Qaa'id gai,' the sentry said. White nearly leapt to his feet then remembered that jundis tended to call every white officer over the rank of major, Qaa'id ... a general. Peter White smiled and slumped back against the sangar wall to watch his commanding officer labouring up the rock-strewn slope towards him.

Colonel Alastair had lain awake on this camp-bed for most of the night. Today was no less trying. He had spent an unhappy morning arguing with the officer commanding Two Company, who was remonstrating over every decision he had made the day before. Then there was his Adjutant and Operations Officer, Mike Cook. Mike sought to lighten the burdens of his job by adopting various eccentricities of dress and behaviour. The wearing of the apocryphal Australian bush hat, complete with corks, was an example. Alastair Wilson regarded it as an ill omen for the man's competence if not his sanity. He had decided to escape by visiting the companies when the RSM elected to join him, thereby turning an intended leisurely stroll into a vigorous hike.

Despite the fact that he only carried a holstered pistol, a water-bottle and cased-binoculars on his webbing belt, the Colonel could not keep up with the rangy Baluch. With rifle bouncing on his shoulder, Pathan-style, the RSM loped across the plateau and up the hill to One Company's dominating summit. Alastair Wilson swayed to a stop halfway up, near to where White had halted the day before. His mouth gaped open as he sucked in the flame-hot air which rose from the bare slopes. Something ached in his chest, his eyes, cheeks and neck stung with sweat. His calf muscles and hamstrings demanding relief, he sat down.

'You rest, Sah'b?' asked the RSM from somewhere above.

'No, no, RSM. I just want to see the position from here,' he croaked. He groped his binoculars from their case and pointed a finger accusingly at them, as if he had no choice in the matter. 'You go on,' he added. 'I'll be up in a minute.'

The Baluch nodded, turned and resumed his loping ascent. Alastair turned and lay back with an unseen theatrical sigh. If he had known that it was going to be like this he would have opted for gardening leave. Those bastards in his regimental secretariat department must have known all along. He wiped his face with the loose end of the headcloth which swathed his head. Then he put the binoculars to his eyes and watched the activity down below. As the helicopters were now tasked with bringing in underslung loads, they were observing a pause throughout the hottest part of the day. Lifts would resume in the late afternoon when cooler air allowed more fuel-efficient payloads. This also allowed the marshalling teams the time to disperse the loads to their respective storage bays.

He could see the squat form of WO2 Thompson pushing and pulling bemused jundis into a human conveyor belt for the purpose of moving his precious shells to the gunline.

'For all his awful Geordie mannerisms, he was bloody good when it came to working the boys!' The Colonel sighed again, and noticed that his chest had now stopped hurting as had his legs and that his breathing had now returned to normal. He cast an eye left and right over the ranks of ridges and the same hazy blue horizon being more professionally observed by Peter White. He wished that the haze was over some part of Salisbury Plain and that all he had to do this coming afternoon was sip a few gin and tonics and perhaps harangue a class of Junior Staff College students on their lack of military perspicacity. 'Now that was soldiering.' He stood up and, stuffing the binoculars in their case, he resumed his plod up the hill to where Peter White was contemplating the GPLF.

Across the broad flanks of the Jebel, beyond the battalion headquarters and the gunline, the feature dropped away sharply into a wide, flat-bottomed wadi. The slopes of this eastern flank of the feature were corrugated by rounded spurs and narrow, dry stream beds where, once or twice in every good year, torrents of muddy water bounced down to the surging foam below. Two Company was perched above it at a point where the spurs started to spread out like fingers. The forward sections tentatively extended a few dozen yards down each one.

Giles Denby-Smith stopped on the newly worn track which was being created by the scores of jundis portering stores from the landing site. He stepped aside just in time to avoid being run down by half a dozen, crate-bearing soldiers scuttling like foraging ants back to the nest. He watched them go, stumbling and slipping, down the rock-strewn slopes and then disappear amongst the stone-walled stores tents. He looked around at the half-completed sangars in the headquarters position and then out to the finished sangars of the platoon positions.

'For a company of a hundred and thirty men, there seems to be remarkably little activity,' he observed to himself. Slinging his rifle on to his shoulder, he started down the path with long, meaningful strides towards the sangar he shared with his second-in-command. Stopping at his roofless sangar he bawled at it.

'Where the hell are they all?' Captain Alan Primmer's head bobbed up from between the timber roof supports.

'Who?'

'The fucking jundis, of course!' Giles yelled, his face turning red by blotches. He threw an arm out behind him. 'Three Company has nearly finished its wiring and we haven't even got the pissing roof on yet. I told Wakeel to keep four boys on this sangar till it was done.' His face now completely red and flecks of foam glistened at the corners of his mouth.

'They went for ghadaa,' offered Primmer, using their Arabic colloquial for lunch.

'And you let them?' fumed Giles. 'Jee-sus?' He turned away from the nearly apologetic Primmer and took a few steps towards the huddle of stone shanties that comprised the remainder of the headquarters. 'Wakeel!'

When the hapless Baluch emerged, blinking into the light, he was roundly berated, mainly in English, as to the general idleness and indiscipline of the Arabian and Indian races. The sergeant major then ran all over the position, from section to section, to raise workers, willing and unwilling, from their lunches. Giles stalked along in his wake; joining in with the odd word of encouragement such as 'feesah' and 'dalheen'.

Alan Primmer watched the double-act for a minute or so and then sat down on one of the low parapets he had made to take their camp beds. He reached into his shirt pocket, extracted a cigarette and lit it with his Zippo. Drawing on the filter tip, he stared at the engraving on the lighter. 'To Captain A M Primmer R Irish, From C Coy 1 Royal Irish Rangers —'Faugh a Balagh.' He looked up at the sky through the roof beams and wished that he was second-in-command to anyone but Giles. The jundis just did not like him which was hardly surprising considering that he loathed and despised them to such a degree. Alan wondered why Giles had volunteered to second in the first place. Thinking about that, he could not even remember why he had contracted-in himself some thirty months ago.

A sound of hurried steps and muttered Arabic returned him to the present.

'Sah'b!' A brown face appeared over the beams. 'Ajeeb saqf? sah'b,' it said and the rattle of corrugated iron followed like stage thunder.

'Tamaam, Jeebu,' replied the ex-Ranger, carefully pinching out the half-smoked Triple Five. Within seconds the skeleton spars were crowded with jundis wrestling with six-foot angle iron rods and sheets of shiny, galvanised metal. Alan Primmer stood in the middle of the sangar directing where the iron cross-members should go and where each sheet should be nailed down.

'Wiggly teen,' said one of the younger boys peering down at him.

'What?'

'Wiggly teen!' the boy said again pointing a red-brown finger nail at the corrugated iron. Primmer puckered his eye-brows to indicated puzzlement. 'Wig-ell-ee tee-een!' the boy exaggerated, looking slightly desperate, as if his life might depend upon Primmer's comprehension. By this time all of the others had stopped working and were looking on intently. Then the painfully pronounced syllables came together in his head.

'Wriggly tin! Yes.' He nodded, smiling broadly. The tension broken, the boy and the other jundis joined in a celebratory chorus of 'wreegellee teen, wreegellee teen!'

Primmer found himself joining in, laughing at their efforts to use British Army slang. The chorus became a work chant and within a few minutes Primmer was in semi-darkness listening to the steady thumps of filled sandbags being packed on top of the tin roof. He sat down again and lit the remaining length of his interrupted Triple-Five.

Irving Ross had parted company with the irascible Denby-Smith just as they reached the gun-line. Giles had been pestering the Colonel to shorten his company's sector as he regarded his position as being, "by far, the most vulnerable". Irving smiled as he strolled along, recalling how Colonel Alastair had even resorted to crude flattery in a vain attempt to appease the indignant Giles.

'Well, it's not by accident that as senior company commander you have got the most difficult sector, Giles, y'know.'

Irving had let the argument reach the "you can have my resignation in the morning point" when he magnanimously offered to move one of his reserve platoons over to cover an isolated part of Giles' sector. It meant that his own position would lack some depth but as most of Three Company were looking over a sheer cliff he felt in no danger of being bounced in the night. Irving unslung his American M2 carbine as he reached the flank sangars of his reserve platoon. A sentry lounging behind a tripod-mounted machine-gun hailed him as he passed.

'Shoo akhbar, Sah'b?'

'Kull shee zayn, Hamed,' replied Ross raising an open right palm.

'Hamdu Li'llah,' intoned Hamed in the time-honoured fashion. Hamed would have praised Allah regardless of the state of the news for it was just ritual but one which could not be ignored.

After negotiating the steep, zig-zag track that his own portering jundis had made, Irving reached his command post. The sangar was so low that Irving could rest his elbows on the edge of the roof to steady his binoculars. Two boulder and sandbag wings swept round from the rear walls of the sangar to enclose a small space. Open-ended boxes were set into the walls, filled with primed grenades, rifle magazines, illuminating cartridges and flares. The sangar was low only because Irving's second-in-command had managed to excavate a deep enough hole with a few well-placed charges of plastic explosive. Irving gazed in admiration at his co-patriot's handiwork. On the left parapet by the dark entrance lay a carefully-arranged belt order with a loaded Belgium FAL propped beside it.

'Looks great Shanksy.' He paused to listen for a response. 'You there?'

'In here,' came the reply, the tone indicating that the speaker was being disturbed. Irving dropped down onto the first step and peered blindly into the gloom.

'What are you doing?' There was another pause.

'Putting the Claymores through one box. The illums are on it too ... there.'

'Didn't see any wires?'

'Buried,' the voice in the dark replied.

'Efficient bugger!' Irving started to back out as Shanksy made coming out motions. 'Just hope you don't go sick or something, otherwise I might decimate the company turning on the news.'

'No you won't, I've labelled each one for you and ...' Irving had started beating Shanksy about the head with his bush hat.

'Stop! ... I don't want to hear anymore ... enough!'

'And,' continued the emerging 'Shanksy'. 'I've drawn a map.'

'A map?' echoed Irving, mimicking the other's flat East Midland vowels. 'Well, then, who cares if you go sick.' The two men laughed and flopped down; Irving on the wall, his second-in-command hoisting himself onto the roof-parapet.

Ross recounted the outcome of the meeting with the Colonel and Denby-Smith whilst Shanksy casually scanned the wadis below through his binoculars which he had extracted from his webbing.

'The way Giles goes on you'd think we were expecting human waves of Chinese or something,' said Ross. 'Of course, you know what will happen. We'll just get settled in and they'll move us, just you wait.' Edward Shanks made no comment but had turned over and was now steadying his optics by resting his elbows on the roof-top sandbags. 'Are you listening?'

'Irv. Do the Hawaafi lead or follow their goats?'

'What?' Shanks turned round.

'Do the goat-herds lead or follow their goats?'

'No idea. Why?'

'Well, I can make out about a dozen goats but no goatherd.'

'Let's have a shoofti.' Irving Ross drew his binos and clambered up alongside Shanks. 'Where are we looking?'

'Two ridges back from the main wadi, just below the crest of the left ridge.' There was a pause till Irving found the ridge.

'Got 'em!' he announced. 'Must be a boy somewhere about, a couple, more likely.' They lay still for a minute or so while they examined every crag, cave and bush for a tell-tale sign of human presence.

'Well, then, the news will be out soon enough,' Irving declared, sitting up. 'You'd better tell Mike Cook. Something for the log I suppose; first sighting of the enemy, ten to twelve goats.' They laughed and dropped down into the fighting bay behind the sangar.

Irving made a move up towards the platoon which was to go under command of Two Company.

'I'll go and break the good news to Darweesh and get things along.' Irving picked up his carbine. 'See you for "ackle".'

Edward Shanks watched him go and then picked up the handset of the field telephone and cranked the handle to make contact with the battalion headquarters. Irving Ross whistled softly to himself as he traversed up the steep slope to his left rear platoon headquarters. He had joined the Emirate's Defence Force, as it then was, whilst still on terminal leave from the British Army. He had enjoyed his five year commission but saw the withdrawal from Aden and the Far East as being the end of the good times for the infantry officer. Northern Ireland erupted over a flat-footed Labour Government a few weeks after he had flown into the Emirate's "International" airstrip but he still felt no pang of regret in having gone.

CHAPTER SIX

Three hundred miles South of the Lion Jebel and two hundred miles inland from the aquamarine shallows of the Gulf lay a gravel plain which marked the western borders of the Emirate. There was no border fence or markers of any kind. Nor were there any customs posts or regular patrols by border police for all that was between the Emirate and the Holy Cities of Islam was rock, gravel and sand; the Rub al Khali, the Empty Quarter. The only inhabitants of this gravel strip were the perpetually wandering Bedu and a team of an oil exploration rig which had been drilling and sampling its way across it for the past two years. Neither had found any reason to stay longer than strictly necessary. The midday sun made the landscape dance to a constantly shimmering rhythm in a temperature averaging 120°F; the glass-clear nights stilled the air to a chill pre-dawn 50°F.

On the morning of D+1 of Operation Saladin fifteen camels swayed gently to a halt. Ten of the camels had riders. Though no two were dressed the same, their bearing and manner distinguished them as not being just a party of Bedu. Three wore cotton fatigue trousers, the remainder were bare-legged under faded, grey or khaki dishdashes; the traditional ankle length cotton shirt of the region. Each wore a headcloth but again some wore it khaifaya style, secured with the black agal rope around their heads and draped across their faces and shoulders. Others wore it as a turban, the tasselled ends swinging gently with the see-saw motion of the rider. Each carried a rifle, slung across his back. Four different models could be identified; Lee Enfield No. 4s, Belgian FNs, a Garand and an ancient Mannlicher. As much as this little band appeared to be a quartermaster's nightmare, they were, never-the-less, regular soldiers of the Emir's armed forces.

The lead rider turned and gestured to one of those following in his tracks. The fourth rider gently urged his beast forward with a touch of his camel-stick and after a few bouncing strides reigned it in alongside the leader. A word or two later and following some spreading of hands over the plain, the fourth rider urged his mount to kneel. The remainder followed suit with the occasional belching protest from some of the beasts. The riders dismounted and proceeded to follow a ritual of stretching and rubbing themselves whilst they chattered away in their peculiar brand of Arabic. The leader took a few paces away from the group and stood, feet apart, gently tapping his leg with his camel stick. He brought his left hand up to his half-covered face and drew back the khaifaya, flicking it back over his left shoulder. He felt a welcome coolness as the fragile desert wind evaporated the perspiration that had been trapped beneath the chequered cloth. He wetted his right forefinger and held it up to judge what wind there was. Satisfied as to the strength and direction, he took a few paces forward across the blue-grey gravel and looked about him.

'Ya'lla!' he snapped, turning on his heel. The chattering camel-riders were instantly silenced. 'Tarteeb a' Tayarra!' He waved his camel stick to indicate the flat stretch of desert behind him. 'Bin Saad sawee shai.'

The little band erupted into a babble of Bedu chatter as the riders started pulling packs off their mounts and running out to where their leader had pointed; like children out of class. The arrival of an aircraft was still held to be a novelty though they set about clearing and marking the landing strip with practised ease. Khalifa bin Saad squatted down to carry out his privileged task of making tea. The leader came over to him and sank down, cross-legged, opposite. He took out a packet of State Express filter tips. After giving one to bin Saad, he lit both and watched his men clearing away stones.

This was the seventh year in the Emirate for John Rolls and he was enjoying it. As second-in-command of the Border Scout Regiment he was not obliged to do anymore than just visit the patrols. The Bedu officers and wakeels were quite capable but Rolls preferred the hardships of the gravel plains to the tedium of the regimental base even with its newly built swimming pool and barbecue. The patrol's meanderings were rarely interrupted by anything more than the occasional inter-tribal taqlif over well rights. To Rolls the patrols held the dual charms of the desert and the Bedu. The desert, because it held a spiritual fascination for him as it had for generations of travellers before him. The unearthly beauties of the dawn and dusk coming as prologue and epilogue to both the unremitting challenge of the day and the numinous settings of the night. The Bedu, too, held such men in a similar spell. As with other aboriginal people, they lived in a special relationship with their environment which was the envy of men such as Burton, Lawrence and Thessinger, John Rolls was, likewise, entrapped by this two fold enchantment.

Rolls drew deeply on his cigarette and watched the jundis clearing the rudimentary landing strip and putting out marker flares. Another was assembling and testing the VHF radio which he had pulled out of one of the camel's saddle packs. Bin Saad was singing unselfconsciously to himself as he carefully measured water into a blackened pot on top of an old Primus stove. Rolls grinned as bin Saad pulled off his turbaned headcloth to give his collection of tea glasses a cursory wipe. No more than fifteen years old yet the young Bedu affected all of the mannerisms of Arab manhood. His black hair fell over his face and ears in well-oiled ringlets; his beard and moustache still little more than down. The khaki dishdash was belted with a double row of cartridges in hand-tooled leather loops: an ornate khunja sat snugly in its silver inlaid scabbard beneath the buckle. A new Lee Enfield No. 4 rifle lay at this right side.

'Where are you going, bin Da'oud?' he asked in his guttural tribal dialect.

'The General wishes to see me,' Rolls replied.

'God willing, he will make you a colonel,' the young man surmised.

Rolls laughed. 'God willing, but then perhaps tomorrow there may be apricots.'

Bin Saad rocked back with laughter, nearly upsetting the water pot and laughing all the more. Rolls watched him, marvelling that anyone could find such an obscure proverb so funny. An afterthought of sadness soured the joke for him. He felt that the summons to Ayun Rashid and by such expeditious means would signify a one-way trip. He would miss this rag-tag little force. In what army in the world could a senior major be called 'David's son' by his tea-boy and not lose one ounce of respect.

By the time bin Saad had recovered and had poured the boiling water into his assortment of glasses, the other soldiers had gathered round. Rolls lifted out the little teabag by its labelled string and added a lump of sugar from the box in the centre.

'Do you like red tea, Sah'b?' asked one of the jundis, using the more conventional term of respect.

'Yes, when in the mess I have white tea but with the Bedu, red only.'

They continued such banter till a pilot's blasé tones came from the radio set. Rolls leaned over and replied as two of the jundis got up to run over and light the flares. The De Haviland Beaver appeared out of the blue haze after about five minutes. It circled once and came in to a bouncy landing between the smoking flares. Two soldiers lugged Rolls' saddle bags and bed roll over to it.

The pilot sat quietly in the doorway, not wanting to intrude on the Bedus' farewells. The little party formed an untidy line as Rolls walked past unhurriedly, shaking leathery hands, pressing nose to cheeks and clasping their shoulders. The Bedus' love for Rolls ascended to something close to that between parent and child. They followed him to the door and stood in a tight half-circle. There was another long round of hand-shaking and benedictions. John Rolls gave the senior Bedu a mock admonition not to go raiding the Saudis while he was away and climbed up into the rear cabin. His saddle bags and bed-roll were pushed in after him. The Bedu went back to steady their mounts while the Beaver trundled off down wind before turning for take-off. With a juddering roar of its single prop, it charged forward. As the ageing mono-plane lifted wearily into the air, John Rolls exchanged waves with the men crouching by their camels. He felt a desperate pang of leaving within himself and a feeling that he would never see them or the gravel plain again.

CHAPTER SEVEN

According to the Foster's Lager calendar it was 1 September, 1973, but Mike Cook's entry on the command post log sheet had it down as D+4. It was 9.30am and the Australian had just returned from his first civilised breakfast that week. The arrival of the HQ company elements the day before signalled a return to centralised messing for the officers. It was the general practice throughout the Gulf to rise just before dawn and get a useful three hours work done before the sun smothered all motivation.

The ex-patriot's practice of taking a full English breakfast at 9.00 served a secondary purpose of convening the officers without recourse to the radio. The Colonel had, indeed, used this first congregation to remind them of the General's impending visit. WO2 Thompson promptly jumped in with his own reminders about the adjusting of gun and mortar fire onto preselected targets in each company's sector. In minutes the makeshift breakfast-room resembled the floor of the Stockmarket after a devaluation. Mike Cook had sauntered off wondering what they would have left to say at the daily conference proper at 5.00.

The command post was made up of two walls of stone-filled ammunition boxes with a stone and sandbag roof. The open ends were shielded by free-standing blast walls, also made from ammunition boxes. In one half sat Mike Cook, or Ali Mohammed the Regimental Adjutant, at a table cluttered with radio and field telephone handsets. The walls were hung with maps and diagrams showing all of the frequencies, codes and nicknames used to shroud the mundane radio traffic of the day with a modest semblance of secrecy. Partitioned off by a square of black hessian, at Colonel Alastair's insistence, the other half served as the CO's office and briefing room. The notion of formal briefings had disgusted the young Australian who, pointing to his Vietnam experience, suggested that any significant orders were likely to be done face down into a radio handset in between the 'big jobs'.

An overpowering wave of cheap cologne presaged the arrival of Mohammed Zur, the Punjabi chief clerk. The little staff sergeant bowed his glistening curls as he stepped through the blast-wall chicane. An immaculate figure in starched and pressed, green, cotton-drill fatigues, he presented Cook with a plastic tray of papers.

'Signals in, signals out and company returns, siddee,' he announced proudly, flashing a dazzling array of white and gold teeth.

'Oh shit, Chief!' Cook whined, his voice rising.

'Captain Meadows, Sah'b, says no returns, no rations.' The chief clerk rocked his head from side to side.

'Don't wag yer head,' scolded Cook taking the tray.

'Sorry, Sah'b,' said the chief, this time nodding furiously. 'Must remember not to wag head.'

'Jesus.' Cook swung back to his table. The chief backed out into the sunlight. 'Bloody Stan thinks he's back in Blighty.' Cook complained to the silent, uncomprehending signaller at his side. The source of this irritation in his life was the battalion quartermaster, now holding the whip-hand of the supply chain at Harrow. Stan Meadows was an ex-Coldstream Guards quartermaster who had no intention of letting a small matter of operations get in the way of proper stores accounting. His sworn enemies were the three company commanders and their chief negotiator and Trojan Horse, Mike Cook.

Mike was staring at the columns of letters and numbers which composed the strength returns when Colonel Alastair's red face appeared over the blast wall.

'Mike, I'm off to meet the General.' He frowned. 'Aren't you going to change?' Mike Cook looked down to somewhere in the region of his navel then up again at his CO.

'Into what, sir?' The Colonel's eyes bulged slightly, his lips pursing in to words.

'Into ... Into ... Oh never mind!' He turned away and disappeared.

'Am I going to change?' muttered Mike as if green singlet, khaki cut-offs and chukka boots without socks were de rigueur for operations officers the world over. Not that a set of pressed fatigues would have made very much difference to the gangling Aussie graced as he was with over-large forehead, close-set eyes and a sparse tooth-brush moustache. The Colonel was forced to tolerate the ex-Royal Australian Regiment officer's eccentricities simply because the job required the continuity of experience which only the contract personnel could acquire.

The Jet Ranger's skids had barely touched the dust-brown rock of the landing site before Colonel Alastair was trundling forward; bent over almost double as if the slashing blades were threatening inches from his skull. With eyes half shut from the dust, he fumbled with the handle, only succeeding in preventing the General from opening the door from the inside. The omnipresent Chief-of-Staff restrained his continuance and released the General. Alastair Wilson compounded this flustering by trying to begin the briefing before the helicopter had lifted off to re-fuel. All of his opening lines were drowned by engine noise.

The General, himself, ruined Alastair's next move by insisting on going to the gunline instead of to the mess for coffee. He seethed inwardly when the General went straight over to the sergeant-major and greeted him like a long, lost friend. Mr Thompson was stripped to the waist in shorts, a white Beanie hat shading his head. The gunline consisted of four Indian 75mm howitzers and a mixture of British 81mm and American 4.2 inch mortars. The Arab and Baluchi crews were closed up around their oddly matched pieces patiently awaiting Mr Thompson's next utterance.

'We al'as do a spot o' drill' fore we touch the real stuff, sir,' Thompson was explaining, flicking his camel stick towards the waiting gunners.

'How do you manage the plotting with the mortars as well?' the General asked looking round at the proud faces beaming back at him.

'Oh, I've got the wakeel there and three good sharweeshes.' The artillery warrant officer pointed to an ammunition box structure in rear which resembled a fairground shooting gallery with its front open onto the gunline. Brown faces with flashing white teeth could be discerned in the shadows. 'They're not bad in slow time and they're getting better,' he added with a knowing wink.

On leaving the gunline the little party wound its way on towards the headquarters. Colonel Alastair felt it necessary to explain the various factors which influenced his decision to site everything where it was. To spare his General any more of this tedious explanation, Gilbert Dixon diverted his charge in the direction of a row of sandbag-walled tents which house the regimental aid post.

'Is this your RAP, Alastair?' Dixon asked rhetorically.

'Er, yes but would you not ... ?'

'Let's go in and see Panda,' the General offered to his Chief of Staff as if Alastair had disappeared. With a hot, frustrated Wilson in tow the pair strode over to the tent at the end of the line. The end-flaps were rolled back at both ends so they could see a squat, powerfully-built man in silhouette at a trestle table. 'Salaams, Panda,' opened General Welles entering the tent.

'General, I am honoured. Please come inside,' beckoned the occupant, standing up.

Arvin Sadrapandi was the Battalion Medical Officer and a representative of the only other army which seconded its officers to the Emir's forces. Arvin or Sad Panda as he was known to the British ex-patriots was one of those rare professional people who had genuinely put his talents at the service of other people before his own interests. Consequently, at the age of forty two, he was still a captain in the Indian Army Medical Services. Panda had that healthy roundness of most higher caste Hindus. His chubbiness disguised a wrestler's compact muscle groups which packed the sturdy, sixteen stone frame. Born in the Sind, partition had all but ruined his proud family and it was in the sweat and dust of a hundred bazaars that the young Panda fought to pay his way through medical school. His infinite patience and aura of semi-mystical calm contributed more to the morale and welfare of the jundis than any of the Brits would realise; that is with the exception of Harry Shaw.

The General might also have had an inkling of this for, after having sipped his tea, he asked Panda about the morale of the soldiers. The Indian captain thought carefully before answering; aware, perhaps, that his CO was beginning to squirm a little in his canvas chair. He said, in reply, that the younger soldiers were afraid of the Adoo's reputation but it was always the same before first contact. General Welles nodded, not wishing to push him or show over-concern in front of Wilson. He knew that Panda would not be afraid of voicing his concern if it were otherwise. The dark almond-shaped eyes had seen enough action in Kashmir and on the high plateaux of Ladakh, not to be coy in such matters.

After tea in the Medical Officer's tent, the General again

frustrated Alastair's attempts to steer him into the mess by this time electing to climb the hill to One Company's position. The Commander and Colonel Dixon started up the now well-worn path leaving Alastair Wilson to stumble along behind. All three gained the top, their shirts dark and glistening wet. Alastair felt near collapse as his chest pounded and his vision swam. He allowed Peter White to introduce himself and guide the party off to the vantage point of the command-post roof.

The lack of any obvious threat had persuaded Peter White to convert the roof of his command post into a sort of promenade deck complete with canvas chairs, coffee table made from an empty flare box, and a curious railing around two sides made from scaffolding. When asked the purpose of the railing, Peter, rather smugly, explained that he and his second-in-command had taken to watching the sun go down over a gin and tonic and that the railing had become a vital piece of furniture. As if on cue the long blond locks of Faulkener appeared over the rim of the roof followed by a tray on which were four tumblers containing gin and ice cubes. Alongside were jugs of what was assumed to be tonic water and lime juice.

'Well, that's what I call style,' enthused the General pouring some tonic into a glass.

'How the devil do you get the ice?'

'James has a little box of chemicals he bought in Harrods. He makes the tonic water too but it tastes odd to me.'

'Oh, it's jolly good, Peter,' the General said. 'To tell you the truth I was dreading another cardamom tea.' Everyone laughed and even Alastair Wilson looked less anxious. Peter White then proceeded to orientate the two senior officers by pointing out the major features around them. After a few more minutes of general chat about the state of the company, Peter got the impression that the General wanted to be alone with his Chief of Staff and Alastair Wilson. He excused himself to go and start to record artillery and mortar targets from the forward positions.

General Welles began by asking Alastair what his intentions were as far as operations off the jebel were concerned. Alastair felt trapped. With the General lounging in one of the canvas chairs and Dixon leaning back against the cocktail bar, they seemed to stalk him like wolves after a straggling sheep. One reason was that he had been so preoccupied with the defence of the jebel, he had given, virtually no thought to anything else. All of the patrols business was organised by Mike Cook. Past lectures and seminars on minor tactics sprang to mind.

'Well, our exit route will have to be secured,' he spurted out. 'Mine clearance patrols, then some OP's out ...' He was stopped midflow by the General's upraised hand.

'Alastair, you were told that the aim of this little evolution is to place a manned barrier across the adoo's main supply route South.' The General watched for some sign of dissent before continuing. 'You're not going to do it by footling around in your backyard.'

'But we have no idea of the enemy's strength?' pleaded Alastair; now well and truly cornered.

'Which is a good sign, is it not?' Welles continued. 'It's obvious that if the adoo were out there in any numbers at all, he would have hit you by now, yes?'

'I suppose so, but ...'

'But nothing Alastair,' Welles gestured to Gilbert Dixon. 'Gilbert, point out Cub on the map.'

Gilbert Dixon jerked himself upright and, producing a plastic-film covered map from a slim, canvas attaché case, laid it before the unhappy Wilson. The map was neatly overprinted in blue and green ink. He recognised the now familiar contours of the Jebel Assaad, decorated with blue circles. Dixon's finger traced a line eastwards across three grid squares to a small, closely-contoured feature.

'Lion Cub,' he said quietly. Then turning and pointing out at the blue haze over the cocktail bar. 'Not too clear at the moment, but you should have a better view as the sun goes down.' The Force Commander continued as if he and Dixon were selling a car.

'What I want you to do, Alastair, is put a strong platoon out on Cub. Gilbert will lay on extra cabs and the jets will provide a CAP if you want.' Alastair looked stunned.

'What had he been sold?' his mind asked.

'Today is September the first, let's say dawn the third. No, let's say last light tomorrow. Then, that will give them a whole day to dig in. Yes?' Alastair had recovered sufficiently to nod. The General continued, this time to Gilbert Dixon who appeared to be scribbling the details down in his note-book. 'Gilbert, you jack up the nitty-gritty with Mike Cook and I'll nip round the other companies.' Gilbert Dixon smiled, recognising his cue to leave the new owner with the chief salesman for a bit of after-care.

When his chief of staff had disappeared over the brow of the hill, Stewart Welles stood up and went to lean on the cocktail bar.

'Don't worry, Alastair. You've got some first-rate operators here, Primmer, Cook, the young Marine Shanks, they won't let you down.'

'Sir, it's ...' Alastair hesitated. 'It's just that I don't feel that I've had time to consolidate our position ...'

'Consolidate!' the General interrupted, his tone now more menacing than conciliatory. If the young buggers here have had time to think about having sun-downers, it's high time they got off their arses.'

To this, Alastair had no reply. He merely puckered his brow and tried to look as concerned as possible.

'As soon as you have got Cub secured, we'll get the Engineers in and whack up a fence and minefield,' General Welles declared. 'And when that's done we'll crack on and put another out to the West.' He turned to face Alastair. 'Don't worry, Alastair. For God's sake, we're right behind you. No-one expects you to do it all by yourself.'

'Yes, thank you,' was all the unhappy man could muster.

The two men started down the steps when General Welles stopped and turned to him.

'I'm sending you a replacement for Irving Ross. Good man, 2 IC of Border Scouts; very experienced.' He turned to continue his descent. 'Then Irving can go and get himself married at long last.'

CHAPTER EIGHT

John Rolls had been given 48 hours in which to report himself to the Commander, so he had persuaded the Beaver pilot to stay overnight at the Border Scouts' headquarters. This allowed him time to devest himself of a fortnight's worth of dust and grime and to catch up a little on the affairs of the regiment. He was puzzled when his CO told him that he was likely to be transferred to another unit. Normally the only inter-unit transfers for the contract officers occurred when one of their number was killed, injured or sacked. Their equivalent of the bush telegraph had revealed no such reason, so he was naturally curious as to why he was being summoned so expeditiously.

The Border Scout's Regiment was a very small outfit: five squadrons, three camel and two horse, together with a small headquarters element. As with so many of the military organisations in the Gulf it was born out of a long forgotten need and some individual's particular idea of how to fill it. In this case an ex-Trucial Oman Scouts' officer called Buffy Hancock, who at the time was looking for a way of extending his service in the region. The result was a group of British officers who were so individual that they were probably unemployable anywhere else on the planet.

Well paid, they certainly were, by the standards of their contemporaries at home but money was the last reason why they were there. In any case, there was little to spend money on in the regiment's scattered camps and outposts. For some it was a refuge from suburban obligation and the genteel treadmill of middle class existence, for others it was the Shangri La of military life. It was private army where the only laws were that of the sun and the sands.

That afternoon the squadron officers arrived by camel, horse and landrover from all along the Emirate's southern border. The early ones basked in the garden beneath the date palms or found relief in the small swimming pool. In the evening, dressed in the green, white and gold of their mess undress uniforms they would re-create a little of the splendour of a bygone imperial age. The evening had developed from the post-prandial ports to a heavy whisky and brandy session well into the early hours as the ex-patriot officers of the regiment bade farewell to their Mess President. It was as well that Rolls had a full 48 hours because his pilot did not emerge from his bed till past 11.00 the next morning and did not declare himself fit to fly till 3.00 p.m. So it was as the sun was casting deep shadows over Eyoon a'Rashid that the Beaver banked for its approach to the oiled-sand strip which ran parallel to the approach road. The liaison plane bounced down the runway and taxied to a halt. The shame-faced pilot apologised for the landing. A battered Landrover, aimed rather than driven by an ageing Baluch, stopped in a cloud of dust alongside the Beaver.

The saa'iq loaded Roll's cases, bergen and bedroll into the back as John, stiff from the two hour flight, eased himself into the front passenger seat. His bearer, a sullen, bearded man, lifted his own kit into the Rover and climbed into the back. The Rover then hurtled off towards the mess.

The colourful, if perfunctorily swift, tropical twilight combined with the often primitive lighting conditions had presented generations of foreign and colonial Brits with the excuse to drink earlier than would be considered proper at home. The mess members at Eyoon a'Rashid were no exception. The coloured lights strung around the garden bar drew not only the staff officers from the headquarters and the training depot but ex-patriots, service and civilian, from a twenty mile radius of the capital. The hard core of the advance guard would seize the favoured vantage points from which to catch the barman's eye soon after 5.00 p.m. Laying-in a reserve of horse's necks, gin and lime or lagers, they would await the main force of staff officers and service corps advisers who trooped in by department. The work groups would spend half an hour together before members slipped away to re-enforce other groups or spontaneously coalesced to form special interest parties. Mess boys in long white dishdashes and red sashes, glided under and between rising elbows and clenched glasses till 7.00 when the officers started to melt away into the darkness. By 7.30 here would be just Ghulam, the barman, and the hard corps; a valiant rearguard awaiting the return of re-enforcements who were dining-in.

The last vestiges of John Roll's hangover disappeared with his first gin and loomee of the evening. The western sky was fading after a brief spectacle in red and yellow over the Central Plateau and sun-downers was in full stride. Rolls was still in his day dress of bush-jacket and slacks as were most of the officers on the patio. He had never felt at ease in the headquarters. The austerity of the desert living made his tall frame gaunt and he seemed to tower over the generally plumper specimens here in Eyoon a'Rashid. He felt disapproval in older staffers' eyes at his beard and darkly sunburned skin. He wanted to tell them that he would have shaved but for the fact that he would then be left with a two-tone face; for he really was white underneath.

'It's alright, I haven't gone native just yet,' he nearly re-assured every new face to whom he was introduced. No-one had ever stopped Arab Officers from attending sundowners, it was just that they never came. Most of the locals did drink despite the prohibitions of the Koran but they preferred to be more discreet. Rolls had begun to feel of late, more at ease in the company of Arabs than he did with these headquarters lurkers.

It was 18.50 hours. Rolls glanced at the wall clock over the head of the ordnance major who was informing him of the introduction of new, boxed dry-rations from Pakistan. A squarely built man with a balding head and a Pancho Villa moustache caught his eye. The man's eyes smiled and his right hand rose in front of the moustache and flicked an invisible glass. Rolls excused himself to the self-absorbed commissary and made his way to the bar.

'One with loomee and one with tonic, Ghulam.' The moustachioed officer turned to Rolls, jabbing out his hand.

'Johno, Keyf haal? How's the border?'

'Fine, Hank, see you're still in this circus.' Roll's eyes indicated the hubbub behind him. The ends of Hanks moustache tweaked up as he grinned.

'Gives you something to look forward to, when you wake up. What's Buffy doing these days?'

'Hawking.' Rolls watched a look of surprise raise Hank's eyebrows. 'The Wali of Shahaboon gave him a Saker and he's becoming quite an expert.' Hank motioned him with an inclination of his head towards the edge of the patio.

'I suppose you know what's on the cards for you?' he said quietly.

'I presumed it was to take over from someone in the "geysh",' Rolls answered using the colloquial term for regular army units.

'Well, I shouldn't want to give anything away,' Hank started. The staff officer glanced carefully left and right melodramatically. 'You're to replace Irving Ross in Third Battalion.' Hank watched for reaction in the tall major's pale eyes. John Rolls stared back blankly.

'So what's happened to Irving?'

'Nothing!' Rolls smiled weakly and made to turn away from what was developing into a non-conversation. Hank grasped his forearm and added desperately. 'He's on Saladin!' Hank scrutinised John's face for any further sign of cognisance. Then in exasperated tones, 'God! Don't you people read any signals?' Rolls shrugged.

'I've been out in the Jalaahat for two weeks.' Hank groaned and taking Rolls in a fresh grip around the shoulders steered him back towards the bar.

'After you've seen the Old Man, pop in for an Int brief. I'll fill you in then. Hey, its gone seven; I've got drinks downtown. He drained his glass and releasing Rolls made for the main hall.

'See you' bukra.' John Rolls raised his glass to Hank's back and watched him disappear.

The patio was beginning to empty, so Rolls made his way through the gardens towards a line of chalets that served as accommodation. A figure came swiftly and silently out of the deep shadows by the end wall. It stopped a yard short of Rolls and leaned forward from the waist, hands proffered forward, a thin bundle of letters between the fingers.

'Thank you, Din,' Rolls said, not in Arabic but in Urdu, 'I have to see the General at eight, wake me at six.' The man nodded. 'You have a bed?' The silent man nodded again. 'God be with you, Din.' Din bowed, turned and merged again with the shadows.

After showering Rolls sat in his towel on the edge of the bed and stared at the total sum of his possessions; a folding suitcase, a bergen rucksack, a set of personalised webbing equipment and a cardboard box of books. Not much for a colonel's eldest son at thirty-five. He leaned forward and picked up the still unopened letters. Discarding the monthly demands of his book club and American Express, he held the other two, one in each hand. One was addressed in the deliberate and precise backhand of his former wife, Caroline. The other was in the carefully fashioned scrawl of his daughter Miranda, now in her third term at boarding school. He squeezed both envelopes between his fingers, no photographs. He tossed them onto the writing table in no good mood for reading, God, he hoped Hank Mullen was right and that he was to replace Irving Ross. He couldn't stand to be a lurker here at Eyoon. That was, above all, the best aspect of the desert; you never looked back. No time for anything but the job.'

He checked his watch and made a move to finish drying himself and get dressed. Thirty-five years old. What would he have been if he had stayed in the Brigade. Company commander? perhaps, staff doggy in Brigade or Hong Kong Garrison more likely? And Caroline, dear Caroline, an embryonic Colonel's lady since puberty. Her face when he told her he was leaving! He smiled painfully at the image whilst tying his tie. 'Yes, why did he leave, now? Winding up of Confrontation? Cutting back of the Gurkha Brigade? Returning to England to take one's place in the mainstream of army life; School of Infantry, Staff College, desk job in the MOD. Or was it something else? He picked up a red bandana handkerchief, thrust it into his pocket and stepped out into the scented air of the garden.

'Sod it! A bottle of wine with 'dins' and then find some pilots to drink with; then I'll think no more till morning.' He strode off towards the brightly lit veranda of the mess.

By 11.30 he was indeed in the company of pilots and had ceased to ponder the mistakes of his past or concern himself very much with anything more than his immediate future. The assembled company had advanced to the stage where they thought nearly anything was funny. The star attraction at that moment was a helicopter pilot who was attempting to balance on twin columns of lager cans in emulation of a circus trick he claimed to have once seen. Wobbling furiously three cans high, he was trying to place a fourth under his left foot with the aid of his assistant's head. The sound of splashing and high-pitched, female laughter suddenly distracted his audience. The erstwhile circus star sprawled backwards into the flower beds; empty lager cans scattered over the concrete.

'God! Fanny!' exclaimed one pilot, craning his neck for a confirmatory sighting. The assembled rose almost as one. The sound of splashing and female laughter continued. Like pilgrims drawn to the sight of a miracle, they made their way slowly yet purposefully towards the pool.

The drinking party re-assembled in the light at the end of the pool; blinking in the glare of the sodium lights. Two young, white females in bikinis frolicked with three young men in the flashing greens and blues of the pool. A collective groan rose from at least half the drinkers.

'It's Sally and Kate.' With the exception of John Rolls they drifted back into the darkness.

'Rolly.' A cry of recognition came from the water. A shapely silhouette carved a wake through the phosphorescent green. A round-faced, near-naked nymph pulled herself from the water, slicked back her long hair and bounded towards him. 'Rolly, where have you been?' Rolls felt a shock of cold as Sally Welles flung her arms around his neck and pressed her wet body against him. She strained up and planted a cold, wet kiss on his lips. 'Are you staying?' she asked, arching her head back. Recovering from the initial shock of impact, Rolls enclosed his arms around her firm waist. She felt like a wet, inflated inner tube.

'Sally, good to see you.' She kissed him again and then a broad grin broke across her sea-sprite's face. The little, bobbed nose wrinkled as her large, glassy eyes examined his face. She shook her head.

'Say you are staying.'

'I don't know. Have to see your dad tomorrow.'

'I'll tell him to post you here ... as my personal bodyguard!' She allowed her front teeth to peek coyly over her lip.

'C'mon Sal! He's not your personal property yet.'

'Hi, Kate!' Rolls looked around Sal's head to see her older sister looking up from the side of the pool. Kate had the same wide mouth and large eyes as Sally but was darker and had better facial bones. She offered up a slim hand.

'Besides, I get first choice; privilege of rank.' Sally released her grip on Roll's neck to allow him to reach down and grasp Kate's hand. He pulled and she rose halfway out before lodging a foot on the side. 'Now!' she cried, heaving herself backwards. Rolls felt himself arch forwards. A shriek and a push from behind and his world turned a swirling universe of green. Chlorinated water filled his nose and mouth. He thrashed about briefly. He surfaced, mouth full of water. Kate pounced on him, sucking at his lips and running her fingers through his beard.

* * *

Under a single 40-watt bulb in the battalion command post Mike Cook and Alan Primmer sat in front of the main map.

'Have another?' Mike Cook offered, holding out a half-empty bottle of Glenmorangie.

'No, thanks.' Alan Primmer shook his head. 'Haven't finished this one yet.' He put his glass down and picked up a note pad in front of him. 'Got to get my head down too.' His finger stopped on one of the underlined sub headings on the grimy lined paper.

'Don't worry about fire support,' the Australian said. 'Eddie Shanks will stay with you till the last lift. He'll adjust any targets for you and bring the jets in should you get bounced. Harry will take care of loading your boys and all the stores from this end and so just take your time over there, okay?'

'Harry's quite an operator isn't he?' said Alan relaxing in his chair.

'Too right, and he doesn't make a show of it either,' added Mike. 'Right, is that all I can do for you.' Alan glanced through the notes in front of him.

'Yes, that's about it. I wish the Old Man had let on a bit sooner.'

'Don't think he knew himself till the Commander came. Been in a bluey all afternoon.'

'Operation Cub then.' Alan raised his glass before draining it.

'Here's luck to you.' Mike raised his glass, then added, 'And to roulement; I'm bored with this one already.'

Thirty yards away Colonel Wilson put down his wife's letter and watched the date on his watch change to 3 Sept. He turned the paraffin storm lamp out and lay back in the inky darkness. He thought of his cottage in Fife, his rosy cheeked wife, his two Springer spaniels and wondered if an eternity on gardening leave was not better than another day on Jebel Assaad.

CHAPTER NINE

John Rolls downed the milky tea which Din Mohammed had placed on the bedside table. His head throbbed and he felt slightly nauseous. Reaching for his towel, he lurched across the room to the sliding glass door. He pulled it open to suck in the moist, early morning air. The gardens were already washed pink by the, as yet, unrisen sun. Recovering a little, he retreated back into the bathroom to wash away his hangover under the shower.

By 06.30 all but the most senior officers on Eyoon a'Rashid were in or around their offices. The little colonial fort was a living hive of clerks, messengers and drivers. Rolls made his way up onto the balcony. Dressed in the light sand-coloured barrack dress of the Scouts, complete with blue- and white-checked shemargh and camel stick, he felt awkward and conspicuous, amongst the olive green geysh. He found the office of the General's aide, a seconded Irish Hussar with a mop of dark curls.

'By God! It must be Lawrence!' the young captain cried, cheekily.

'That's enough from you, Donal, I feel like I'm from a different planet as it is,' Rolls replied wearily.

'Come in, do,' said Donal sweeping a hand invitingly towards a cane chair. 'Shai? The Old Man's not in yet.' Rolls flipped up a social salute as he entered and sat down. He drew back the ends of the shemargh and flicked them back over his shoulders while the aide organised his clerks next door into bringing morning tea.

'Any idea what this is about, Donal?' Rolls fished.

'No.' Donal shook his head, smiling blandly. 'and I wouldn't tell you if I did, would I now?' Rolls smiled.

'I don't know how you keep this job down. I really don't.'

'Sally needs my body.'

'Dirty little devil.'

'Who, me or Sally?' Donal grinned. 'You've been too long in the desert. Anyway, perhaps you're to be added to the collection.'

'Collection?'

'Yes, Sally and Kate's.' Rolls laughed at the thought.

'You're disgusting, Donal. A disgrace to your race.'

Their banter was interrupted as a large figure flashed across the doorway. They heard the door open in the adjacent office.

'Tea, Donal?'

'Coming, sir.' Donal made a knowing face and leapt smartly up from his desk to open the inter-office door, just in time, to allow the tray-bearing teaboy an unimpeded journey. Rolls smiled in appreciation at such a polished routine. 'Major Rolls is here, sir,' Donal announced from the doorway.

'Has he got tea, yet?' Donal turned his head in time to see one of the clerks holding out a cup and saucer.

'Of course, sir.'

'Well, send him in then.' John Rolls stood up, took the tea from the clerk and strode into the General's office.

'Good morning, sir,' he opened. The General came from behind his desk and indicated two chairs by a coffee table.

'Good to see you, John. Sit down.' His smile was cordial, his tone tentative. The General was leafing through a signal pack. ''S'cuse me, a moment,' he said, without looking up.

John looked around the office; plain, white wall, issue furniture, a few plaques, photographs and other momentos of past Force commanders and their visitors. There was very little of General Welles about the room; almost as if he preferred to be anonymous. The General scribbled occasionally with a red ballpoint pen and folded the annotated sheet back so that it would stick out; all in silence. Coming to the end of the second pack he spoke again.

'How's Buffy.' He stood up and returned the signal pack to Donal's office. 'How are the Saudis behaving?' rummaging through his desk for a small cigar. He continued in this vain until he was sitting again across the coffee table from Rolls. He paused to draw deeply on the cigar and appeared to be deciding how to frame his next remark.

'You were hoping to take over from Buffy when he retires next year, weren't you?' he asked quietly. John felt a sudden emptiness in his stomach.

'Well, yes I presumed so; being 2 IC.' He was stopped by a raised forefinger.

'That's fine,' Welles said. 'Nothing has changed. I just want to use your experience to help us through a tricky patch.' He watched for signs of relief or protest in the major's eyes. 'You'll know that we have a largish op on right now. Third Battalion has been dropped out some eighty miles north of Harrow to put in a wire and mine barrier.' Rolls nodded. 'I want you to take over from Irving Ross. Nothing wrong with Irving, except he had to postpone his wedding.' Again Rolls nodded. The General drew on his cigar and leaned forward. 'Nothing wrong with Third Battalion; good officers, good unit. It's just that they were only brought up to strength in March and this is their first show. You've seen action with One Battalion in the Wadi Naqeed.' Rolls nodded again, now feeling a faint thrill dancing through him. 'There's been no contacts yet, but shouldn't be too long in coming.' The General paused. He leaned back and jabbed out the crux of the message. 'I want you in there as my belt and braces, John, just in case.'

The interview ended shortly afterwards and Rolls found himself out on the balcony, faintly intoxicated by the prospect of action once more. He had reached the double offices by the first flight of stairs when Hank Mullen barred his way with his bulk and diverted him through a door and a bead curtain into a brightly lit, windowless room. Maps and charts covered the walls and desks. The far end of the room looked like a drawing office. Two Baluchi clerks poured over maps and air photographs, in a far corner. The only other occupant was as tall and as thin as Hank was not. He wore gold-rimmed glasses and had the hands of a concert pianist.

After ushering John through the door, Hank appeared at his side and swept the room with a imperial hand.

'Welcome to the shop,' he beamed up at Rolls. 'That's Geoff, he's a professional; Int Corps.'

'Geoff Pullen,' said the thin, young intelligence officer, walking between the desks to shake hands.

'Taking over Two Company from Irving, right?' Hank bubbled.

'Yes, just for the duration of ... What's this thing called?'

'Saladin.' Hank's little round eyes blazed with enthusiasm. 'Great, now we're getting somewhere.' Rolls felt as if he was a precision tool suddenly thrust into the hands of some impoverished inventor. Hank rubbed his chubby hands together then hooked Roll's arm and drew him away to a corner desk whilst looking over his shoulder at the Baluchi clerks with theatrical wariness.

'What do you know about the North-West sector?'

'Not a lot.' John allowed himself to be seated in front of a large-scale map.

'Geoff, give him the business.' The Intelligence Corps officer gave Rolls a short but comprehensive account of events leading up to the mounting of Operation Saladin. The geysh had spent four grim seasons between the summer rains and the winter drought trying to dislodge the Hawaafi from the southern bounds of their domain. It was as futile as punching fog. The mountain men on the other hand, used their mortars and rocket launchers to maximum effect on the villages and towns of the fertile Plain of Sweet Water. Most of the contract officers had began to accept the stalemate with the same fatalism of their jundis but now there was an impatient optimism in the air. Even Hank was infected with it.

When he had finished, Hank Mullen drew his chair closer to Rolls and became conspiratorial once more.

'The strange thing is that the decision to put the line through Jebel 'Assaad was made over the head of the Old Man. In fact, Chief of Staff has got us trying to find out why.'

'What do you think?' asked Rolls.

'I think that as Third Battalion makes us up to a brigade, his Nibs wants to show off to his relatives and do a brigade size op.' Hank leaned back, satisfied with his perception.

'What's the CO like?' This made Hank sit upright again, spittle bubbling at his lips. An angry V-shaped furrow appeared in the middle of his brow.

'A right tosser!' he hissed. 'Came in here last May for his joining brief. Didn't listen to a word. I got the whole story of him and his jocks in the Radfan; how they sorted out Aden, Sharjah, Bloody Wilson Pasha, I call him.' Hank paused to appreciate the look of resigned horror spreading over Roll's face. He leaned forward and gently tapped the desk in front of Rolls. 'But, come the brief for Saladin ... all changed. He was shitting himself ... I can tell you, but for Mike Cook and their QM, they wouldn't have got as far as Harrow. You've got your work cut out there, Johno.' Rolls leaned back and rubbed his beard.

'Is Harry Shaw still 2IC?' he asked.

'Yes, just about. Wilson Pasha can't stand him but the Old Man won't hear of a posting.'

'Good.' John Rolls stood up and stretched. 'At least I'm not going to be lurking around here.'

'You'll be pleading to be my Shai-wallah within a week,' rejoined Mullen following him to the door. Rolls had just reached the threshold when the metal-sheeted door swung slowly inwards. A small figure in tribal dress, complete with slung Lee Enfield stood half-framed against the sky.

'Abu Issa!' exclaimed Mullen moving forward to grasp a leathery right hand. The old man wished peace upon Mullen and half-turned to Rolls.

'Major Rolls of the Border Scouts, I believe.' John Rolls felt his mouth fall open with shock. The shaiba continued in faultless and accentless English. 'The Beni Qaisaa have told me of your wisdom and justice, Major. They hold you in high regard.'

'Well, thank you,' Rolls managed to say. The old Arab in tribesman's clothes shook his hand with more than perfunctory warmth. 'Where did you learn your English, if I may ask?'

'My father believed that education was a form of family investment and sent me to England when I was twelve. He wanted me to be a doctor so that he would be looked after in his old age.' He held out his arms to indicate his clothes. 'Alas! I wandered from my appointed path.'

'Abu Issa's come down to fill us in on the Adoo,' explained Hank.

'I'd like to stay,' said Rolls, 'but I've got to catch the midday Islander.'

'Cheers! Hank, Geoff.' He shook hands with the smiling Abu Issa. 'Ba'ashoof'ak, ya Sheik,' he promised.

'In sha'allah,' replied the old man.

* * *

Aside from Rolls and his bearer, Din Mohammed, the only other passenger was a young Briton who had been bundled aboard just as the Islander was about to taxi out onto the runway. The noise of the twin props drowned all but shouted hellos. The young man had then spent the entire two hour flight with his nose pressed against his window; so it was only after they had landed and disembarked that the lad introduced himself.

'Hello, Richard Callender. I've just come out.'

'John Rolls.' They shook hands and then loaded their baggage onto the back of a Landrover which had drawn up alongside the Islander. Rolls sat beside the driver, Callender clambered onto the back of the open Landrover with Din. Rolls was immediately conscious of being carefully scrutinised along with Din, their weapons and equipment. The driver roared off across the landing strip and into a maze of tents and tin-roofed huts. They stopped in a cloud of dust outside one of the larger, single storey huts. With some attempt at a garden around the front door, it could only have been the Officers' Mess.

Leaving Din to sort out rooms for Callender and himself, Rolls led the way through a small entrance lobby into a long dark room dominated by a spacious and well-stocked bar. Rolls shivered in the chill of the air conditioning. The two occupants of the bar looked up from the backgammon board between them. The barman stiffened to attention and displayed a yellow, toothy grin. His silver haired opponent half-turned on his bar stool and took the cigarette off his lower lip.

'Ali, a beer for the major,' he croaked. The barman, whose actual given name was Masool, ducked down and delved into a cool-box behind him.

'Stan, Keyf haal?' asked Rolls.

Stan Meadows had retired from the British Army after a distinguished thirty-seven years; from drummer boy to Regimental Sergeant-Major and then through a Quarter-Masters' Commission to Major. For the last ten years of his service he toyed with and then treasured the idea of owning a profitable, little newsagents and tobacconists. He lasted six months. He was never quite sure what had been worse; the trivia-bound world of his customers or a wife whose constant company he had never known for more than six weeks without a break since they married. He escaped back into a world he knew and understood.

Resigned to die in harness, he was happy; so was his wife. Stan smoked as if tar and nicotine were his life force; a smoker's smoker. Every afternoon he would settle onto the corner barstool to smoke, drink, talk and play backgammon through to the small hours, pausing only to shower or dine. Perched on his stool, squinting through the smoke and railing against the world, he had always reminded Rolls of Lewis Carroll's pontificating caterpillar.

'Stan, this is Richard Callender,' Rolls said, suddenly remembering the young man behind him.

'Pleased to meet you, sir,' Callender said, reaching around Rolls to offer his hand.

'You a flyer, then?' rasped Stan.

'Oh no, I'm Ordnance.' Stan look non-plussed.

'I didn't know we had any?' The young officer laughed as if it were a common misunderstanding.

'No, I've come to join the Battalion; number three, isn't it?' Stan turned to Rolls.

'Nobody said ow't to me?' Stan said as if apologising to Rolls. Calender's face clouded in doubt. John Rolls shrugged and picked up the glass that Masool had just poured.

'I don't think he'd lie about it, Stan.' Stan turned back to Callender.

'You'd better have a beer then.' He gestured towards his heart. 'Bloody Rag And Oil Company! Do you think I'm being sacked?' The tension in Callender's face broke a little. 'Ali, another beer.' He lit another cigarette from the butt of the first. He leaned out from the bar and made a show of looking Callender up and down. 'We'll have to dig out a set of kit then.'

'Do me one too, Stan,' said Rolls. 'All I've got is Scout's "theeyab".'

'Ok, I'll ring the RQ.' Stan peered up at the brass-cased clock over the spirit racks. 'Half three. I'll get a Rover here at five!' He gestured to Masool for a battered field telephone which lay beneath the counter. Rolls turned to the much relieved Callender.

'Well, here's to us new boys. Sihaatak!'

'Cheers.' Calender smiled, happy that he had found some friendship, some acceptance.

Stan was having difficulty in making himself understood to whoever was on the other end of the field telephone line. Promising to "sort the stupid Babu out", he downed his beer in a fierce gulp and stalked out.

Callender became more relaxed and over a second and third beer attempted to regale Rolls with personal experiences of school, Sandhurst and life as a subaltern in the Ordnance Corps. Rolls indulged him by listening patiently, only interrupting to verify the existence of mutual acquaintances. It then occurred to him that these men whom he once knew as lieutenants and junior captains were now majors and lieutenant-colonels. Was he that old? What must he seem to them? Some kind of military Peter Pan? He remembered the letters in his pocket and felt the urge to read them.

'Look Richard, it's half four. I want to check that Din's got my kit organised,' he lied. 'Let's find your room and I'll meet you out front at five.' The very voluble Callender agreed and followed him out.

* * *

The last of the AB 205s released its cargo net and with a clattering roar began its spiralling climb to join the remainder of the squadron. Alan Primmer sat back against the edge of the shallow hole which was to be his refuge for the coming night. The throb of the departing helicopter was rapidly fading to a hum as it reached 3000 feet. The rest of the squadron was orbiting in a sequence of changing formations; three Vs, echelon, arrowhead.

'Must be bored,' thought Primmer.

'Hello, Man Cub. This is the vet. How's your balls?' Alan reached forward and picked up the Panasonic.

'Okay, Mike, last Hotel clear of my location, over.' He looked instinctively towards the setting sun, seeing the main feature of Lion as a grey-blue silhouette against a furnace glow of red and orange.

'Roger, Alan.' Mike Cook's voice settled down to his usual, laconic, Melbourne drawl. 'You do your DFs now, Sheldrake acknowledge, over.'

'Roger,' Alan answered.

'Copied!' chipped in Mr Thompson. Alan scrambled forward to the edge of his shellscape.

'Stand-to!' he shouted, holding up his carbine. Every man stopped what he was doing; heads bobbed up out of half-finished sangars. 'Stand-to!' he yelled again this time turning to his left. One or two of the jundis dived for their weapons and equipment. For a second Alan wondered why they looked so shocked. Then he realised what they were thinking and shouted again, 'Stand-to, Tamreen al midfaryah.' He felt a wave of relief flood back to him as the jundis relaxed and immediately scrambled into their shell-scrapes and sangars, pulling on their webbing, grabbing their weapons. Artillery practice was, on the whole, a fair description of what he was about to do. He tugged his map-case out of its niche in the parapet wall and selected one of the blue crosses onto which he would call down gun and mortar fire from Lion. He had never had to bring down defensive fire for real and even doubted how effective it would be in such a broken landscape. It was a comforting ritual, all the same.

Picking up the transceiver, he spoke the short liturgy of his fire order and then waited for the familiar Geordie tones of Mr Thompson to read it back. He looked out towards Lion, now indistinguishable against an indigo skyline. He saw a flash. A dull plume of smoke in the distance. A rolling bang followed.

'Shot one, two zero,' intoned the Panasonic.

'Shot one, two five,' responded Alan. He turned and looked out over the dull outlines of his right forward section across to a parallel ridge. He held his breath in child-like anticipation. An orange flash, an instant cloud of black smoke on the pink-brown slopes. A sharp crump. He took a deep breath and held up the Panasonic. 'On! One round fire for effect.' He turned to Mohammed Sadeek, his senior platoon commander and second-in-command.

'Watch this, Mohammed,' he said in Arabic. Four flashes flickered against the now uniformly dark, mass of the Assaad. Mr Thompson's controlled voice announced the shells' departure with a curt 'Shot out.' The rumbling report echoed around the hillside. The target hillside erupted in a short, shaking chaos of orange and black.

Alan Primmer was heartened by the sight. Though he was now well into the third year of his contract, he never felt completely secure when he was alone with the soldiers. It was always a comfort to have another Brit around; even if it was Giles. He despised himself for what he recognised as a fundamental weakness. Resolving to shake off his secret fears, he buckled on his belt order and leaving Mohammed Sadeek in charge of the headquarters, went off to check the mortar targets from the forward section's positions.

CHAPTER TEN

John Rolls was woken by the sound of his door being carefully closed. The first glimmering of dawn brought dim colour to the thin, cotton curtains. He sat up, grimacing at the sour after taste of the previous night's drinking. He caught the sweet smell of tea on his bedside table. Reaching out he felt for the cup. A neat pile of clothing lay beside the cup. Switching on the bed-side light, he found his new, green fatigue dress freshly washed and pressed; on top lay the green and white chequered shemargh of the Third Battalion; the edges now neatly fringed, the corners drawn skilfully into horse-tail tassels.

'Silly Sod,' thought Rolls affectionately. 'Must have been up all night.' Putting aside Din Mohammed's handiwork, he swung his feet out onto the matted floor and went over to peer into the dark mirror over the wash basin. It had been a good night. Stan had ruthlessly hammered all-comers at his beloved backgammon. The Huey pilots were in high spirits: Jebel Assaad was just a milk run now.

Rolls emerged into a fresh-aired dawn to find Din and a driver waiting in an open Landrover. Both greeted him in their respective tongues. As Rolls took the front passenger seat, he exchanged his small field pack for a webbing belt slung with ammunition and water-bottle pouches.

'Where's Mr Callender?' asked Rolls.

Din tipped his head towards the airstrip. 'He has walked, Sah'b,' he added. Then he passed Rolls a canvas gun-case.

As the Rover meandered through the camp towards the strip, Rolls extracted a gleaming Kalashnikov, its shining black metal flashing in the rays of the climbing sun. The red-brown stain of the stock and butt shone warmly.

'Tamaam bundokeeya, Siddi,' commented the driver. It was indeed. A brand new AKM (Avtomat Kalashnikova Modernaya), dated 1972, that the Scouts had found in an arms cache near the border. Rolls handed the case back to Din. He pulled a pair of motor-cycle goggles from one of the pouches on his belt and settled them over his shemargh.

'Thank you for doing my shemargh, Din,' he said, turning round.

'No thanks required, Sahib, my duty,' Din replied, bowing his head.

'You spoil me, Din.'

The helicopters were dispersed along the far side of the landing strip, each half-hidden in makeshift bays made from sand-filled oil drums. On the camp side were lines of boxes, barrels and other stores, all sorted into rows by commodity; at right-angles to the runway like passengers waiting to board. Here and there jundis, faces swathed in their headcloths against the comparative chill of the morning, moved slowly about carrying boxes or trailing cargo nets. A dust coloured tanker hummed amidst a crowd of black plastic barrels; its attendant lethargically distributing water with a hose. An aging Bedford whined along unnecessarily in four-wheeled drive; its open back packed with boxes and a cold, pathetic huddle of soldiers. A Landrover crossed its tracks and jolted to a halt, a clutch of stiff-limbed, bleary-eyed pilots stumbled awkwardly from the back and made their separate ways towards their machines. It was a scene repeated daily in varying forms on small military airfields around the world.

Rolls' Landrover pulled up alongside a makeshift shelter constructed out of filled ammunition boxes and corrugated iron. Callender was sitting in the middle of a group of soldiers who seemed more than usually animated for that time of the morning. One of the privates was binding the long edge of a stiff, new shemargh around Callender's brow. The soldier shook his head in frustration as he tried to tuck away the unyielding corners to the accompanying shrieks of laughter from his companions. He gave up, fluttering his hands about his head. Callender smiled at Rolls.

'You don't speak Arabic?'

'Not a word, only on attachment, you see. Not worth it for the time,' Callender explained. Rolls laughed.

'They were saying that you looked like a 'magnoon,' a lunatic.'

'I gathered that,' grinned Callender. 'Magnoon, I'll remember that,' he said in mock reproval of the surrounding jundis.

Just then a canvas-topped Landrover roared into view from behind a row of bundled sandbags. It was followed by a large Dodge pick-up. The jundis stiffened at the sight and scuttled away to where their packs and rifles lay. Their alarm was contagious for out of hiding-holes and gaps in the rows of stores emerged sleepy-eyed and yawning, a horde of green and khaki figures. The two vehicles stopped in front of the make-shift caboose. Stan climbed out of the Landrover and motioned to the passenger in the front of the Dodge. The Regimental Quarter-Master Sergeant eased his awesome bulk out of the cab and waddled round to where Stan stood with Rolls.

'Kanda Bux,' said Stan. 'You know Major Rolls and Mr Callender?' The Baluch warrant officer bowed his head as much as his chins would allow.

'Good morning, Sahibs, I trust the uniforms are fitting?'

'Tutori, Wakeel,' replied Rolls. 'Thank you, they are fine.' Kanda Bux smiled.

'Right Kandy, get'em going,' snapped Stan. The fat man spun round and started bellowing in deep, bullfrog belches and waving his fleshy arms about. The assembled horde of stores handlers dived away to carry out his bidding. Kanda Bux turned back to the Englishmen. Stan stood inside the shelter undoing a flask of tea. He thrust a mill-board out at the RQMS.

'Here you are, Kandy. Put the Major's party on number one,' and then to Rolls and Callender, 'You'll make breakfast on Lion then.' The Baluch scanned the manifest sheets and then stumped off to give terse directions to a handful of stores NCOs who in turned doubled away to their respective dumps.

'I think I'll have to put old Kandy Box on a diet,' mused Stan, staring out through the steam of his tea. 'If he has a heart attack or anything now, I'd be well and truly up shit creek, I can tell you.'

Rolls smoked and watched as the daily routine of the air-head got off into first gear. Cargo nets were laid put by the NCOs at set intervals between the oiled landing strip and the rows of stores. Jundis then trotted or staggered out, depending on the weight of the load, and placed their burdens in the nets. Everything to sustain five hundred fighting men, from their food and water to bullets in their rifles and the sandbags they hid behind, had to be flown in. Stan and Callender were already deep in discussion about the technicalities of resupply. Callender was undergoing a form of culture shock when he learnt that instead of individual ration packs the companies received their portion of rations by weight according to the number of soldiers. The young supply officer stared increduously at the grinning Quartermaster.

'But what can they do with 100 gramms of flour?' he asked.

'They don't get it themselves,' Stan said, as if the whole system was axiomatic. 'The comapnies cook centrally or by platoons. They only do two menus so even they can't cock it up.' Callender looked terrified at the thought. Rolls turned back to watch as the first of the Agusta-Bells started up. The other pilots were still walking round their machines, mechanically running through the list of physical checks.

Stan consulted his day-sheet and then pointed out a spot to them. They picked up their weapons and equipment and stumbled over the rough earth to where the RQMS was standing by a pile of crates and boxes. The first helicopter roared and rose up in its bay, throwing up a curtain of dust. It then dipped its nose and emerged to skim across the airfield and settle alongside them. Callender was instantly blinded. He found himself being bundled forward and lifted bodily into the Huey. Only when he had wiped his eyes with the loose end of his headcloth did he realise that everyone else was wearing goggles of some description. He was pushed onto a canvas bench with his back to the green domed heads of the pilots. He felt for his seat belt but there was nothing there. His FN rifle was thrust into his hands. The cabin space began to fill up with crates and boxes. Then just before the door slid shut the giant RQMS appeared. A broad grin creased his chubby, begoggled face as he dumped four, writhing, plastic bags on the only remaining floor space at their feet. A black, lop-eared head protruded from each bag.

'Goats!' Callender shouted into the roar of the rotors. The Baluch waved benignly and slid the door shut. The engine note changed and the vibration increased as he felt the machine lurch then lift smoothly off the ground. He felt lost and panicky; his head battered by the noise of the engine, his nose assailed by the mixture of kerosene and goats. He was hot and sticky with sweat and grime. His eyes were gritty and sore from the dust. He felt trapped and claustrophobic. Rolls was no less sweaty and cramped but he was spared the racket of the engines because the crewmen had given him a set of headphones with a boom microphone. He was talking to the squadron commander and the co-pilot.

'Sorry we can't offer you a lefthand seat, Johno, but we're on combat rules. Two up anywhere north of Harrow.'

'S'okay, Mike, I'll put my little friend on, talk him through the route. I think he needs the diversion.' Without waiting for a reply, Rolls lifted off the earphones and placed them over Callender's head. The boy smiled in gratitude.

As soon as Callender seemed happy Rolls settled back into his corner and opened his letters; still unread from the previous night. The first was from his daughter, Miranda. Now in her first year as a boarder, her letter bubbled over with the carefree non-sense of a happy and secure little schoolgirl who accepted an episodic relationship with her father. She, non-too-secretly, revelled in his romantic status and life-style and looked forward to their promised winter holiday together. The second letter was a cool page and a half from Caroline, now his ex-wife, who detested her own status and life-style. She had insisted on remaining in the pretty Wiltshire village where he had bought a cottage shortly before leaving the Army. The problem which he could foresee and she could not was that it was deep in the British Army's backyard. With Tidworth and Bulford within cocktail party range, Caroline was constantly in touch with a society to which she no longer belonged as of right. He had offered to resettle her nearer London but she refused and so was reminded daily of what she thought could have been. Rolls folded up the letters and smiled at the doomed goats. He offered the nearest goat Caroline's letter. It sniffed the blue paper and turned its head away to ruminate on an earlier morsel. Rolls tucked the letter away in his shirt pocket, and, closing his eyes, allowed the hammering of the rotor blades to shake his mind into neutral. He was once more the happy warrior, off to war.

The morning after the successful occupation of Lion Cub had led to a sudden relaxing of the atmosphere. Having neither heard nor seen any sign of adoo during the previous week, the head-quarters had assumed all the bustle and genial confusion of a small town suq. They even had time to catch up on some of the trivia of battalion administration, NCO promotion conferences and the like. Giles Denby-Smith had concreted the re-arrange-ment of the morning routine by persuading the Colonel to switch the officers' daily conference from its traditional early evening time to the half-hour before breakfast. Mike Cook had protested on the grounds that he had enough to do in the mornings, running the helicopter re-supply, without having to prepare operation and intelligence briefs as well. Giles voiced his concerns that without a second-in-command he would not have sufficient time to check his positions before evening stand-to and therefore would imperil the entire southern flank. His shrill English tones prevailed over Cook's Antipodean mutterings about OC Two Company's fear of being shot in the dark by his own men. The Colonel expected an outbreak of personal abuse leading to physical violence at one point only to be rescued by Harry Shaw, who offered to take over the responsibility for the re-supply. So now all of the British company officers except Shanks and Primmer were still lingering over toast and old air-mail copies of The Times when the first two re-supply Hueys appeared as specks on the southern horizon.

The 205s had no sooner touched the swirling dust of the landing site when they were besieged by begoggled headquarters wallahs, heads swathed like Berbers against the stinging cloud. Doors pulled back on both sides, the porters stripped the cabin of boxes, barrels and goats in seconds. Then another swarm of porters jostled around, packing the cabin with empty plastic water barrels and any other item for the return trip to Harrow. Rolls and Calender found themselves being all but carried to the edge of the dust cloud. Din Mohammed and their baggage joined them in similar fashion. A small, muffled jundi waved his hand under Roll's chin, his voice lost in the chop-chop of the idling rotors. He bobbed down and came up staggering under the weight of Rolls' bergan. Another wave and he staggered off towards the headquarter's sangered tents.

'My saviour!' cried Irving Ross, leaping up from a semi-reclining position behind a copy of Autocar. The little guide dropped Rolls' bergan gratefully in front of the mess tent, waved another salute and trotted away. 'John, good to see you.' Irving strode out from under the awning and grasped Roll's hand.

'Irving ...' Rolls smiled. 'What's this about you deserting the ranks of the young and free?'

The two contract majors continued their exchange as they went into the mess tent. Callender remained standing in the middle of what had become the main track through the headquarters. His eyes flicked from tent to tent; the orderly room with its ancient Punjabi clerks tapping away at antique Imperial typewriters, mess boys of no more than eleven or twelve being harangued by a fat Goan chef. The kampodas of the Medical Squadron laying out sheets to dry in the sun.

'A real Fred Karno's outfit, eh?' Callender spun round to behold Mike Cook, decked out in green singlet, long shorts, flip-flops and his morning headdress: a blue and white shemargh worn Arafat-style. 'Mike Cook, I'm the Ops O.'

'Richard Callender.'

'Been expectin' yah, Dicky.' Cook lapsed into his Bondi lifeguard accent. 'Who you from?'

'Ordnance, I'm afraid.'

'Don't worry,' Cook said, throwing an arm around his shoulders. 'Anyone who's been in the Brit Army more than two weeks knows more than these buggers'll know in a life-time.' He was about to steer his new found charge up to the make-shift veranda of the mess when Callender stiffened under his touch.

'Listen!' Callender said. 'Funny, sounds like geese?'

'Geese?' Cook's face frowned a fraction then his eyes sprang wide. 'Incomers,' he yelled to the tent. 'Incomers!'

A short, faint whistle then ... Crump. Callender ducked from the waist. Cook bolted away over a wall, into the command post.

'Qumbula! Kull wahed, taht!' someone shouted. Crump. Another loud, flat explosion ripped the air. Then silence. Then bedlam. Three or four bodies leapt from behind the veranda wall and sprinted past the dazed lieutenant.

'Here, come inside.' He saw Rolls beckon him from behind a sandbag wall. More geese, more whistles ... Crump, Crump. Strong hands propelled him up and over the wall, a hard, angular body crushed him into the dust floor and rolled away. Bang. The air popped in his ears. The ground shook. Magazines and papers flopped down around him.

'Bloody Hell!' exclaimed Rolls. 'That was close.' Callender looked up to find everything dark, then grey, then sunshine again. A cloud of dust settled on and around them. 'Get over by the CP,' Rolls motioned. They all scuttled, crabwise across the floor towards the overhead cover of the shelter.

'Eddie, can you give me a bearing?' Mike Cook was asking on his radio. A flat, calm voice gave a 'Wait out'.

Rolls, Callender and Din Mohammed sat in the entrance lobby of the Command Post and listened for the arrival of more incomers. None came. After a few minutes, Rolls eased himself up and leaned inside.

'Do you lay this on for all your new boys, or just me?'

'I think we should send you back on the next chopper or throw you overboard, bloody Jonah, that's what you are.' The Australian winked as "no further contact" reports filled his earphones. 'Well, it looks like range practise is over for the morning.' He leaned back. 'Can we stand-down, Colonel?' There was a pause and then from the adjoining room; 'If you think that was it, Mike?' a voice returned, heavy with tension.

'What about the re-supply?'

'I've info'd Stan and he'll tell the squadron,' the Ops officer replied. 'I'll get them to run into Three Company's landing site for the rest of the day. Do you want the jets to fly a CAP?'

The figure of Alastair Wilson filled the opposite entrance to where Rolls stood.

'It wouldn't do any harm, I suppose,' then noticing Rolls, 'Oh, Hello. You must be the new chaps?' Rolls braced up and smiled.

'John Rolls, Colonel.'

'Alastair Wilson.' The Colonel grinned sheepishly and waved his hand towards the sandbags. 'Sorry about this.' He felt a little off-guard in front of Rolls, especially as Mike Cook and Harry Shaw had been reminiscing over his part glories for most of the previous night. The Colonel stared intently at the wall-map whilst Mike relayed information and requests to the Force Headquarters. After a few minutes of rapid, radio traffic, Mike leaned back.

'Jets'll be overhead in fifteen minutes, Colonel. The Hueys'll stand off till then.'

'Err'fine, Mike. Any casualties?'

'No, Colonel, and no damage.'

'Well, let's hope they're all like that.' The portly lieutenant-colonel smiled benignly at Rolls. 'Find yourself a cup of tea or something and come through, er … John, isn't it?'

The interview was brief and to the point. The Colonel expressed his misgivings about Roll's replacement of Irving Ross, his anxiety about the Battalion's mission and firm disapproval of Roll's beard. He listened patiently while Rolls told him of his previous career details. Indeed, the mention of his service in the Gurkhas seemed to prompt the Colonel into asking more details of his campaign service. When John left the tent, Alastair Wilson sat in an attitude of troubled contemplation; his mind frantically trying to recall names and dates from the past.

Rolls and his bearer, Din Mohammed picked up their webbing and packs and made their way towards the gun-line and Three Company's positions. Richard Callender had gone to have his interview with the Commanding Officer prior to joining Two Company as 'Third-in-Command.' Mike Cook had observed to Rolls that the boy would be better off joining the adoo.

Rolls spent the rest of the day going over the company position with Irving Ross. As the operation was only a week old there was little to do in the manner of formal handover. The minutiae of ammunition scales, ration states and minefield maps were left to the company 2IC. Rolls knew that his immediate task was to maintain continuity of leadership. Both Arab and Baluchi soldiers came from small rural villages and, as such, were accustomed to a patriarchal way of life. The bond that developed between the company commander and his soldiers did have some shortcomings; chiefly the virtual exclusion of the platoon officers and the company 2IC from the chain of command. Officers and NCOs were frequently played against each other, sometimes with Byzantine cunning. The transition of loyalty between patriarches was difficult enough in barracks but on a isolated hillside, in the face of an unknown enemy, it could be disastrous.

The two contract majors strolled from sangar to sangar all afternoon. Rolls taking care to shake the hand and ask the name and village of every man. It was easier because they all knew that Ross was returning to England to marry; an important enough reason to leave in their eyes. They would then sit for twenty minutes or so in the smoky, man-made caves, drink tea, eat fresh dates and talk idly of other times. The sun was just beginning to float downwards to the western hills when Rolls and Ross left the last section which was part of the platoon that had been placed on Two Company's exposed right flank.

'What's OC Two Company like?' John asked as they breasted the spine-backed ridge separating the two sub-units.

'God, he's a case!' said Irving. 'Donkey-Walloper, same push as the General. Hates the boys … Don't know why he volunteered.'

'Perhaps he's after a gong?'

'Wouldn't be surprised. He drives Al Primmer up the wall.'

'Hmm.' Rolls felt a sudden concern for Richard Callender. 'Where's your 2IC?'

'Eddie? He went off with Mr Thompson, the shelldrake. Got very excited over the incomers this morning. I think they went digging up the craters for bits.' Ross chuckled to himself.

'What's he like?'

'Eddie? Absolutely shit-hot! Deadly serious and very professional.'

'Marine, isn't he?'

'Yeah, keeps calling the floor a deck, has dog-watches and all that sort of thing.' They both laughed.

'Anyway, Matey ... Oh-crack-sparrow ... bukra it's all yours. I'm on the first chopper out and then ...' He paused as he vaulted the low wall of the company command post. 'Big silver bird takes me to London ... and Mrs Gillian Ross!' He leaned back to acknowledge applause.

'You'll have to grow up then, young Irving, my boy,' said Rolls with all the mock seriousness he could muster. Ross turned to a thin, scruffy waif with a cast in his left eye.

'What's for dinner, Saif?' The waif shrugged and announced that it would be goat stew and rice in harsh, guttural Arabic.

'Just for a change, eh Saif,' Ross said in English. Saif nodded without comprehension, then turned and disappeared into a natural cleft in the rocks which served as his kitchen.

As the glimmering red disc of the setting sun began to cut into the blue-grey hills in front of them, the jundis began to observe the British Army ritual of stand-to. The change from light to dark and dark to light had been regarded as a propitious time for an enemy attack since before the Boer war. Standing-to served many other purposes though; not least to break the monotony of defence for an hour or so each day. During their communal supper, Shanks, the second-in-command came up on the transceiver radio to say that he would eat with Four Platoon in the depth position and would remain with them throughout stand-to. Rolls and Ross now moved quietly from sangar to sangar amongst the forward platoons. The jundis crouched behind their stone and sandbag ramparts watching the last red and purple streaks fade from the jagged horizon. Rolls was gratified to find such a high standard of discipline being observed. All the soldiers were correctly dressed and equipped even to the extent of having full water bottles on their belts and spare batteries placed next to radios.

'They're pretty sharp, Irv,' whispered Rolls, as they climbed the slope towards Four Platoon.

'Can't take all the credit, I'm afraid, Old Boy,' Irving confided. 'Young Shanks is your man there. Keen as mustard ... really got a grip when we were working up.'

The two majors wound their way slowly through the rear sections to find that Shanks had moved up to a point just below the crestline of the ridge.

'I'd say you were fairly secure here,' said Rolls as they neared the crest. 'What's the drop at the lowest point?'

'Shanksy climbed down the other day,' answered Ross. 'Said it was about 80 foot shear and another 150 at one in two. No one's going to come rushing up; that's for sure.' He stopped just short of a roughly crenallated outcrop. 'There he is. What you doing, Shanksy?'

The figure squatting in the darkness did not answer straight away. He was holding a short, black, tube-like instrument to his right eye. He lowered it and half-turned to face them. 'Hi, boss, come and look at this.' As Ross scrambled up beside him, Shanks acknowledged Roll's presence. 'Eddie Shanks,' he said quietly; offering his hand.

'John Rolls.' The soft, silvery glow of the desert starlight was good enough to give Rolls the impression of a squat, powerfully built man with an unruly shock of blond hair. Rolls was at once struck by his eyes which were shallow set and protruded to give Shanks the immediate impression of being startled. The eyes flicked slightly as if to take measure of him.

'What do you make of this then?' Shanks flicked a small switch on top of the tube and pressed the rubber eye-piece to Ross' eye in the manner one would demonstrate a kaleidoscope to a small child. The instrument whined softly and Rolls could see a green glow around Ross' right eye.

'Lummy!' Ross exclaimed in his odd mock-cockney way. He took hold of the image-intensifier himself and swept the landscape. 'What are they?' Then without waiting a reply. 'Hey Johno? Take a look.' He passed the 'scope to Rolls who put his eye against the rubber cup.

'It's blank.'

'Push against it,' advised Shanks. As he did so the inner lips opened and an eery green landscape glowed back at him. He focused on and recognised the distant skyline and then dipped the 'scope to find another point of reference. The line of sangars rose with view. He went up again and slowly panned the middle distance.

Little pinpricks of light glowed where to the naked eye there was only the uniform greyness of a moonless night. The points of light were grouped in a band across the arc he swept. Some bright, some dim. Twenty, thirty, perhaps fifty.

'Fires,' said Shanks, flatly. 'We can't see them 'cos they're in caves, but the IWS picks it up.'

'Lummy,' Ross repeated lamely. 'And I thought we were alone.'

CHAPTER ELEVEN

The revelation of the campfires had occupied Roll's wakeful mind as his body sought the refuge of sleep till well after midnight. He was sleeping soundly when a hand shook his foot firmly.

'Sah'b, stand to,' Din Mohammed whispered hoarsely. He was awake and alert in an instant, being immediately aware of his surroundings. Irving groaned on the campbed alongside. Rolls shivered in the crisp, morning chill.

'You'll miss all this next week, Irving.' He leaned over and pulled the thin blanket off the sleeping figure.

'Oh, Oh God,' moaned the now shivering hump. Rolls slipped his feet into his chukka boots and picking up his AKM, he felt his way to the hessian-strip covered doorway. The waning moon glared triumphantly down on both him and the barren rocks with a ghostly sheen. Already the jundis were picking their way over to their shallow, open sangers. Irving stumbled noisily about behind him yawning and shivering.

'I'll go down to Two Platoon,' Rolls said. Irving nodded in mid-yawn, and then started rummaging around for his webbing.

As the sun rose up behind the position, the wadis and ridges to the west were shown up in sharp relief. Rolls sat in a sangar in one of the forward section positions slowly scanning each feature with his binoculars. Din Mohammed sat silently behind him.

'Nothing, Din,' he said as he continued to scan. 'I cannot even see any caves.' He strained to penetrate the thorn trees which marked a steep-sided ridge about a thousand metres away. He sensed the Pathan move up behind him.

'See, sah'b, birds.' Rolls looked up from the eye pieces to see where Din pointed. Then he saw them, five or six wheeling birds, large enough to be seen with the naked eye.

'Kites, Din?'

'Perhaps.' He looked again through the binoculars.

They were kites. The aerial opportunists and general scavengers of the jebel. They would spot any carelessly discarded bones or offal and then circle lazily for the chance to swoop down and carry it away. He checked the area beneath minutely but saw nothing else. He marked the spot mentally and then sought it out on a small scale map laid out on the sangar wall.

'Adoo? Sahb.'

'Yes Din, we saw their fires last night. A lot of adoo.'

Following stand down Rolls dug out his razor from the depths of his bergan and set about removing his beard in accordance with his new colonel's wishes. As he was finishing Irving Ross returned from saying his farewell salaams to individuals in the company.

'That's an improvement, now what about that big brush under your nose?'

'Don't you think I've sacrificed enough,' Rolls replied.

He ran his fingers over the now smooth and white skin of his jaw line. He peered at his reflection in the small steel mirror propped against the sandbag sangar. 'I look ridiculous!' he said.

'Nonsense,' Irving chirped. 'Look like a real soldier now, not like one of your camel bandits.' Rolls made to hurl his basin at him and Ross ducked into the shelter bay.

Ross had just started tossing his baggage up from the bay when Shanks appeared on the parapet. Daylight filled in the shadowy impression Rolls had received in their encounter on the ridge. The Marine officer was shorter than himself but much broader across the shoulders and altogether sturdier in the arms and legs. His eyes still dominated his facial features, light blue and lemur-like.

'One company has been warned off for a patrol this morning and Mike wants me to do anchor OP, if that's okay by you?' he said in a flat matter of fact tone as if Rolls had been his superior for months and not minutes.

'Yes, that's fine.' Rolls paused. 'What do you like to be called? Not Shanksy, surely?' The Marine dropped to his haunches and flashed what Rolls guessed was a rare smile.

'Eddie's fine.'

'He'll always be Shanksy to me,' Ross chimed in, emerging from the blackness of the shelter. He brandished his small American-made carbine. 'Who wants me M1?'

'No thanks,' said Shanks. 'And it's an M2, not an M1.'

'Seven months as his guide and mentor and what abuse I get from the boy?' Irving appealed. Picking up items of Irving's kit, the officers trooped off towards the headquarters.

All the white officers attended that first morning conference with the exception of Alan Primmer who was up on Lion Cub. Rolls introduced himself to those officer's he had not met, and settled himself down in one of the folding canvas chairs reserved for the company commanders. He stood up as the heavy figure of Alastair Wilson trundled into the tent followed by Mike Cook and Harry Shaw. Mike Cook immediately launched into a summary of the activities of the previous day and night. It had been confirmed that the position had been hit by eight mortar rounds, one had failed to explode. Mr Thompson stood up at this juncture and passed round pieces of jagged, silvery metal. His undulating Tyne-side accent cut through the resulting murmurings.

'Chinese 82 millimetre, Gen'almen. Range about three Ks.' He held up a metallic green tailfin and continued as though he was on the Demo Park at Larkhill. 'Not very ac'rate and even less so when fired off an unprepared baseplate. Yesterday 'e bounced 'em all over the shop.'

'Thank you Sergeant Major,' Mike Cook injected to regain control of the orders group. After some amplification of the sightings of camp fires during the night, Mike Cook stepped back to a large scale map pinned to a crate top against the poles of the marquee. Alastair Wilson stepped forward. He appeared hesitant as though he'd been roused from deep thought. He started by formally introducing John Rolls as the new officer commanding Three Company. His manner made Rolls feel almost apologetic for merely being there. The Colonel then outlined his plan to link up with Lion Cub. All three companies would push out daylight patrols in half company strength, to survey the intervening ground. He expected the Force Engineers to arrive within the week to start the erection of a full wire and minefield barrier. In spite of the low key manner of his delivery a buzz of excitement began to fill the group. After a short address by Harry Shaw on water and ration conservation, the 'O' group disgorged into the mess tent for breakfast.

Rolls waited for the rush to subside. Giles Denby-Smith also waited. With his large Roman nose and his long blond hair unfashionably slicked back off his forehead, he reminded Rolls of one of the officer types of the Jon wartime cartoons.

'I say, Rolls, do you mind awfully if I send young Callender along with Shanks this morning. Doesn't know a lot about fire control and I thought Shanks might show him the basics.'

'Rolls smiled at the hussar major's style of personal address and expressions. He was tempted to reply 'Denby-Smith' but settled for 'Fine, Giles, I'll tell Eddie.' Giles smiled politely and rose.

'What push were you with before you came out here?'

'Gurkhas.'

'Oh, little brown men to little brown men, what?'

Giles flashed his "Must make an effort not to patronize the poor blighter" smile again and left Rolls in no doubt why he was not the most popular man in the battalion.

Breakfast had been a boisterous affair. Irving produced a crate of Dutch beer and would have extended the proceedings into lunchtime had Mike Cook not put his baggage on the second flight of supply helicopters. Irving, terrified of being separated from his kit, had leapt aboard still waving two empty cans. The officers dispersed once more to their separate domains.

The temperature at midday was 104°F. Shanks and Callender sat on top of Two Company's command post. They were watching the progress of three platoons of One Company across the wadi floor. The heat haze made the tiny figures dance in time with the surrounding thorn trees.

'I think they will start working their way back now,' said Shanks.

'Can I do another target,' asked Callender, picking up the map which lay between them.

'Wait till they're back, clear of the wadi.' Shanks scanned the scene through his binoculars and then stopped as he recognized the slim figure of Faulkner waving his rifle in the air. He switched left to see what was happening. A string of jundis had changed direction and were now turning down the wadi.

'They're turning now,' he commented. A purring sound like a distant train made him look up. A thin trail of smoke. 'Incomers,' he yelled to a startled Callander. A crump! A ringing, metallic bang behind them. Rolling backwards, he fell in a heap in the firing bay. Callender sprawled beside him.

Prrrrt. Silence then another bang. Shanks held his breath. A distant rumble to the right. A loud bang behind him. He bobbed up. A small grey and brown cloud drifted up the hillside and dispersed in thin strands of yellow and grey. He snatched at the transceiver mike dangling from his belt. '39A, two incomers, Two's location.'

'Roger, seven. Acknowledge.'

'Roger, 39A,' Mr Thompson's voice burst in, breathlessly. Shanks spun round on his knees and grabbed at the compass around his neck. He stared out to the hills on the far side of the big wadi: Prrrrt. He looked up another trail of smoke. He clenched his teeth. Bang, then another distant rumble. He came up again, to the level of the sandbags. Callender watched him, eyes wide, mouth gaping; helpless. Shanks brought the prism block to his eyes and read aloud the bearing.

'Can you see them?' asked Callender, his voice tremulous with shock.

'No, but I heard them,' Shanks replied as he scribbled the bearing on his hand. He picked up his mike and relayed the bearings to the gun line. 'From your bearing I would say that they're in that narrow wadi in square 59' 60.'

The Sergeant Major came back. 'I've no idea what 'es usin' but I'll give him a couple of rounds anyway.' Prrrrt! Bang! another incomer impacted on the hillside this time below their sangar. The dust cloud drifted over them depositing a thin layer on their hands and shoulders. Shanks looked down at Callender who seemed to be holding his breath.

'Should we move?' Callender asked, in a weak, little boy voice. Shanks cocked his head in an effort to listen out for the tell-tale flight of the incoming projectiles. Then he looked straight at Callender.

'No, you're better off inside,' he said, reaching out to yank Callender up out of the corner. They wormed their way into the dusty gloom of the sangar. Bang! No whistle, no Prrrt. They dropped flat, then lay panting, breathless, then choking in dust. Eyes and mouth streaming, Shanks pulled himself up to an embrasure and glanced over the rim. 'That was just in front.' Instantaneously he heard the brittle crack of one of the Indian 75s then a second, then a third, then a fourth. The shells whizzed overhead. Three more shells hummed out towards the unseen enemy.

'Shot, three five,' an Indian sing song accent broke in over the transceiver. Shanks checked the second sweep of his watch. He peered over the ledge of the embrasure. Nothing moved. Then he heard a faraway rumble and echo. Seconds later another. Then a thin trail of smoke rose from behind a ridge in the distance. He checked the bearing and permitted himself a grim smile of satisfaction. An image of startled adoo gunners crouching out in some distant wadi sent a glow through him.

After waiting for five minutes, Shanks and Callender scrambled up from the dug out shelter and back on to the roof. A roar of jet engines made them look up in time to see a pale crucifix wing over and wheel around over the suspected enemy firing point.

'Strikeys,' said Shanks. 'Looks good but it's not much cop really.'

'Why's that,' asked Callender, who, till then, felt a great sense of comfort in the appearance of any friendly aircraft.

'Only carries two bombs, and the grounds too broken for them to be all that effective. Besides the crabs are a bit hit and miss as well.' Callender's face fell a little. Shanks was busy scanning the wadi where One Company were sitting out the bombardment. He spotted Peter White waving at the thin stretch of thorn and scrub. Jundis appeared from out of the undulating valley floor. They spread out hoisting their FN rifles over their shoulders, holding them by the muzzles.

The company had only moved a matter of yards when the platoon lines suddenly scattered; seeking cover. An explosion echoed back to the Jebel. Shanks scanned right. A sandy cloud rose and mushroomed away.

'Contact. Mortars. No, two men down. I think it's a mine.' The transceivers crackled their urgent calls. Shanks felt a stab of impotence as he watched a ring of soldiers develop around the site. Then he saw the tall figure of Faulkner move right into the centre. Shanks and everyone else within earshot of a transceiver on Jebel Assaad listened hard for long minutes. Faulkner's laconic voice broke the sequence. 'Two cas, frag wounds; legs and back I think they'll be alright.'

An hour later Alvin Sadrapandi and his kampodas gently loaded the two lacerated soldiers onto the cabin floor of an AB 205. The crewman took the bottles of plasma expander and carefully hooked them up above each stretcher. Peter White, still rigged, hands bloodied, leaned in to give a valedictory grip to the shoulders of the stoically impassive jundis. The crewman slid the door shut and with a clattering roar the Huey rose and careered forward before the broad blades pulled the blunt nose up into the late afternoon sky.

That afternoon, after stand-to the company commanders had been called to the headquarters to discuss alterations to the patrol programme. The soldiers who tripped the stick mine in the wadi had survived through a stroke of unbelievable luck. Half of the mine's shrapnel jacket had failed to fragment and was found buried in a tree trunk nearby. The Colonel was also concerned about the shelling of Two Company's position. Mr Thompson by means of his diligent detective work, had identified the incomers as 76 millimetre anti-tank rounds. Despite the fact that the battalion had taken its first casualties and that the adoo appeared to be able to shell them with accuracy and impunity, the mood of the officers was pragmatically optimistic. As they all sat down together at the trestle table in the tented mess there was a general consent that they had come through their first blooding well.

The company commanders and headquarter's officers lingered over their simple meal. Talk took a step back to previous experiences. Aside from recalling a patrol action in Cyprus, Alastair Wilson was content to listen as the conversation leapt from war to war. Mike Cox was being skillfully cornered over Vietnam by White and Denby-Smith. Mike turned to his fellow contract officer, Rolls,

'You were in Borneo, weren't you? Johno, tell these drongos 'bout panji traps.' Rolls stroked his moustache with his thumb. Before he could speak Mr Thompson spoke up.

'Which division were you in, Major?'

'Two Division,' answered Rolls.

'I was there 64/65,' chirped Mr Thompson glad to have found something in common with at least one of the officers. Rolls elaborated for him. '65, we were at Kampong Surugai. I was second dickie to A company on the river section.'

Thompson must have had some mutual connection with the area for he was about to speak when he noticed everyone was looking at the end of the table. Colonel Alastair was standing; his fists clenched, knuckles down, on the table. His face was contorted, his cheeks throbbed purpley-red. He glowered at Rolls and began to tremble.

'You!' he burst out, his voice guttural, grunting. 'You murdered my men!' Rolls looked blanched with shock. 'It was you. You are the one.' The other officers sat immobilized mouths open. 'You watched them murder my jocks and you did nothing. You used us as bloody bait!' He stopped and reeled back a pace, frothy specs spotted his shirt. 'Well, didn't you!' he bawled. Rolls mind raced, the strands of an appalling coincidence came together. He took in an intake of breath but remained mute. The Colonel staggered backwards a bit more, a choking sob convulsed him.

'Bloody murderer,' he cried, and lunged forward to sweep glasses and plates from the end of the table. 'Bloody murderer,' he screamed, eye-balls, glassy, straining. He spun round unsteadily and lurched through the double flap-ends of the marquee.

Harry Shaw was the first to speak. He stood up.

'I think we'd best be about our business, Gentlemen.' His normally thin voice, calm and resolute. 'I'll see the Colonel's alright.' There was some murmuring as chairs were eased back.

'What was that all about?' enquired Mike Cook leaning across to Rolls.

'I'll tell you sometime, Mike,' answered Rolls quietly, he felt other eyes burning into him.

'I think you'd better tell me now, Sport,' said Mike earnestly. 'I got enough hassle with the adoo, let 'lone you an' the Old Man.' Rolls thought for a moment.

'Okay, come back to my place and I'll fill you in.' Rolls stood up and made his way out into the night air. The sudden chill told him how flushed he must have been inside.

He felt slightly queasy, his throat felt tight and full. Hoisting his AKM onto his shoulder he waited for Mike to emerge. Mike came out of the CP entrance, buckling on his pistol belt. The full moon was just clearing the eastern horizon as they passed the low light and chatter of the gun-line.

CHAPTER TWELVE

News of Colonel Wilson's outburst reached Force Headquarters in the late afternoon of the following day. After a long talk with Rolls, Mike Cook had penned a lengthy, handwritten note which he despatched by hand of one of the re-supply pilots. The General paced up and down his office stopping occasionally at the open window to watch the sky darken the waters of the Gulf to indigo.

'Isn't that just typical?' he threw at Gilbert Dixon, who watched him from the cane armchair by the desk. 'I send him the one man who can help him pull himself together and he accuses him of murder or some such.' Gilbert said nothing. General Welles stopped pacing, returned to his desk and sat down. 'Where was it again?'

'Two Div. Alastair's company were at Kampong Bariti.'

Gilbert Dixon paused to check his General's reaction from over his half-rims. He removed them. 'I seem to recall the incident myself; I was at Far East Land Forces at the time.' The General leaned forward, his elbows on his blotting pad, and proceeded to pick at his thumbnails while his Chief of Staff reminisced. 'Rolls' Gurkhas were a river patrol down on the border, the Sungai Bariti itself, when they cut the tracks of a large force of Indons; KKO I believe. Anyway, they followed them up, thinking they would run them into the other half of the company who were in ambush on the main route north.'

'So what went wrong?'

'The Indons turned at right-angles off the track and went straight across the boundary with Alastair's push.' Alastair Wilson had just made company commander and, well, to be honest they were a bit on the slack side.' Dixon stopped, as if he had told enough tales out of school for one day.

'Well, what happened?'

'Afternoon of the next day, the Jocks took six dead and about eighteen wounded. Most of them pretty badly too.' Dixon stopped again, this time as if the memory itself was too painful to recall. 'It was a Saturday and most were paralytic at the time; on their beds mainly. Mortared from close range. They were all pretty torn about, bed springs in the gut and that sort of thing.' He paused again. 'Well, anyway, Rolls heard the firing and guessing what had happened, nipped back to the river. He assumed, naturally, that a company position was fairly secure and they could take care of themselves. He caught the Indons just as they were crossing back. His boys killed all but a couple; he was recommended for the MC.'

'He didn't get one,' the General observed drily.

'No, bit of a stink because of Alastair's people. The Jocks claimed that Rolls knew what was on and deliberately held back to catch the Indons on their withdrawal.'

'Did he?'

'No, I don't think so. Like I said, one would assume that a firebase could look after itself. He was certainly quick about getting to the river but he told his own people as soon as he cut the Indons track. It just never got passed on. Brigade's fault, if anyones'; but you know how people are. They tend to believe only what they want to believe.'

'So what do we do now? I expect to have Alastair pounding my ear at any moment.'

'If Wilson's as shaky as you think, you can't afford to pull Rolls out,' Gilbert suggested.

'No, they will just have to get on with it. What was the form today?'

'About twenty incomers, mortar and SPG 9s. No cas. Patrols out from the main position and Lion Cub: no contacts,' Dixon read from a millboard on his knee.

'What about the Engineers?'

'Advance party in tomorrow, stores lift over the next five days.' The General abandoned his nails and leaned back.

'Well, it's some progress I suppose.' He checked his watch. 'Let's go and have a gin before the wives come.' They rose, wished Donal the aide "Goodnight" and strolled out into the starlit night.

* * *

The situation on Jebel Assaad over the next few days had progressed but not in the manner envisaged by the Force Commander. The bombardment by mortars and anti-tank rockets increased daily. The adoo gunners changed directions, targets and the times of day they fired. At the end of seven days, the daily incomer rate had topped one hundred. The battalion had in general taken the daily pounding with stoicism and not a little good humour. The exception was Alastair Wilson, who since his verbal onslaught on Rolls had confined himself to his dugout. His sole appearance during daylight hours was to give a terse oration to the orders group each morning. Though Rolls sat in the front row with the other company commanders, Wilson resolutely avoided eye contact. In fact, he even avoided mention of Three Company all together to the dismay of White and Denby-Smith who found themselves more often out on patrol than in.

The unit had also taken its first fatality. A signaller had lingered over his chapati and corned mutton breakfast instead of taking cover. Taking a large mortar splinter through the chest he bled to death, unheard and unseen by his comrades safe inside their sangars. So far, all enemy action had been limited to the daylight hours. The result of this had been a change to a nocturnal pattern of life for the occupants of the Jebel.

The evening air was still, full of mixed aroma of the desert night-flowering shrubs and the field cooking of the soldiers. Instead of congregating in their sangars, smoking, sipping tea and talking the early evening away, the jundis squatted silently against the rock and sandbag blast walls which curved like arms round their sangars. Many used the hushed atmosphere to pay their ageless obedience to the "One God" standing, kneeling and bowing in the manner prescribed by Mohammed, his prophet. The headquarters officers would linger over their supper in the mess tent. Harry Shaw, Mike Cook and Mr Thompson worked out their priorities and timings for the next day's resupply over a can of lager or glass or two of port. The Colonel would sit quietly, nursing a whisky and a cigar or two before going back to his sangar. There he would sit on the blast wall looking out towards Lion Cub, his cigar glowing occasionally against the black mass of the structure.

Two company had been detailed off for an all-night fighting patrol into the wadi between Assaad and Cub. The CO had given up the staff college ideal of setting a precise mission for every patrol and merely directed that the patrol was to return by first light. Giles was less than happy as he had been the first to observe

Three Company's exclusion from these daily excursions. John Rolls, feeling just as aggrieved, attempted to compensate by offering the services of Shanks to "baby sit" Giles's position while he was out.

At about midnight Rolls paused on the crest overlooking Two Company's lines. He held the microphone of his transceiver close to his mouth and announced his approach to Shanks. Exchanging whispered salaams with a handful of watchful jundis on his way down, he found Shanks sitting with one of the platoon commanders who was left behind as rear party.

'Salaam Alaykum, yaa Raa'id,' said the lieutenant with a brief nod and a dazzling smile.

'Haatha, Salim Murbarak,' said Shanks by way of introduction. Rolls found out that Salim was a hillman from the south and had been in the Army sixteen years. With courtesy satisfied, Salim excused himself and disappeared towards the platoon positions.

'I can't get over how old the subbys are,' said Shanks showing one of his rare smiles.

'It's a hangover from the old Levi days,' Rolls explained. 'It was all British-officered then. To fill the gap when they left, they promoted the sergeants, and no one has seen fit to change it.'

'Seems to work very well.'

'Meritocracy, can't beat it!' Rolls took a tin mug of tea offered up from inside the command post by a signaller 'Shukran'.

Shanks craned his neck to look behind Rolls and then either side of the blast walls.

'Where's your shadow?'

'Din?' Rolls laughed. 'He doesn't come out on social calls.'

'He's more than just a bearer, isn't he?' said Shanks, a note of professional admiration in his voice.

'Well, of course,' said Rolls, lightly. 'He's my Akharbij.'

'A what?'

'Akharbij, Battle brother.' Rolls settled down against the blast wall. 'Din is a Pathan. It's the custom with some of the warrior tribes for the orphaned sons to be adopted as sort of lifetime companion to one of the chief's sons. They grow together, fight together, and one acts as bodyguard to the other.'

'Have you adopted Din?' interjected Shanks.

'I'm not sure,' said Rolls, grinning broadly in the darkness. 'He may have adopted me.' Again Shanks face creased with an uncharacteristic show of humour.

Rolls had at first thought that his sudden replacement of Irving Ross was the cause of Shanks's dourness. As he was to find out over the following weeks the young Marine officer was shy; by the standard of the other captains anyway. Shanks appeared to only have two facial expressions. One of intense professional concentration, when he was working., The other, an impassive frozen mask of meditation. The latter was assumed whenever he was listening to the conversations of others. Rolls noticed that he rarely joined in conversation with the other officers or when fuddled round a pot of tea with the jundis. He would speak only when it was absolutely necessary, to avoid awkward silences or to draw more conversation. But, Rolls had no complaints. He was a genial, if quiet companion, and one of the most competent operators that Rolls had ever seen in this or any other army.

'Are all Bootys as sharp as you?' he suddenly asked. Shanks was scanning the wadi through his starlight 'scope. He stopped and turned towards Rolls.

'Pardon.' Rolls immediately wished he had not asked. He felt he had touched a raw nerve.

'Professional, Eddie. Are all Marines like you? I'm serious!'

'How do you mean?' Shanks seemed more than a little embarrassed as he slid down the sangar wall to squat behind the blast wall.

'I'm not being funny,' Rolls began. 'But, you leave the rest of us in the shade. You're all about on mortars, you do all the demolitions. You produced that thing from nowhere,' indicating the 'scope, 'How long have you been in?' Shanks seemed to relax and settled down to sit.

'Seven years. I'm still a lieutenant,' he admitted shyly. 'Navy rank system, you know?'

'But you've done much more regimental time that your average infanteer surely.'

'Yeah, I suppose we're lucky in the Corps, we never get garrison duty.'

'But you take things more seriously than most, don't you?'

Shanks did not answer for such a long time that Rolls wondered if he had offended him or not.

'I must be a bit of a pain at times,' came back the sad confession.

'It's just …' he paused as if to choose his words. 'Well, I don't want to let anyone down …' Rolls started to pooh-pooh the notion when an up raised palm appeared before his face.

'I did once … just once.' Rolls instantly wished that he had not prompted a hand wringing session. Seemingly oblivious to Rolls' discomfort Shanks continued. 'I did my first tour in the Far East, Singapore. I was a troop commander and like the other subbys I used to go ashore all night. Y'know Singers, Start off down Orchard Road and end up down Bugis Street. Well one morning the company drove across the Straits and up Kota Tinggi for a week's jungle bashing. I was so badly hungover I left half my kit behind, worse still we were to march in twelve K by half troops to RV with the rest of the company.' He paused. 'I got my lot half lost … marched about for six hours, didn't know where the hell I was. This old corporal came up to me and said "We're lost, aren't we, sir?" He took my compass and map and took us straight through the ulu, no following tracks or streams. Straight through. We hit the RV just before last light.'

Rolls was about to express the sympathy of a fellow traveller but Shanks continued with his atonement. 'Just before we hit the perimeter, the corporal gave me back my map and compass and told me to lead the way.' He paused again. Then he said, very quietly.

"You're a fucking wanker, sir. Buck up." Rolls held his breath not knowing whether the anecdote was supposed to be funny or not. Then he heard Shanks chuckling quietly to himself.

'I told myself right then that no-one would have cause to say that again.'

'Is that why you volunteered for secondment?' asked Rolls relieved by the Shanks recognition of the humorous side of life.

Shanks stood and hoisted his 'scope up onto the sandbagged edge of the roof. He seemed unsettled by the question. 'Sort of … it's a change from Northern Ireland anyway.'

Rolls stood up and joined his observation of the wadi. Deciding to change the track of the conversation. He said, 'How's the campfire club?'

'About the same, the fires are getting bigger, I think.'

Rolls pulled his binoculars from their case on his belt. Resting his elbows on the sandbag, he stared out at the blue, grey landscape.

'There are no wild camels, are there?' asked Shanks.

'Not really, no.'

'I can see a camel, I think. Have a shuft.' Shanks passed the 'scope to Rolls. Pushing his eye into the rubber eyepiece opened up the ghostly green world of the starlight 'scope. Shanks directed the lens.

'Up a bit, middle of the wadi, passing in front of the spine back.' The picture became more grainy as Rolls tried to focus into the middle of the mile-wide wadi.

'It's not much cop past 600. But I thought I saw something moving.' He panned left and strained to put form on the pale, green, fuzzy shapes. Then one moved, a dipping, swaying step; then another. He panned left a touch. Another shape swayed forward. The rhythm identical to the first.

'Camels!'

'Must be half a dozen, at least.'

'Where the Hell's Giles?' hissed Rolls passing the 'scope back to Shanks, who was busy taking a bearing. 'They must be right in front of him!'

Shanks lifted his head up from the prismatic compass. He shook his head slightly. 'No, Two Company can't see them.'

Rolls stared increduously at him. 'But they must be damn nearly on top of them. It's the main track?'

Shanks pursed his lips as though debating on some point of ethics. He passed the 'scope back to Rolls. 'No, he can't. He's just down there at the foot of this spur.'

Rolls grabbed the 'scope and crawled higher up the wall to take a look down the spur features in front of him.

Shanks gave quiet measured directions. 'Bottom of the left hand spur … Two hundred out, a big tree … go left. You can see a couple of jundis.'

Rolls followed. He focused in, the picture becoming clearer as he zoomed the lens in. He could not identify any shape at first, then there was a movement. A man's head. The hunched head and shoulders of two men focused in his mind.

'The fucker. How long have you known?' he snapped at Shanks.

'Since I came down, I watched them go.'

'Why didn't you …' Rolls stopped. His initial anger cooled as a wave of rationale swept over it. 'We can't report the camels now, can we?'

Shanks took back the 'scope offering no comment.

Rolls slid back onto the blast wall. He dropped his chin onto the back of his hands. 'To tell or not to tell,' he said half to himself. 'I've had this hassle before "Taqleaf" between contracts and seconded. Accusations, denials, bad blood all round. As if we didn't have enough already.'

'What are you going to do?' asked Shanks. Rolls bit the back of his knuckle.

'I'll tell Mike Cook in confidence, I think. I don't fancy telling the Colonel; that's for sure.' He looked at the hunched figure cradling the starlight 'scope. He smiled at Shanks and dropped down from the wall.

'Tell me what happens, Eddie ... We'll see what tomorrow brings.' He picked up his Kalashnikov and threaded his way out of the bay and off towards the headquarters.

* * *

The morning briefing had been brought forward by an hour to seven thirty as it had become evident that the adoo gunners had more civilised working hours. Giles reported that his long night's vigil was fruitless and in his opinion "a waste of a man's sleep". He sat down with an air of self-satisfaction unaware that two people in the tent were wise to his deceit. The officers broke up from their now customary breakfast at eight thirty and had just started to make their way back to their respective sub-units to await the first of the daily schedule of incomers. Peter White paused on the crest of the feature before taking the now well trodden path to his command post. A noise like a tube train in the distance caused him to look up. A white plume arched gracefully towards the gunlines. Kawump. The shock wave tipped him backwards. He sprawled in the dust; mouth open, gasping.

'Bloody hell!' A column of dust rose into the air. It formed a billowing oozing mushroom. He saw figures running.

'Zero, this is one. Contact ... I saw the bastard!' The radio slung from his neck squeaked to life with Faulkner's voice.

Mike Cook answered, 'Zero, roger. Hello 7. You alright?'

Mr Thompson came back. 'Just about. That was a Kat-yousha; that was.'

Peter White looked down to see a smoking crater a full six foot across between the Sergeant Major's sangar and the number two gun. He scrambled up and pelted down the path to his sangar.

Another "tube" noisily clattered by. Ker-wump. He reached the sangar and fell gasping within the shelter of the blast walls. James Faulkner had abandoned his usual languid pose and was bouncing up and down with excitement. He spun round to White.

'I've spotted the bastards,' he yelled. 'Jets'll be on them in a flash.' He was waving his hand-sized beacon radio up and down.

White recovered himself and moved up alongside the ecstatic Guards officer. Another "tube" thundered by, leaving its characteristic white plume in its wake. The explosion rumbled round the hill to shake the ground beneath them. 'Look, see that cloud. That's the firing point.' White peered through his Zeiss lenses and saw a grey ball of dust rolling up a distant hillside.

'The jets'll spot him,' yelled the gleeful Faulkner. A noise came from Faulkner's Sarbe like someone talking into a paper bag.

'Hello, Gravelbelly, this is Skyman confirm grid, over.'

Faulkner snatched up his map and read out a series of co-ordinates which he had scribbled on the top. 'Roger, Gravelbelly, I have visual. Commencing attack run now.'

Faulkner and White looked up as another Katyusha hammered by. The first Strikemaster appeared over the top of the feature and tore away in a long swinging arc towards the offending launcher. The wingman followed, higher and to the leader's left. The officers watched with breathless anticipation as the first Strikemaster levelled off. It pulled up, swinging back towards the Jebel Assaad. A gray-brown cloud sprang from the rear slope of the distant ridge.

'Round again for number twos,' the Sarbe squawked. The Strikemaster rolled wing over to its right. A thin line of white smoke streaked up to meet it. A white feather of smoke burst on its tail. The little jet appeared to drop pieces of tail-fin; tail plane. It yawed and spun over. 'Oh Shit!' crackled the Sarbe. The plane turned over and over again. Then it arced belly up and vanished down behind a low crest.

'It's gone,' whispered Faulkner hoarsely. A thick pall of black smoke and yellow dust billowed into view. The wingman swung his mini-fighter up and pulled a tight circle over the site.

'Sams!' The word came over tense and sharp. 'Sorry, Guys. Nothing we can do.' The Sarbe cut out sharply as the pilot switched to his base control channel. The Strikemaster dropped low over the ridge where his leader had crashed and accelerated down into the broad wadi to the east of Assaad. It skimmed low over the acacias and out of sight as its sand and green camouflage merged with the wadi sides.

James Faulkner sat down and dejectedly switched off his Sarbe.

'It's not your fault, James,' said White. 'It was always on the cards sooner or later.'

Faulkner nodded silently; his eyes glazed with tears.

CHAPTER THIRTEEN

The sudden and unexpected use of a surface-to-air missile had brought about a drastic alteration in the helicopter re-supply schedules. The squadron flew in en masse just before dawn and just after last light. Consequently, they could only replenish the battalion with the bare essentials of life and combat; the slender reserve stocks of food, water and ammunition already on the position would now only diminish. The staff officers in the Force Headquarters set to work on alternative options. Doubts were now openly expressed about the feasibility of constructing the proposed barrier minefield or even the continued viability of holding Assaad itself.

Colonel Alastair awoke with the dull hammering of a whisky hangover deep inside his skull. His mess boy hovered in the darkness of his dugout after placing a mug of tea beside his camp-bed.

'Moo haadha, boy?' he croaked grumpily , reaching for the reading lamp set into the sandbags above his head.

'Maktoob, Sidi.' The light illuminated the dusty interior in a blinding glare. Alastair blinked painfully before catching sight of the cream, crest-embossed envelope sticking up from between the boy's grubby fingers and thumb. Dismissing the lad Alastair hungrily tore open the flap and, after finding his glasses, examined the contents.

It was a brief demi-official from the General. In it, he regretted any embarrassment to Alastair, he really appreciated the additional strain and "at such a difficult time but he knew that he could rely on Alastair's leadership and magnanimity". Alastair gave out a snort of anger, disgust and impotence. Screwing the letter and envelope up together, he hurled them at the wall; all of three feet away. Ignoring the shooting pains behind his eyes, he leaned forward; his fingers searching the dusty floor between the ammunition boxes which supported his bed. Unscrewing the cap he stopped only to gauge the remaining volume of amber liquid before thrusting the neck to his lips and allowing the sharp taste and peaty aroma to retake his numbed senses.

At the officers' mess that morning WO2 Thompson held up what looked like a section of drainpipe.

'Kat-yoosh-ka, Gentlemen,' he announced in his "Let me brighten your darkness" pitch. His audience found their "darkness" little improved as he rattled out the performance statistics of the Soviet-made rocket. 'Warhead about forty pounds but the good news is …' He mimed a music-hall comedian's punchline stance. 'It's not guided!'

'Nearly blew your little house down, 'major,' heckled Giles.

'Beginner's luck!' quipped Mr Thompson, with a cheek-swelling smile. The Colonel put paid to any further jesting by standing up.

'Gentlemen,' he began, looking round lugubriously at the assembly. 'in the light of the appearance of these new factors in this operation, I am cancelling all further patrol activity until we have regained a measure of combat air support.' He allowed the announcement to sink in. 'I want you to look at ways of re-enforcing your sangars.' The Colonel made to sit down but was stopped by a raised finger gesture from the front row. It was John Rolls. A flicker of pain pinched at the wrinkles at the corners of the Colonel's eyes.

'Colonel,' opened Rolls. 'surely if the adoo see that we are not patrolling then, that leaves them free to concentrate on Lion Cub. They will have all the initiative.' Alastair Wilson looked numbed at first. Then he seemed to compose himself with a long intake of breath.

'Major Rolls,' he said, his Calodonian roots suddenly quite evident in his voice. 'In the British Army, orders are not given as a topic for general discussion. We, in the Headquarters, are fully aware of the situation and are able to make the correct decisions accordingly.' He sat down. Rolls felt himself redden. The following silence lasted for an eternity.

'Thank you, Gentlemen,' Mike Cook broke in. 'Just tell your jundis to keep their water use down to a gallon a day, okay?' The officers stirred in a hum of small talk and gradually dispersed. Out in the morning sunlight, Giles fell in alongside Rolls.

'I say, Rolls Old Chap, that was a bit off, y'know.'

'What do you want me to do, Giles?' asked Rolls, without stopping. 'Say yes, sir; no sir and fudge my patrols like you do.' Instant regret stopped him short but it was too late.

'I beg your pardon!' A heavy-fingered hand arrested his progress. Rolls turned and looked directly into Denby-Smith's angry, guilty eyes. He waited for the verbal tactics to form in his mind. He detected a flicker in the skin below Giles' left eye. Giles had coloured up.

'Fudge your patrols, Giles.' Rolls spoke quietly and deliberately. 'Like you did the other night.'

'What do you mean?' blustered Giles. 'I was out all night.'

'Yes, you were,' agreed Rolls. 'But if you had been where you said you'd been, you would have bumped a camel train.'

'Camel train?'

'Yes, twenty or so. I saw them through Eddie Shanks's night 'scope. I saw where you were, too.' The angry flush in Giles' face gave way to the pale mask of denouncement.

'But you didn't tell anyone, did you?' he asked; his voice faltering in pitch. Rolls turned towards the gun-lines and the path to his company.

'I don't tell tales, even if I'm not in the British Army.' He walked on. Giles watched him go before making his own way, the weight of his guilt like lead upon his spirit.

Mike Cook was in the middle of squaring away the command post in readiness for the, now, daily bombardment, when the square shoulders and rounded features of the Medical Officer filled the doorway.

"Panda, what's up? Out of laughing gas!' Panda ignored the joke and perched himself on the edge of the ops table, hands clasped in his lap; thick brows knitted.

'I have a problem, Mike.'

'Haven't we all, Sport?'

'No, this I feel is serious.' Mike Cook stopped rolling up the blinds on one of the back windows.

'Okay,' he said. 'Go get a couple of 'shai's,' Gulor.' The English-speaking Baluch signaller half bowed and disappeared. Mike took station on another table opposite the powerfully built Indian. 'What's up?' Panda fidgeted and shrugged his shoulders as if unsure where to start.

'On Sunday, the Colonel told me that the platoon on Lion Cub needed morphine.'

'That's fair enough,' said Mike. 'Alan could be in deep shit if he gets any cas.' Panda shook his head.

'No, No. I agree and I gave the Colonel a box of twenty syrettes to take over on the re-supply.' Panda broke off.

'So what's wrong? Primmer taken a trip?'

'No, no, on the logreq, last night, he asked for morphine.'

'He wants more!'

'No, he did not receive any from the Colonel. I called him this morning on the radio to ask.' Mike Cook tipped his hat to one side, to scratch his ear.

'Sounds like the Old Man forgot. Got a lot on his plate with one thing and another.' He smiled, knowingly at the MO, 'I'll check it out and let you know.'

'Thank you,' said Panda, and pushing himself from the table he lumbered off into the sun. Mike scribbled a note on the top of his message pad and started his radio checks.

The shelling that day was as heavy as any they had received so far. One sangar in Two Company took a direct hit from a mortar bomb. The roof had partly collapsed but apart from shock, deafness and bruising the occupants escaped. Spurred by the news of this incident much frantic re-enforcement of sangars was carried out in the pauses between incomers. Dusk still brought a respite from the shelling just as the cool, moonlit nights were regarded as a God-given relief from the open-furnace heat of the day. Colonel Alastair had left his spartan supper of tinned tuna and rice half-eaten. He stopped briefly in the command post to flick through the thin sheaf of signals received that day and then retired to his shelter. At his insistence that morning, a work party of jundis had built up the roof protection and had constructed an extra blast wall around the entrance. The structure resembled a bee-hive in shape and he now had difficulty squeezing in and out.

He slumped down in the canvas chair by a crudely-made writing table. The unit carpenter had made the item according to the Colonel's own design. It had a hinged lid which folded back to serve as a map board and stationery holder. Aside from a small-scale map of the jebel, it now held two colour photographs. One showed a smart woman in her forties wearing country-set uniform of green, quilted jacket, tweed skirt and headscarf. She was standing inside a flower-filled marquee; a display of labelled pot-plants in front of her. The other print was of two teenagers lounging against the bonnet of a Volvo estate with a granite-stoned cottage in the background. He flicked on the single, naked bulb fastened to one of the roof beams. He looked at the pictures and felt very home-sick, very alone. Reaching down under the desk he found an occupied segment in the cardboard box and pulled out a bottle of malt whisky. Holding the bottle under the bulb for a second, he watched the light playing on the golden liquid. He picked up a smudgy glass from his bedside table, cracked the seal and poured himself a generous measure. The sweet, smoky tang assailed him momentarily before he drained the glass in one slow, deliberate swallow. A glowing fire warmed his seemingly fish-cold innards as he quickly splashed out another.

It was painful to face, too, bloody painful without a drink. He first realised he had the problem in his second term at Sandhurst. Everybody thought that it was hilarious then, he thought it funny too. His training platoon were creeping around Pirbright Common at the time, clearing the heathland of "pockets of enemy resistance". They had Lee Enfield Number Fours then, and .303 Brens. The enemy, ludicrously over enthusiastic in the face of blank cartridges, were recruits from the Guards Depot. Alastair's section was patrolling a shallow defile at the time. A cry of "Fire" and a volley of blank shots and Bren gun bursts leapt from the thicket on the right-hand side of the track. 'Ambush left' bawled Alastair and eight startled cadets turned their backs to the enemy and charged off all over the common. Oh, everyone laughed then, even the instructors, but Alastair knew the truth. He could feel panic rising through himself at the first inkling of action and there was nothing he could do to stop it.

About twenty minutes later he heard someone feeling their way down the rough hewn steps in the dark. Colonel Alastair had lost track of time.

'Who's that?' he called out in surprise.

'Only me, Colonel.' The thin face of Harry Shaw appeared in the glow of the bulb. Harry Shaw was a solitary, nocturnal drinker of some fifteen years standing and this sudden act of sociability should have rung warning bells in Alastair Wilson's mind. But not tonight. He felt so isolated from all he knew and trusted that even Harry's company was a welcome relief.

'Find yourself a seat, Harry. Sorry about the mess.' His voice was thick and slurred.

Harry pulled up one of the metal ammunition boxes which had

contained the Colonel's few mess traps. He sat down with a false sigh.

It had only been Mike Cook's insistence which had brought him here. The Australian had expressed his concern at the CO's reclusiveness following his accusation of Rolls. Harry had half promised to speak to the Colonel but had otherwise avoided the issue. Harry knew that Alastair Wilson despised him as a "pathetic, drunken queer". Why shouldn't he? Harry despised himself for those same reasons. He was weak morally, physically and, probably, in any other way too. He had found a haven free from the pressures of confrontation and argument in the Emir's service. In this part of the world only Allah, the all-powerful, the all-seeing, made judgements. For man it was all written. In sha'-Allah. Telling one's Commanding Officer that he was neglecting his duties was not conducive to a conflict-free life.

Mike Cook was not a man to be put off by feeble excuses. Earlier that evening, he had cornered Harry in the command post and virtually ordered him to go and "talk it over with the Old Man." Having steeled himself with half of his nightly bottle, he had now reluctantly complied. Harry nervously looked about the cramped compartment while the Colonel rummaged for a glass.

'Not very clean, I'm afraid, Harry,' the Colonel said setting down a cloudy tumbler.

'Glenmorangie alright?'

'Yes, thank you, Colonel,' Harry replied, thinking that so far was so good. The Colonel charged his own glass to the half-way point and gestured a toast.

'Cheers!' He took a gulp, his eyes, heavy-lidded, fixed on Harry's face. Harry drank but the Colonel's dull-eyed stare took away his remaining nerve. His mind ran from excuse to excuse to explain his visit.

'Been looking at the map,' Wilson slurred, his eyes still fixed on Harry. There was a leaden moment which Harry felt compelled to break. Before he could, the Colonel turned away and jabbed unsteadily at the map. 'Bloody hopeless,' he said, shaking his large head. 'Typical of bloody staff officers. Tell the General what he wants to hear, not what the bloody tru …' He stumbled verbally. 'Bloody facts are. We've seen it before, haven't we?'

'What?' Harry's mind was suddenly blanked by his apparent shared experience.

'Bloody staff johnnies!' said the Colonel, annoyed with Harry's obtuseness. He jabbed the map again with one of his stubby digits.

'Brigade task, this, y'know. A full brigade orbat, too. Proper artillery. I should have a BC and a couple of OP parties; not some Geordie buffoon with his toy guns.' Wilson stopped abruptly and sat staring at Harry in mute appeal for agreement.

'Well, now you come to mention it, Colonel,' Harry started meekly.

'And then they take away one of my best company commanders and send me that bloody Gurkha bastard.' Wilson swayed backwards and half-drained his glass. 'Comes in here like a bloody Bedouin, telling me ...' He pointed to his chest with his free hand, eyes now bulging with indignation. 'Me, how to do my bloody business.' Harry sat immobilised by the tirade. The double chink of bottle on glass signalled more of the same. Harry's remaining resolve evaporated. All he could do now was to sit and let the torrent flow over and around him.

High above the Colonel's dugout the soldiers of One Company sat around their firing bays, enjoying the cool peace of the night. Peter White and James Faulkner had begun to settle in for what they expected to be a protracted stay on the jebel. They had built up the sides of their sangar roof initially for use as an observation point from where they could direct mortar and artillery fire. The sand-bag enclosed bay now served as a patio on which the two officers could while away the long, starry nights. They lounged in canvas chairs each with a chunky cocktail glass of gin and tonic water, complete with ice and lemon. The ice now came from a paraffin-run 'fridge grudgingly despatched by the Quartermaster.

'This could be an interesting little war, James,' said White, with a deliberate touch of whimsy. Peter White was relaxed and happy. He had found the ideal war at last. None of the gnawing uncertainty of Ulster here. No doubt about who the enemy was; even if you couldn't see him. No pink cards. No white or yellow cards telling you when you could open fire, whom you could search. This was what he was trained for. True he missed his dour, North-Country Toms but then again, there was certain glamour, a special flair in commanding Arab troops. He would be the only officer with genuine combat experience in his Regiment when he got back.

'A bit worrying about the jets, don't you think?' Faulkner's languid tones broke in on his contemplation.

'Oh, I don't know,' replied White, still partially musing on his heroic homecoming. 'I don't think they made that much difference. Anymore G and T?' Faulkner leaned forward and picked up the plastic jug in front of them.

'What do you think of this chap, Rolls?' asked Faulkner, refilling both of their glasses.

'Like all bloody "Gurks"; bloody arrogant!' pronounced White, without hesitation. 'The way he went off at the CO today.' The young Guards officer frowned and stared out into the gloom as if to define an alternative answer.

'Eddie says that he is very experienced,' Faulkner put in. 'I believe he led the first company into the Jaheed.' Peter White broke out with a braying cackle and then sat up.

'God, James, haven't you heard the expression "tell it to the Marines".' He laughed at his own witticism until he almost choked. 'Oh, dear me.' He recovered himself, stood up and stretched. 'Did you check the Claymores?'

'No, you said you'd do it,' said James, sourly. He was still smarting from his company commander's cavalier dismissiveness.

'Okay, where's the doobly-flick?' said White, wearily looking around for the test unit. He found it unaided and proceeded to disconnect the command wires of each of the six directional mines in turn to check the integrity of their electrical circuits. 'Shit!' he announced. 'Number four's off.' He tested the remaining pair. 'Probably one of Kamil Rashid's boys kicking up the wire.'

'It goes through their boule area,' suggested Faulkner, referring to the designated latrine areas in the shallow re-entrants between the platoons. 'I'll go if you like.'

'No, I want to check the boys out anyway.' Peter White clipped on his webbing belt and slung his FAL onto one shoulder. 'Get the egg banjoes on and I'll be back in ten.' He stepped over the wall and dropped down into the bay.

It was past eleven and all but the sentries had withdrawn into their shelter sangars to curl up and sleep on their banduris, thick cotton sleeping-mats, until the time for their watch or the morning stand-to. Peter White ambled down to Two Platoon and, after a brief word to the sentry, picked up the twin wires to the unresponsive mine. It was impossible to bury the firing cable so they ran over the rocky surface pinned under sizeable rocks at regular intervals. White wrinkled his nose with distaste as he passed through the boule area; choosing to lean down and peer closely at the wire rather than to run along it with his fingers. At last, he came to the skeletal shadows of the coiled-wire fence. The wires led to what looked like a miniature radar scanner standing, immobile, on matchstick legs. It stood there exuding silent menace like some alien, robot intruder. Peter shuddered inwardly at the thought of its destructive potential. He saw immediately that one of the wires had come free of its plastic socket. The wire had been pulled free of its anchoring rock so Peter deduced that it had indeed been inadvertently kicked by some defecating jundi.

He fixed the wire and stood up. He looked round and scanned the position. ' From an attackers' point of view it was a tough proposition,' he thought. 'Bare, rounded slopes, devoid of cover, the approaches to each platoon position more than adequately covered by fire from one or two of the others. The wire fence covered by the claymores, machine-gun and mortar fire.'

'Bloody text book,' he thought. 'Must get some pictures tomorrow. Bound to be asked to give a presentation when I get back.' He followed the course of the perimeter wire west along the front of Two Platoon.

White had gone about thirty yards when he stopped. A movement out beyond the wire caught his eye; no, a light. He turned and stared at the distant twinkling. It was high up on the skyline of one of the middle-distance ridges.

'Could be a torch, no ... Venus more than likely.' He mentally ticked off the possibilities. Then he stepped back to get a better look. Crack. A blaze of light to his right the steady roar of burning magnesium. A taut wire bit into his ankle. He spun round, mouth wide. 'Tripflare!' A hammer-blow sent him sprawling backwards. Crackling fire, thunder-clapped above him. Winded, he could not breath. He tried to turn over but could not move. The Dannert wire snared his shirt; tore at his neck and head. The sharp, staccato cracks went on above. The short, echoing rattle of machine-guns' rattling reports followed.

'God, I've been shot,' he thought. A numbness spread outwards from his groin. He felt his fingers moving: to do what he did not know. Blood, he felt it on his hands; slick, wet, warm. It trickled down his back to pool in the seat of his trousers. He felt numb and cold.

The firing stopped. He became aware of shouting.

'Help! I've been shot!' he called. At least he thought he did but not a sound passed his moving lips. He could see the sky and the stars crossed by bands of spikes; the wire, he was in the wire. Shapes appeared over him, touching, lifting, turning him. One loomed nearer, blotting out the stars.

'Peter, Peter,' it was saying. 'You're going to be alright.' Peter White nodded or at least he imagined that he did. He felt himself being lifted, then he was floating up and up …

* * *

'Mike, we've got a 'taqleef' in One Platoon.' Faulkner's voice sounded edged with concern over the field telephone.

'What's up, Matey?' Mike asked.

'The jundi who shot the boss has got together with some of his relatives. They've convinced themselves that we are planning some sought of reprisal.' Faulkner's voice had regained some of its laconic calm. 'I've tried to calm them down but I'm afraid that I don't seem to be making much of an impression.'

'Roger that, Sport, hang-on.' Mike Cook lowered the phone to listen to a message coming over the unit rear link. The night-time atmosphere had a peculiar effect on the high-frequency radio circuits. In this case, it was making the Airhead Duty Officer sound like Donald Duck on barbiturates. Mike heard the message out and then lifted the field telephone handset.

'Hey, Jimbo. I got to jack up the lights for the casevac chopper.'

'I'll send the Second in Command down; Harry's good at sorting "Rubshas". Okay?'

'Okay. How's Peter?'

'Panda reckons he'll make it.'

'Fine. I'll wait here in the CP for Harry.' Faulkner rang off.

'Shit!' he swore. 'Everything's at the fucking treble.' He gave terse instructions to the signals lieutenant who was acting as duty officer and then ducked under the black-out to find Harry. It was not until he stuck his head into the 2i/c's sangar that he remembered that he still had not told the Colonel. The CO's increasing abrogation of responsibility over the last fortnight had led Mike to run things as if he did not exist. The Australian back-tracked to the Colonel's dugout. He felt his way down the steps and pushed through the sacking curtain.

The air inside was hot, fetid and whisky laden. The Colonel was slumped at his desk, head on his arms snoring loudly. Harry lolled against one of the side walls, a glass in his hand.

'Hello, Mike, Old Thing,' he slurred, thickly.

'Harry,' Mike began. 'Peter White's been shot.'

'Shot!' Harry repeated in inebriated disbelief.

'Yes, shot.' Mike dropped to his haunches and gently relieved Harry of his glass.

'Sentry opened up on a tripflare.'

'Flare?'

'Oh Christ, Harry, what a time to get shit-faced.' The shit-faced Harry nodded agreement at Mike Cook's departing back.

'Sorry, Old Thing, awfully sorry.'

CHAPTER FOURTEEN

Peter White survived the night to receive emergency surgery at the hands of an RAF Field Surgical Team at Harrow. Two 7.62 millimetre bullets had ploughed their way through his abdomen without damaging any vital organs, main blood vessels or nerve centres. Once he was restabilised from surgery he would be medevaced to an RAF hospital in Wiltshire and a hero's welcome; albeit a discreet one.

Major White unwittingly left a sense of irrevocably deepening crisis in his wake. When Colonel Wilson woke, soreheaded and nauseated, the following morning, he found himself as besieged by his own sense of hopelessness as his unit was besieged by the adoo. Mike Cook had spent the night calming down the frightened and agitated jundis in One Company with the stolid support of the RSM. He had lost any pretence of respect or loyalty to his Commanding Officer. The Colonel attempted to purge his shame by spending the day drafting a long, disjointed letter to the General. He managed to regurgitate some of the sentiments which he had expressed to Harry Shaw the previous evening; not that he remembered.

As if privy to the events of that night, the adoo added a new tactic to their already extensive repertoire. For the first time the forward positions came under small-arms fire. At first it was a lone sniper or perhaps a pair, later a light machine-gun. The enemy remained as remote and as invisible as before but to the jundis, in the forward sangars something had changed: now they could imagine a man behind a gun. The helicopter re-supply, already constrained by the frequency of the shelling and the threat of SAMs, now became fleeting, furtive drops; the Huey's skids barely touching the ground before the crewmen were frantically kicking out the precious stores. Operation Saladin had suddenly taken on the aspect of long and grim investment.

Alan Primmer sat on the command post wall tossing a stone in his hand. It had been nearly a week since the main position had last come under small arms fire. So far, Cub had been left alone. They had received their quota of mortar rounds and SPG rockets but nothing more. Alan was now happy in his isolation. He looked about at the two platoons of jundis preparing for the evening stand-to. The position was so compact that he felt that he could hit any one of the sangars with his stone, that was how he liked it; tight, compact, no complications.

That was one reason why he was glad to be detached. Not content with just being an opinionated bore and an intolerable snob, Giles Denby-Smith was, in Alan's mind, unbelievably incompetent. Wrong decisions and errors of judgement, Alan understood, and could readily forgive, but Giles would never admit that he was wrong, and, even worse, would change his mind, direction and plans regardless of the effect. He had intended asking for a transfer within a month of Giles' arrival but changed his mind when the warning order for Operation Saladin was given. Seven years in and had never a shot fired in anger, he could not miss this one.

The undulating accent of Mr Thompson, responding to an unheard fire request, told him that "Mother", his private name for the main position was standing-to. He leaned down and told the signaller, sitting in the gloom below, to pass "stand-to". Buckling on his webbing, he picked up his rifle and began his rounds. He felt fortunate in that he could walk to his outer positions and not have to creep and crawl along communication trenches like Giles and James had to do on their positions. He stopped at a shallow white and pink scar in the bare rock surface. Stirring the pulverised stone in the middle with his toe, he exposed a few silver shards of metal; SPG 9. He reflected on his luck so far. Perhaps it was because Cub was so narrow; the flat top only sixty metres across at the widest point. The edges dropped away steeply on three sides. It was a difficult target even if you had plotting computers and experienced artillery spotters. Cub was certainly too small for the Katyushas; he shuddered at the prospect.

On reaching the first sangar he did a cursory check to make sure that everyone was present, well, and by the standards of the day, happy. Walking on to the next section, he inwardly marvelled at the stoicism and hardiness of his soldiers. The jundis were mostly from the villages of the coastal strip and fertile wadis of the south. Violence was virtually unknown in their society unlike the wild-eyed camel and goat herders of the northern uplands. To the latter, the blood feud was a part of daily life. Of course, the adoo came from the heart of these uplands where he was now. He smiled at the irony. Not that he was not proud of his own boys.

Within the bounds of their physical and mental capacities, they gave their best and complained very little. A British battalion fed on nothing but corned mutton and tuna with not a can of beer or a film show in sight would have gone "over the hill" a month ago. He was happy too that he never had to worry about sleeping sentries. In his two years in the Emirate he had never heard of any Arab or Baluch dozing off. He grinned at the possible explanation; to a man, they were fervent believers in the "demons of the night", despite being devout Muslims. They were also avid listeners to dramatic renditions of popular Arabian fantasy stories broadcast nightly from Radio Cairo. That seemed to re-enforce their nocturnal fear of djinns and the like.

The last rosiness of the evening sky gave way to uniform blue-grey as Alan Primmer stepped over the low wall of his Second Platoon's headquarters sangar.

'The night is peaceful, Sah'b,' said the platoon commander in ritual greeting.

'Praise be to Allah,' Alan replied, his right hand automatically moving over his heart. The gesture had now become natural to him. He squatted down placing his rifle between his knees. 'Kayf Haalkum?' he asked the little group who sat round their commander, Ali Khamess. A straggling litany of 'Zayns,' 'Mabsoots' and 'Handu l'illah's' followed. He looked around. One or two smiled shyly under his gaze.

'Kull she zayn, Ali?' he asked of the diminutive Arab Officer. Ali smiled and nodded.

'Kull she zayn, Sah'b.' Every thing is well. Not that Ali Khamees would say otherwise, Alan thought. As a strict Muslim, he believed that life and every occurrence in it was God-given. He would have praised Allah and have been 'Mabsoot' even if he had been slowly starving to death. Alan asked a number of questions about the ammunition and ration states. Ali rattled off his precise holdings without hesitation. Alan smiled in secret admiration of the lieutenant's conscientiousness; but then he had to know all such minutiae by rote as he could neither read nor write.

Alan knew Ali Khamees when he was still a Naqeeb, staff-sergeant. Though only thirty, this was Ali's twentieth year in the Emir's service. The third son of one Khamees Mohammed al

Rakura, a date farmer in the Wadi Dhalheen, his fortunes lay in the Army or the Mosque. The family eeked out a living from land first irrigated by Persian engineers eleven hundred years before the Prophet. The field systems had shrunk back over the millennia and now yielded barely a quarter of what was harvested under the rule of the Satrap.

At a fraction below five foot four and lean eight stone, Ali was of average size for the Arab part of the army. With raven black curling hair and dark, deep set eyes he had retained his boyish good looks. His brothers were prematurely bent and aged with rough leathery skins from the rigours of work in the field and a diet dependant on capricious harvest fortunes. Given early schooling and encouragement Ali could have entered almost any profession of his choice. Only the concept of choice would never occur to him. Personal ambition was not in keeping with the strict Islamic perception of life in the Wadi Dhalheen. Allah would provide and Ali Khamees would be grateful.

Alan left the platoon commander with a short word of praise which set him glowing with pride. Since joining the Emir's forces Alan had been amazed how much the jundis appreciate a little praise for their efforts. Giles judged them by the standards of his technology born and bred hussars and harangued them day and night. That was one of the lessons which the seconded officers rarely learnt in time, he thought, to adjust to the change of pace. He recalled his first week when he arrived in the Emirate as a contract officer. Something for which his five year commission in the British Army could never had prepared him: a step back into the 19th century and sometimes beyond. When he wrote and told his father that his battalion maintained a donkey platoon he felt like he was writing fiction.

On reaching his own command post he checked the communications link with Assaad. Mike Cook's bored drawl confirmed his signal strength and wished him a 'quiet night'. Alan stripped off his webbing and settled into a corner of the sangar. The temperature was still about 20 °C; too hot to try to sleep in the stifling pit of the shelter. He took out a small transistor radio from which a white ear-piece dangled on a thin umbilical cord. Fitting the plug into his ear, he searched the short wave band for the BBC World Service. The prim tones of Jean Chalice filled far more functions to isolated ex-patriots like Primmer than ever envisaged by the directors of the Overseas Service. Apart from the BBC and the terse, procedural English of the unit radio net, the only time that Alan heard English was when he was occasionally visited by the CO during re-supply. He had not seen the Colonel now for a week or more, but with the increase in enemy activity he was not unduly alarmed. He looked up at the stars twinkling above and savoured libidinous thoughts around the disembodied voice of Miss Chalice.

Had he not had the earpiece in he might have heard the ripple of distant thumps. Instead a lightning flash blinded him, a hurricane blew him flat, stones and sand stung his face, debris clattered down. Silence for a long second. He felt warm, comfortable. Then he fought to move. He shrugged off burst sandbags, stones and dirt. Men coughed and groaned in the settling dust cloud. His ears rang. He blew his nose with his hand to clear his breathing. His command post was a shambles of dust, debris and slowly moving bodies.

Wham, bang. The air was savagely split, the ground heaved, he fell over again. More debris pattered down on his back. He fought to stand up, no rifle to hand, no radio, everything was buried. He clawed away in the dark feeling for familiar shapes. He found his FAL and stood up. More squawks, more whooshing air.

'Incomers!' he shouted out at the deaf and silent stars.

Primmer struggled forward to the roof of his sangar. He pushed himself up and lay there trying to order his mind. The blast from a quartet of bombs on Three Platoon whipped at his face and arms. His mind raced, 'night attack; first one. Adoo assault.' He drew himself up onto his knees. Turning left and right he shouted out. 'Shoof minshaan adoo!' Watch for the enemy. He prayed that the sections had not bolted down into their shelters. No answer came back. Then another idea stuck him.

'Any casualties?' he yelled in Arabic. This time voices floated back.

'Marshay, marshay.'

'None,' he thought. 'Good, they're still out in the sangars.' A groan followed by a word of re-assurance in Arabic below brought his attention back to his own headquarters. He was about to move when the combined whistle and purring sound of mortars and rockets flattened him again. Another salvo beat a vicious, earth-shaking tattoo along the ridge.

'Bloody Hell!' exclaimed Mike Cook. 'Where's that?' The echo of the incomers on Cub reverberated out from across the wadi. He jumped up from the Ops desk and stepped out into the night air. Harry Shaw came down from the mess veranda with Panda.

'It's Cub,' said Mike. 'I hope this is not going to become a habit.'

'I'm surprised they haven't shelled us at night before,' said Harry. 'Have you told the Colonel?'

'He can hear it for himself, can't he?' Mike replied tartly. He was going to add, 'If he's sober?' but refrained in front of Panda.

They stood watching in silence for a moment. The faint thump of mortars reached them from some distant wadi. They waited, breathing stilled, for a full half minute, then saw the bright yellow flashes jump about on the dark hump across the big wadi to the east. Seconds later the echoing drumbeats of the explosions confirmed what they had seen. Mr Thompson's voice on Mike Cook's transceiver broke their fascination. 'Zero, this is 79 standing by. No word with 29A, over.' Mike Cook lowered his head and spoke into the microphone clipped to his lapel.

'Roger, can you eye-dent the incomers?'

'Mor'ers,' the Geordie lilt putting in a glottal stop. 'Baseplate somewhere around Redesdale. If you hear a flat bang that'll be the SPG. Might spot the backblast too.'

'Roger 79,' Mike replied, 'You copy that Sunrays?' he added, for the benefit of the company commanders. His pocketphone confirmed that they were listening. Mike turned towards the CP.

'Be a good 'un, Harry and tell the "Old Man". I'll be up in the tower.' Harry nodded sadly and with some resignation went off to tell the Colonel what was happening. Mike had the signallers remote his main radio sets up to the small observation sangar on top of the CP. There he pored over the map looking for Redesdale, in the thin spot of a pencil torch.

The Gulf Arabs were less than sentimental over the naming of small geographical features, so the sergeant major had named a number of prominent ridges and wadis to act as reference points. In retaliation for the naming of all the Emirate's airfields after English public schools, he used the placenames from his hometown area of Hexham.

The flashes on Cub increased steadily as did the rumbling echoes that followed. Mike repeatedly called 29A on the main Racal set but there was no answer. He tried his Panasonic but there was nothing. A grunting and wheezing behind him announced the ascent of the CO followed by Harry Shaw.

'Any word from Primmer?' asked the Colonel, slumping down on the makeshift bench beside Mike. The sweet smell of whisky assailed him like a blanket.

'No, Colonel,' he replied, making an effort to keep the disgust out of his voice. All three sat for a moment, as yet another cascade of flashes swept across the black ridge. 'They're getting a real bloody pounding,' said Mike. 'I think this is an assault.' The Colonel gave a slurred murmur of doubt. Inside an old nightmare of chaos and shame rose up through the well of his subconscious. Neither expecting nor receiving any form of direction or advice from his CO, Mike took the initiative and ordered the gunline to lay every weapon onto Cub's defensive fire targets.

They continued to watch the flashes leaping about in a grotesque light show for a few more minutes. Mike tried to call 29A again when the Eastern sky lit up with a strobe ripple of light. The air jumped with a cacophony of sharp explosions.

'Jesus Christ! What's that?' exclaimed Mike, rising from his bench. The hammering of distant automatic fire followed. 'It is an assault,' he yelled in Alastair Wilson's ear. Wilson stared at him, his eyes bulging in stark terror.

Mike sat down and shone his pen-torch onto his map. Selecting two recorded targets on the north end of Cub he spoke quickly to the gunline. Within seconds the CP was lit by the muzzle flash of the four Indian 75s. Their sharp, cracking report as distinctive as a bugle note. The hollow, drainpipe thump of the medium mortars followed.

'Must have had a direct hit on the CP,' surmised Mike to his dumbstruck audience. The Colonel stirred.

'Are we stood to?' he asked urgently, the slur disappearing fast.

'Yes, we are, Colonel,' snapped Mike, he was staring through his binoculars at the beleaguered outpost. He could see faint stabs of light in between the brighter flashes of the shell-bursts. Mike dropped the glasses and thumped the sandbags in front of him.

'We've got to get a counter-attack ready, Colonel,' he stated in a sharp matter-of-fact tone. 'We've got to assume the worst and get it moving now.' Wilson shook his head, his mouth falling open.

'But what if they attack us as well?' he spluttered out, his jowl quivering. His secret fears now exposed. 'It's out of the question!'

'But we gotta try,' interrupted Mike, ignoring the Colonel's protestations. 'An' better soon than later.' He stood up and spoke quickly into his microphone. '39, are you watching?' John Rolls impassive voice replied.

'Yes, I'm on the crest with 39A.'

Mike continued, 'I've no contact with 29A and assume a hit on his CP. Meet me in five for orders.' Mike Cook picked up his map and binoculars and climbed over the sangar wall. Colonel Wilson remained seated, looking out at the sparking and flashing inferno which was Cub. All the eastern sky now glowed with the light of ignited trip-flares, their smoke reflecting the flashes of the gunfire and explosions. Harry Shaw leaned forward and placed his bony-hand on Wilson's hunched shoulders.

'He's right, Colonel,' he said gently, 'we have to try. We have to send someone.'

By the time John Rolls entered the CP the shelling of Cub had ceased; by the gun-line as well as by the adoo. Sporadic small-arms fire continued. It seemed to observers on Assaad that the only resistance was coming from the southern tip of the feature. Mike Cook had expected a protest from Giles Denby-Smith over the choice of Three Company for the counter-attack or the fact that he would have to thin out his position to cover the vacated flank. Giles concurred without comment and even sent a runner with a rough sketch map of the section positions on Cub. It gave the names of all of the platoon and section commanders. "Good Luck" was scrawled on the bottom.

The plan that Cook and Rolls hastily evolved was that Three Company, less the platoon detailed to Giles, would march out directly to a forming up position, 500 metres south of the feature. They would then assault through the feature and pull out any survivors to await a helicopter lift at first light. The decision to abandon Cub was taken for granted. Force Headquarters merely acknowledged the coded signal outlining the plan. All Mr Thompson's support weapons were laid on the central and northern sectors of Cub. As there had been no signals from Cub for over an hour it was decided to shell them in order to take the pressure off any survivors and to cover the approach march of the relief force.

Rolls had not been gone for more than ten minutes when Colonel Wilson burst through the CP's blanket-curtained door.

He stood there gently swaying and eyeing up his Australian Ops Officer. Mike could smell fresh whisky and steeled himself for a confrontation.

'Why are the guns firing?' he asked; his voice absurdly petulant and slurred.

'To cover Three Company's approach,' Mike replied turning on his canvas seat.

'Call them back!' Wilson snapped. Mike made no movement. The Colonel blinked and he hiccoughed ridiculously. 'I said bloody well call them back!' he tottered forward, a podgy fist thumped down on the signallers table: partly for effect, partly for support. 'It's no use. They're all dead,' he continued in justification.

'No, Colonel,' Mike began, with a calm, deliberate authority. 'We can't assume that and even if they were, we don't leave our men behind, dead or alive, in this army.' He emphasised the 'we' and the 'this' to obvious effect.

Wilson glared at him, his lips a taut line of impotence. His eyes misted over with frustration and panic. He lunged forward and grabbed at the command net radio hand-set. He fumbled the hand set up to his chin.

'Put it down or I'll drop you where you stand!' The Colonel froze in surprise as if a third person had spoken. He turned his head to look into the wide, black muzzle of a Colt .45 auto. It was held rock steady; the foreshortened image made the barrel seem a full inch wide.

'Put the handset down and go to bed.' The strange new voice directed slowly with undisguised threat. The cheery strine replaced by the acidly clipped vowels of the Brisbane waterfront. The Colonel's alcohol-abetted resolution crumbled and fell away leaving him divested of anything save primitive fear. He backed away to the door, his eyes still focused on the Colt. With a baleful moan he turned and fled through the doorway, ripping the blanket away. Mike heard him stumbling down the steps of his shelter. The signaller who had been an immobile and silent witness bent forward and picked up the dropped handset.

'Fetch the Police Sergeant!' Mike ordered, holstering his Colt and resuming his seat. The signaller jumped to obey. Mike took a long, deep reflective breath and pondered on a plausible defence at his forthcoming Court Martial.

'Fuck it!' he thought. 'We'll sort tomorrow out when it comes.'

The signaller returned with a burly, six-foot Baluch sporting handle-bar moustaches and a Stirling sub-machine gun. He was known to the officers as Akhbar Ali or 'Big Ali.

'Ali,' Mike began informally in his version of strine Arabic. 'The Muqaddam has had bad dreams, he may have seen a djinn.' He paused to check the credulity of his story in Ali's face. 'He will sleep again but must not leave his sangar tonight, understood?'

Akhbar Ali glanced at the silent signaller, a sign that he had already been fully and probably more pictorially briefed. He nodded his big, turbanned head; black eyes dull, impassive.

'Afham, Sidi.' He rotated on his heel and walked away. Mike smiled inwardly at the two points in his favour in entrusting his personal security to Akhbar Ali. One, he could connect a dramatic upsurge in attacks on tax collectors and policemen in Ali's home province in Baluchistan with Ali's leave periods. Two, he knew of and contributed to Ali's secret taste for the forbidden lager. The question of a conflict of loyalties did not exist.

* * *

There was no moon that night and now they were on the wadi floor Rolls was dependant on his compass to keep direction. The Cub feature was obscured by a series of low sandstone ridges which sat like islands in the silvery sand river of the wadi. The islands were, by comparison, thickly wooded with thorn bushes and twisted and gnarled dwarf acacias. The company moved in two columns thirty metres apart; Rolls leading one, Shanks the other. Rolls looked right to see Shank's column plainly silhouetted against the sand. He felt the gnawing fear in the pit of his stomach that they could be walking into an ambush. He rationalised the thought away. Surely the adoo would concentrate their forces on Cub. It would stretch even the most sophisticated military mind to ambush the counter-attack. Besides, he thought, he could still hear the tell-tale report of a lonely FAL amidst the light, rapid tapping of Kalahnikovs and RPKs. The shelling from Assaad had dwindled to a couple of mortar rounds per minute. Rolls guessed that Mr Thompson was desperate to conserve ammunition. He looked to his right again and immediately recognised Shanks by the small pack that he habitually wore in addition to his fighting order. He checked the weight once and reckoned that Eddie carried about twice the ammunition of anyone else.

It was 0200 hours and they were nearly across the wadi. The Cub feature flanked by its subsidiary spurs loomed high in front of them like a dark building. Though they had made no transmissions, Rolls knew that he still had radio contact with Assaad. He also knew that there had been no contact with Cub. Now they were in the deep shadow of the run-off wadis which led up to the main ridge. Picking roughly parallel spurs, the two columns moved steadily upwards to their pre-arranged forming-up position. The sporadic shots appeared to come from just over the next crest. Far from being apprehensive Rolls took comfort in the fact that their mission was not to be in vain and that they would have some foothold once over the crest.

The columns converged to the mutual relief of the two white officers, two hundred metres short of the final crest-line. Rolls beckoned each platoon forward and led them to their start-line, pointing the axis of advance to each NCO with a single, strong gesture of his arm and a reassuring grasp of the shoulder. Some smiled nervously, others glowered grimly at the star speckled skyline.

In a matter of minutes the company was shaken out in its assault formation. Two platoons in the first wave, the third and the headquarters elements in the second. Eddie Shanks closed up to Rolls in the centre.

'How do you feel?' asked Rolls.

'Shitting myself!' said Eddie bluntly, though in truth he was not. Tense with the prospect of the ultimate test of battle certainly, but frightened, no. Rolls looked at the prominent eyes, near luminous in the star light. He felt the tension in his partner, not the tension of a coiled spring but the set, reliable tension of a trigger on first pressure. Eddie would not let him down.

'Fight through to the CP,' Rolls instructed. 'If they bug out altogether we'll go on to the platoon on the northern position; if not, pull any wounded out and we'll consolidate on the southern flank. The Adoo will have finished off any wounded, I'm sure.' Eddie nodded, Rolls heard him swallow dryly.

'Good luck, then,' Shanks said. He felt that he should have shook hands with Rolls or something but shyly turned away instead and sought out his assault position. Rolls watched him go, the thought that he might not see him again pricked his brain like a thorn under his skin.

Looking left and right at the tightly packed ranks of jundis kneeling up, alert and braced, gave him a familiar lift. To Rolls this was what life was all about. He held up his right hand and then dramatically drew the stubby Kalashnikov bayonet and fitted it over the muzzle brake with a satisfying metallic click. He heard a succession of clicks as the company obeyed his silent signal and fitted their own socket-bayonets over the flash hiders of their FALs. As he had done ever since joining his first company of Gurkhas in Hong Kong, Rolls' right hand dropped down and felt the gnarled outline of the lion's head on the handle of the heavy-bladed kukri, secured in its scabbard on his right hip. An old Gurkhali benediction flashed through his mind as he slowly rose to his feet: 'Many heads or a quick death.'

Like a slow tide the company crept steadily on towards the crest of the plateau. His senses primed, Rolls felt as though he could hear his own heart-beat pounding out an alarm inside his chest. Here and there a jundi kicked a loose stone whose flinty ring seemed to echo around the hill sides. Just below the crest he dipped his lips towards the microphone clipped to his lapel. He squeezed the transmit switch and whispered the pre-arranged code-word for "crossing the start-line". He had no sooner spoken when he was over the top. A reassuring glance left and right. The company was still there; Shanks pushing slightly ahead to his right. There in front lay the gray mounds of the southern platoons' emplacements. No movement, no sound.

'La irmoo, thalaatha sariyya!' he called in what seemed to him a stage whisper. He felt the young rifleman to his left jump with surprise. He held up his left hand and stopped, uttering a single hiss. The skirmish line juddered to a halt and sank, as one to a crouch, weapons poised. For a moment Rolls clearly imagined an adoo gunner taking first pressure on his RPK, the fore-sight steady on his chest. He took a few paces forward and immediately felt foolish for doing so.

'Ay wahed?' he appealed to the silent grey mounds. 'Haadhu Thalaatha Sariyya!' He waited: nothing. He half turned to wave the company on when a single Arabic voice spoke from his left.

'Sah'b Raa'id! Haadha Darweesh.' Rolls felt an involuntary smile crease his face. He reached the voice in five strides and looked down on a huddled mass of jundis, twenty or thirty. Darweesh the platoon commander of Three Platoon, Two Company reached up a trembling hand. Switching his AK to his left hand, Rolls grasped it.

'Hamdu li'llah, Hamdu li'llah, seedee!' Darweesh cried, nearly pulling Rolls into the pit. Rolls grasped his thin shoulder to calm him.

'Where's the captain?' he hissed in Arabic.

'Dead, Sah'b,' Darweesh answered. 'with many others.' The raw sound of the word stunned him like a blow. He knew, of course, but it was still a shock. The first wave of Three Company flowed over the positions, halted, sank down to merge into the blue-grey landscape.

'What about One Platoon?' Rolls asked.

'Here, Sah'b, Ali Khamees is over there.' Darweesh pointed past Rolls to the next sangar. 'He has many wounded.'

'Where's the Adoo?'

'Over there.' Darweesh pointed unhelpfully northwards. Rolls pondered the risks for a moment and then stood up.

'Stay here, Darweesh. Helicopters are coming.' Without waiting for Darweesh's gratitude to Allah or himself, Rolls trotted forward to his slot in the skirmish line.

With a quick hand signal the company was up and moving. Rolls opened the pace as he crossed the flat plateau. His right thumb pushed the safety bar to "single shots'" on his AK. His eyes strained into the gloom to pick out the command post. Then he saw it. A figure bobbed up from the box-line structure, a stabbing flash in the dark. The air above ripped by angry cracks.

'Standby,' he shouted in English. He stopped, AK rising to his shoulder. 'Bullets!' The AK bucked, rifles crashed left and right. 'Advance.' The tide surged forward to fill the shocked silence. A small, lean shadow sprang up again and disappeared. The sangar loomed up in front of him. The wave split and carried on around it. He heard the sound of desperate running over the measure tread of the company.

'Standby!' he shouted again. 'Bullets!' Another volley of sixty rifles crashed out. To the fleeing handful of tribesmen it was a thunderclap. One fighter threw out his arms and crashed face down in the dust; vertebrae and ribs shattered. His comrades, picking over the debris of One Platoon's position, dropped down into the rubble and squeezed off token bursts of resistance. The company emerged out of the darkness and delivered a third volley in a rippling flash. In an instant, the sweeping wave was an avalanche tipped with a dull, grey steel. The tribesmen took not a second look but simply turned and threaded their way through the wire and away back down into the darkness of the wadi. It was over, Cub had been retaken.

Rolls sat against the sangar wall adding up the sad columns of names which would only inadequately tell the story of Primmer's desperate fight that night. He handed the completed message to his signaller who proceeded to tap out the encoded format on the Morse key strapped to his thigh. Eddie Shanks's tousled head and blackened face appeared over the sandbags.

'Okay, boss, we're all set below,' he stated in his usual deadpan fashion.

'Cheers, Eddie,' Rolls replied suppressing a yawn. He was weary in the anti-climax of the assault. 'Make sure the bodies go off in the third lift.' Shanks nodded sadly; his thoughts like his leader's, on the limp, bloodied body of Alan Primmer.

Atop the battalion command post Cook, Shaw and Denby-Smith sat silently watching the first glimmerings of dawn. A signaller appeared at the roof's edge.

'Message, Sah'b,' he said, handing a flimsy sheet to Mike. The Ops Officer read through the tabulations of letters and numbers and then translated aloud for the other two.

'Killed in Action, fourteen including 29A, Missing five, Wounded six. Fighting strength, forty-five. Three Company, no casualties. Two enemy dead left on the position.' He raised his head. 'Johno added that it was pretty quick and clean for all of them.' Harry and Giles nodded glumly. It was small comfort but it allayed the unspoken fears of almost all of the ex-patriot officers. There had been no mutilation of the dead or wounded. Al hamdhu li'llah.

CHAPTER FIFTEEN

Colonel Dixon woke with a start. He was slumped awkwardly in a cane armchair in his office. His mouth was gummy and dry, his neck ached, still dopey with sleep he raised his left hand and casually noted the time; 0610 hours. Pushing himself up out of the chair, he rubbed his eyes and made his way to the inter-joining door leading to the ADC's office.

Donal was busily supervising an orderly in the preparation of tea and sandwiches. Gilbert Dixon gratefully accepted a cup.

'Any more news, Donal?' He said, after half draining the cup.

'They're on the final lift now, Colonel.' the Aide replied. In spite of having been up all night he was fresh and smart.

'Does the Commander know?' Gilbert asked.

'Just going in now, sir.' Donal snatched up a clipboard of typed signals and reached for the door handle just before the tea-laden orderly. Gilbert Dixon followed, cup in hand.

Major-General Welles raised his head up from his arms. His eyes were puffy and sleep-encrusted. He sat up as the tray was placed before him.

'Damn!' he growled, causing the mess-boy to jump back. The General was feeling the end of his shirt collar. 'Dribbled on me shirt!' He looked up at his Chief-of-staff and Aide and gave them the briefest of smiles. 'Looks like Rolls pulled it off then. Any news of the final bill?' Gilbert took a chair by the desk as Donal placed the clipboard in front of the Commander. Welles perused the list of casualties for a moment and then leaned back. 'Could have been worse, Gilbert.' Dixon nodded. He pursed his lips, steepled his fingers and searched his mind for a suitable reply.

'I suppose the whole concept of Saladin is in the melting pot?' He ventured from behind the steeple. Welles nodded but his eyes wanted more. Gilbert collapsed his steeple. 'The original aim will have to be modified at least.'

'Assuming that what we have been told was the real objective?' Gilbert acknowledged the caveat. Welles sipped his tea and awaited a response.

'We could do well to save that little titbit from Abu Issa for the joint conference.'

'I shall be interested in what Henson has to say,' Welles said leaning back. He looked past Gilbert to his wall clock. 'Right then, I'm off for a shave and a shower.' He rose from his chair and stretched. 'I wonder how Old Alastair's feeling this morning?'

Gilbert rose and opened the door to the balcony.

'Seems to have kept his head well enough last night,' he commented.

'I expected him on the net every other minute.' He shrugged. 'Sensible man left it all to Mike Cook.'

'Aye, I'm quite encouraged.' Welles clapped on his beret and strode purposefully out into the morning sun.

Mike Cook and Harry Shaw watched the last of the Hueys disgorge the rear-guard of Three Company at the LS before clattering away in the usual maelstrom of dust. The little knots of jundis gathered around the landing site began to disperse. Sad Panda's orderlies led away two of the walking wounded. The recently disembarked rear-guard stood in line extracting live rounds from the breeches of their FALs under the eye of their wakeel. Giles Denby-Smith shepherded the last of the survivors from the ill-fated Cub detachment back towards his company position. Harry Shaw had watched these ragged remnants with a wave of emotion straining at the back of his throat. As one of the founding fathers of the Third Battalion he knew every NCO and jundi; some since he took up his first contract back in '68. He watched as Giles took the field pack off one small, limping figure and, slipping an arm around his back, half carried him down the track. Harry sniffed and wiped his glistening eyes with the back of his hand. He turned to Mike Cook.

'Has the Colonel been told?' Mike's face broke into a mask of self-annoyance.

'Shit, no. I forgot all about him.' He hesitated remembering that Akhbar Ali would still be standing guard. Harry sensed Mike's reluctance to embark on any face to face encounter with his CO after the events of the previous night.

'No bother. I'll go,' he said feeling a lift of pride in being able to return favours given.

'Cheers, Harry.' Mike turned towards the CP while Harry

straightened his shirt and headcloth before going to shake the Colonel.

Dismissing the Regimental Police Sergeant from his post, Harry descended into the darkness of the blast shelter. He sensed something different about the air. The dugout was rank with the stale smells of confined, human habitation but there was something else besides. A bitter, acrid odour which filled his nose and mouth. All was black and still inside. He felt around the wooden supports for the light switch. Harry blinked as the naked bulb became a miniature sun. A large, corpulent figure lay motionless on the camp bed covered in a blanket.

'Colonel,' whispered Harry. The figure remained still. 'Colonel,' Harry piped, leaning closer. He stared at the Colonel's face; blanched and bloated, eyes shut, lips parted, a bluish tinge. Harry felt his neck hairs rise. 'Oh no!' he cried. He grabbed the Colonel's hand. It was limp, cold and dry to touch. He dropped it. Stepping back he spun a bottle. It was an empty Malt. Its twin beside it had a puddle of liquor in the bottom. In between lay four or five plastic and metal tubes. Like tiny toothpaste tubes, bent over or squeezed flat. Harry scrambled up the steps and yelled for Mike.

Panda laid the dead Colonel's hands together on his chest before covering the pallid, marbled face with the blanket.

'I would say that he has been dead for four, perhaps five hours,' he declared in a flat, professional manner.

'What was it? The morphine?' asked Mike Cook, his eyes slitted with concern.

'Not directly,' said Panda. He toed one of the whisky bottles. 'I think he may have inhaled his own vomit. A common enough incident in cases of such intoxication.'

'Shitty, fucking death!' Mike burst out. 'I suppose I as good as fucking killed the poor bastard?'

'You cannot blame yourself, Mike,' said Panda, shaking his head.

'You carried him all you could, you know,' added Harry.

'Yeah, but I forgot to track down that bloody morphine when you told me, Panda,' he admitted sadly.

'If it hadn't been this way it might have been worse,' said Harry, his voice assuming a rare philosophical tone. 'Look!' He pointed to the bedside cabinet where the Colonel's Browning automatic lay unholstered; its hammer cocked.

'He was very unhappy, y'know.'

* * *

The Joint Staff's conference was being held in the basement of the old fort in what was, in colonial times, the kitchens. The main room held a long table fashioned from a single plank of mahogany. Matching chairs with rattan seats and backs stood round in attendance. A collection of ancient carpets, swords and antelope heads decorated the white emulsioned walls. Henson arrived five minutes before the appointed hour of eight accompanied by two other Britons. One a boyish-looking graduate on a secondment from the Foreign Office, the other a moustachioed pipe-smoker with collar-length, grey hair called McNaughton. He was head of the Emir's secret service or more prosaically, Defence Research Department. After brief introductions, the party took their places opposite the Commander, Dixon and Mullen, the Force Intelligence Officer.

Welles watched intently as Henson removed some papers from his briefcase. 'Smart as ten and as bright as a new pin. Had he been up all night? Was he feeling as smug and as confident as he did six weeks ago?' Welles stopped musing and glanced at the poker-faced McNaughton and the blank-faced cherub preparing to take notes on the other side of Henson. Henson placed his gold-plated pen precisely across his note pad and returned Welles' enquiring gaze.

'I understand that the outpost on Cub was over-run with heavy casualties?' Henson started as if he were at a share-holder's meeting.

'A counter-attack was mounted at two am,' Welles replied in a matching tone.

'Survivors and the counter-attack force were successfully recovered to Assaad just before dawn. There's the damage.' He pushed across a typed list of casualties. Henson quickly scanned the list and pushed it to the cherubic note-taker.

'Do you concur with our estimate of the enemy's strength around 'Assaad?' Welles braced himself for argument. Henson looked up and blinked.

'Yes,' he said. 'In fact, sources indicate your estimate of 4000 to be a little short. We ...' He caught himself, paused and then continued. 'There are nearer 6000. They also have other artillery equipment which have not been brought to bear.' Welles was staggered and felt that he showed it. He felt a bluster coming on but failed to control it.

'Well, that ...' he started. 'That makes Assaad untenable. They're outnumbered ten to one. Saladin's a lame duck!'

'On the contrary,' picked up Henson. 'Saladin is proceeding exactly as expected.' Welles and now Dixon and Mullen stared at Henson almost unable to believe what he was saying. Henson recognised the impact of his words and steadied himself for his next revelation. He stood up and walked over to the high-windowed alcove at the end of the room. He turned and placed his hands behind his back.

'Gentlemen,' he began. 'I regret to have to tell you that it was necessary to use you as the unwitting partners in an strategy conceived by my department to bring about an end to this war in the shortest possible time.' He paused and searched the faces of the three uniformed officers for reaction. 'The real aim of Operation Saladin is to draw the enemy into a position where he can be destroyed in a single air-mounted operation ...'

'You've used us as bloody bait?' Welles burst in, standing up. Henson put out a hand.

'General,' he said calmly. 'what plans did you make for the next phase of Saladin?' Welles was taken by surprise at the question. His eyes bulged and he felt the veins in his temples throbbing like drums. Gilbert Dixon spared him any further agony.

'We've shipped in extra wire, pickets, mines, sandbags; all we need to construct a barrier minefield.'

'Precisely!' Henson snapped. 'It's all ordered up, loaded and on its way ... and every shipping clerk and stevedore in the Gulf knows it. So too, will the Hawaafi.' He paused to savour his triumph of logic.

'Your battalion is dug in on the Jebel Assaad which is where, about fifty years ago, the Hawaafi defeated the local Turkish garrison and established their first homeland for the better part of four centuries.' He stopped and looked at them as if they were dull primary school children. 'Don't you see? It's like the Mormons setting up shop in the Vatican. The Hawaafi cannot ignore it.'

'You're mad, Henson,' said Welles, sitting down. 'Stark, staring mad.' Henson smiled in an overtly patronising fashion.

'Was McArthur mad to land at Inchon?' Welles looked up as Henson returned to his seat.

'If we are going to swap historical precedents, I could mention Kut and Dien Bien Phu for openers,' Welles said tartly. Henson leaned over interlocked fingers.

'General, before you pass judgement listen to the DDRD here. When you see what assets we've collected, I'm sure you'll think it worth the sacrifices.' As the languid McNaughton stood up to reveal more of Henson's grand designs, Dixon wondered if Henson had ever met Alan Primmer.

McNaughton's briefing was so comprehensive that the meeting broke up within ten minutes of its completion. Times had been fixed for staff co-ordinating conferences, lists of those staffers who needed to share the secrets of the morning were compiled. Henson ushered his supporters to the basement stairs. As they left he turned back.

'By the way,' he said, 'I'm so sorry about young Primmer. He was a damn good chap. Met him once at a Rifle Division dinner. Great shame.' Welles nodded away brief appreciation of his sentiments. Henson left.

'Will that be all, sir?' asked Mullen pulling back from the table.

'Yes, Hank, thank you,' replied the General. 'Warn off the COs for a quick brief this evening. No details, just time and place. I'll want Commander Air Group as well.'

'Very good, sir.' Mullen re-arranged his notes and left.

Welles and Dixon sat in silence. One stared at the trophies along the opposite wall, the other down at the briefing notes passed over by McNaughton.

'I know what you're thinking, Gilbert,' Welles said quietly, without taking his eyes off an oryx head. Not bothering to wait for a reply he continued. 'Should I resign or do I tough it out?' Gilbert Dixon cleared his throat.

'He's got you, either way. I would not be allowed to resign with you so the Op would go ahead.' The Chief of Staff waited for comment but none came. He went on. 'If you go and the Ops fails, you'll be blamed for losing your nerve. If you go and it works then no-one will care why you went and they'll laugh you into a bowler hat.' The Commander turned to face him. His lower teeth gently bit into his top lip.

'Bastard's got us, hasn't he? I'll stay but when this is over, I'll have his skin for this; whatever it costs.' Dixon looked into his Commander's eyes, all optimism was gone, resignation and menace remained.

There was a brief rap on the door, the Force Signals Officer entered, saluted and handed a red-sealed buff envelope to the General. It was stamped SECRET and notated COMMANDER'S EYES ONLY. The signals chief went outside to wait for any reply. Gilbert watched fearful anticipation cross his commander's brow. Welles opened the envelope and read the brief hand-written message.

'Oh my God!' he said softly. He looked up at Dixon. 'Alastair Wilson is dead. Died during the night, vomit inhalation a possibility.'

'I wonder who was running last night's show?'

'Rolls,' the General answered. 'Thank God he was there.'

'Thank God for your intuition.' Welles looked at him thoughtfully. The same thought struck both of them.

'You shouldn't blame yourself, you had no idea about that Borneo thing.'

'I knew Alastair would crack, but ... well ... alright, I knew his track record. I knew that Aussie Opso was running the shop but I couldn't relieve him on suspicion.'

Gilbert nodded reluctant agreement. They sat in silence.

'What about an enquiry?' Gilbert started. Welles shook his head.

'No way. Tell Harry Shaw to bury him at Harrow. As far as the world is concerned Alastair Wilson was a valiant commander, killed in action; mortar strike.' General Welles stood up and Gilbert knew that his commander was back. 'It goes no further than you, me and Jenson out there.'

'Very good.'

'Get the Jet Ranger warned off for three-thirty. I'll go in with the first resup tonight.' He left Gilbert scribbling a hasty signal for Assaad.

Climbing the stairs towards his office, the General stopped at the door of his Director of Supply; a contract Lieutenant-Colonel.

The startled man shot up from his desk, as the General's head poked around the door.

'Give me your slip-ons, Derek.' The lieutenant-colonel's hands went up defensively to the badges of rank on his epaulettes.

'My slip-ons, sir?' he said, his voice cracked with shock.

'Yes, your moon and star, man! Don't fret, you're not being sacked ... just want to borrow them.'

The stunned staffer unbuttoned his shoulder straps and handed the insignia over to his commander. 'Buy yourself a new pair on my mess-bill.' Welles took the stairs two at a time, smiling. 'Always pays to put the wind up 'em now and then.'

CHAPTER SIXTEEN

The temperature on the airstrip at Harrow had fallen to a comparatively cool 90°F by the time the General climbed out of the last resupply chopper back from Assaad. His green bush-jacket clung to him like a hot, wet towel. As he walked away from the whine of the liaison helicopter's dying engines, the night breeze greeted him. It brought a collection of bivouac smells: aromas of goat curry mixed with kerosine, hot engine oil and dried human excrement. Stan Meadows, the Quartermaster, punched out a salute as he approached.

'I've held back the burial party just in case you wanted to say something, sir.'

'Thank you, yes. I won't but thank you for waiting.' Welles replaced the beret which he had carried from the helicopter and fell in alongside the Quartermaster. They walked along the perimeter track towards the dark skyline of the distant Hawaaf Kabeer, the Great Ridge.

'The jundis were buried just before sunset,' Stan explained. 'My RQ did the honours.'

'How is Kandu Bux?'

'Oh, he's fine, fat as ever.' They were near the end of the runway now. Welles could make out a shadowy bunch of figures standing at the bottom of a gentle slope which fell away from the runway. A large, rectangular hole was flanked by mounds of stony soil. Forty yards away, to the right, a line of small cairns marked the Islamic cemetery: milestones on the path to Paradise.

The Arab and Baluchi grave diggers moved a few yards to one side, leaving just the General, Stan and two helicopter pilots. Welles looked down into the grave. Two grey body bags lay side by side; one larger and more humped than the other. They brought the curious image of two courting dolphins to the General's churning mind. The image metamorphosed into soft, abstract, shapes floating together in an infinite void. They stood silently for another minute. Welles dipped his head in a brief neck bow. He saluted the black skyline, turned and walked away. Stan

Meadows and the pilots saluted and followed: no words, no gestures: the soldier's God needing no earthly intercession.

Rolls sat on the edge of the serving table in the mess tent; feet crossed in the dust. On his shoulder the borrowed crescent and stars insignia of lieutenant-colonel in the Emir's Armed Forces. Two rows of tired and dusty faces sat in front of him. Older faces now, eyes bagged through lack of sleep, wrinkles etched in the dirt and the grime. Facial muscles still taut from the teeth-grinding blasts of the day's bombardment and the drama of the previous night.

Rolls had made them privy to the grand design of the Defence Department's plan. He had left out much of the invective which the General had used when briefing him.

'When is this all likely to happen?' Giles demanded to know; his voice shrill and imperious. Giles had spent the day mentally preparing his first orders group as Commanding Officer. Now robbed of what he had regarded as his birthright, he felt aggrieved and hurt to the point of tears.

'You can work it out for yourselves.' Rolls looked at them with the sympathy of a fellow sufferer. 'It will take at least a week for the Crabs to get the Jaguars out here. Then there's the logistic back up to follow, recce, rehearsals. It's not going to happen in the week, that's for certain.'

'Bloody hell!' Giles swung one leg over the other and half turned away. 'We'll all be fucking dead by then.' The other officers sat immobilised; watching to see how their new colonel would meet his first challenge. Rolls waited until Giles had satisfied his sense of theatre and had turned back to face him.

'Listen, I can't pretend that its all going to be plain sailing. We are stuck here like tethered goats but we can still do a lot to help ourselves.' He waited for someone to say "such as" but no such response came. 'There are no rules saying that we can't fight back in any way we can.' He sensed a stirring from Eddie Shanks and Mr Thompson. 'and we'll start tomorrow. In the meantime look at your positions again and start thinking "close quarters". I believe Cub was just a rehearsal.' He felt a jump of hope, a mental lift inside his head. 'Any questions?' A negative murmur hummed back.

'Let's go to it then.' The tent cleared except for Rolls, Harry Shaw and Mike Cook.

'They suit you well,' said Cook, patting Roll's rank badges as he moved back towards the CP.

'What "Starry eyed and down in the mouth" ...' quipped Rolls, repeating an old jest about the origins of the insignia.

'Yeah, something like that.'

* * *

The mood of the following morning's conference was more optimistic. John Rolls had spent the night on a camp bed in the mess tent. He was grateful that the Gulf Arabs had a general taboo against using a dead man's chattels. The prospect of a night in the dark, odiferous hole sent a primeval shudder through him. A party of jundis were at that moment caving it in. He would, for the present, use one of the ridge tents and take his chances in one of the numerous fox holes should they be shelled.

'Colonel!' Rolls looked around instinctively for some other claimant before responding himself. Mr Thompson was barrelling towards him with a map and note-book.

'Sorry, Mr Thompson, not used to it yet.' The square-set Geordie smiled away his embarrassment.

'What you said about hittin' back. I think I've got a worthwhile target for you.' They moved under the lintel of the CP. 'The adoo seem to have plumped for one base plate, at least for their eighty-twos.' He led the way to the Ops desk and spread his map. 'There!' He pressed a grease-ingrained forefinger in the centre of a whorl of brown contour lines. 'They've fired from all round us but since last week only from here.'

Rolls stared at the narrow defile. It lay some two and a half kilometres across the main wadi to the east of their position. Mr Thompson had christened it 'The Great North Road' or more succinctly 'GNR'.

'I wonder why there?' Rolls pondered aloud.

'Wadi looks very steep, too steep for my Seventy-Fives. I can only just reach it with the tubes.'

'What's the range?'

'About three Kay. I got the direction from sound bearings and crater marks.'

'You'd think they would keep moving?' suggested Rolls.

'Ah, then they canna' stock pile the ammunition. They won't

waltz it any further than necessary, no point. If I were them that's where I would go.'

'Okay. What do you think Mike?' Mike Cook had been following the Sergeant-Major's logic from behind. He leaned closer.

'Seems likely. If you could cut the wadi at the top end, you'll see their resup' tracks for sure.'

'Right then,' said Rolls. 'Let's do it.'

CHAPTER SEVENTEEN

Rolls had given the young Marine captain a full 24 hours to mount the operation. He thought that perhaps he was being over-generous and that Shanks might feel patronised. His misgivings were quickly dispelled as the thoroughness of Shanks's preparations became known. Though the mission had been no more exact than to find the enemy mortar line and to destroy it, it was clear that Eddie Shanks was leaving nothing to chance. Routes were planned on the large scale maps and visually checked from the various vantage points in One Company's area. Mines and explosives were drawn and distributed, weapons were checked, zeroed and tested. Rolls felt a little abashed as he realised how much he tended to take for granted and let his professionalism drop by comparison. It was a weakness of nearly all of the contract personnel to deride conscientiousness as merely an inability to cuff it.

The day of the sortie was the second without shelling. Rolls had used the opportunity to get around the jebel and assess for himself the strengths and weaknesses of the position. He was now sitting just above one of the rock-cleared spaces designated as an alternative landing site. Jundis were normally loathe to do any more than was strictly necessary for their own survival and comfort but the weeks of shelling had changed that. Rock and ammunition box shelters now littered the jebel. Rolls was sitting in the shade of one built by the helicopter marshalling teams between resupply sorties. Oven-still, the afternoon air rang and echoed with alternative volleys and burst of rifle and machine-gun fire. Shank's patrol was testing their weaponry and practising their anti-ambush drills.

Boots crunched down on the gravel outside and Rolls turned to find Richard Callender peering under the corrugated iron eaves.

'Hello, sir.' His voice was as light and as optimistic as when they had met on Harrow.

'Popped over to watch the "tamreen".'

'Sure, take a seat.' Rolls watched as the Ordnance Corps

lieutenant squeezed his webbing-laden hips through the narrow doorway.

'How he's changed!' thought Rolls turning back. The youthful chubbiness now given way to an angular leanness: a process accelerated by a six day bout of dysentery. Eyes, bluer, against a deeply tanned skin, were narrowed from squinting into the constant day time glare and by the tense expectancy of shelling. The fair, short bristled moustaches arching down over the corners of his mouth combined with the eyes to make his smile less ingenuous. His conversation was now seasoned with Geysh Arabic.

They watched in silence for a minute as Shank's machine-gunners fired short bursts kneeling and standing from the hip. Their targets, large plastic water barrels filled with stones, rocked with the impact.

'Why do they call them "burmails"?' Callender asked. Rolls grinned, remembering how he had asked the same question of some old Rhodesian some seven years before.

'I think it's because they're similar to forty gallon oil-drums,' Rolls began, tentatively. 'The locals thought that they were the greatest thing since the camel. They had "Burma Oil" on the side in English and Arabic and in Arabic vowels are fairly imprecise.' Callender still looked perplexed. 'Burma Oil ... burmail. All barrels are Burma Oils or burmails.' Rolls completed the circuit. Callender beamed as the simple logic of the language dawned on him.

Callender looked out again at the sturdy figure of Shanks walking up and down a line of jundis.

'When will the rest fire,' he asked.

'That's it,' said Rolls. He checked his watch. 'They are out at seven.'

'But there are only ...' He stopped to count. ' ... twenty there!'

'That's all he wants.' Callender was on the point of saying that Giles never took less than two full platoons. He remembered too that Giles never went further out than half a mile. He had paced it out himself. He recalled too that Two Company never test fired their weapons or had done any practice or rehearsals at all.

'Any chance of going out with Eddie, sir?' Rolls smiled and shook his head.

'Not this one, I'm afraid. Eddie's already got a passenger ...

me.' Callender looked surprised. 'Nothing to say that I have to stay at home now I'm CO., Y'know.' Callender was about to chime in with a comment like, ' ... But what if you're killed?'

He checked himself. Rolls answered his doubts as he rose to leave the shade of the lean-to.

'Besides, it's only the only way a CO gets to see the ground.' He scrambled out into the sun.

* * *

Though the sliver of the waning moon was still below the eastern hills, the star light alone provided sufficient light. The bare rock and silvery sand of the wadis made it possible to move quickly and confidently. Rolls had just finished spreading the last of the dark-earth coloured camouflage cream over the backs of his hands when the first of the fire groups silently rose and moved down through the wire. He and Din Mohammed had attached themselves to the last group.

'How do I look?' said Rolls turning his blackened face towards Din.

'Like a monkey-man!' answered the Pathan using his dialect word for negro.

'You are kind, my Brother.' Rolls grinned as he turned away to see the next two groups disappearing through the wire and down the spur. The Company Sergeant-Major, the lead man of the last group rose silently and motioned them forward with a flicking of his hand. They followed him down to the wire where a guide from One Company held the Dannert coils to one side. Soon they were following a thin, pale track down towards the broad, silvery expanse of the Great North Road.

At the base of the spur the groups stopped in turn besides a knot of prone figures. Kneeling alongside was James Faulkner. The Guards captain had swept the track for mines that afternoon and had remained at the bottom with a small, standing patrol to ensure a safe exit for Shanks. The patrol would remain there to guide them back.

'Well done!' Rolls clapped a startled Guardsman on the arm as he passed. He was another youngster who had become a veteran overnight. Leaving the beleaguered jebel behind Rolls felt a euphoric lift; a taste of freedom. His group's leader moved right until he was parallel to the fourth group. The pace slowed as the jundis opened the spacing between themselves. Now in widely spread, double file, with the lead group in a V-formation, Shanks led them out across the wide valley bottom.

The patrol progressed quickly through the black and silver shadow world of the wadi. Save for the soft crunch of boots on gravel and the occasional clink of ammunition belts, the twenty-odd men moved as spectres through the night. Now and then Shanks would signal a halt with an upraised arm and the two files would stop and sink down, each facing outwards; straining to pierce the gloom for any tell-tale movement or sound. Nothing disturbed the background hiss of the cicadas. Shanks would scan a broad arc to his front with his starlight 'scope. Satisfied that the way ahead was clear he would slowly rise and move off. The rest of the patrol followed, tension growing as they neared the dark shadows of the wadi's opposite side.

A full hour had passed since they had left the standing patrol yet it seemed like minutes to Rolls. The grey-blue mass of the first ridge loomed before them. The patrol stopped astride one of the little rock mounds which protruded from the gravel sea like cartoonist's desert islands. Shanks was scanning a shallow side gully which came down the ridge to feed the main wadi. He rose and walked back between the files hand-signalling with his fist and fingers to the groups, 'final RV' ... 'Two and Three Groups cover the ridge'.

The machine-gunners of the covering groups unslung their pieces. Bipod legs clicked down, bodies shuffled back behind cover. The gunners pushed their weapons up until the foresights were dimly silhouetted against the stars. The number twos unclipped belts from their shoulders and snuggled up alongside their cold and deadly charges.

Without a word Shanks rose and moved on, across the final few yards of gravel and then up onto the hard, brittle sand-stone of the ridge's sides. The remaining groups closed to single file. Up they wound to one side of the gully. A careless foot and the loose rocks rang like tiles; Rolls found himself holding his breath. The skyline suddenly dropped and they stopped. Shanks signalled them down. They waited as he moved forward. Then they moved forwards, this time on the level. An aqabat, a narrow shoulder between two gullies. They crossed the skyline quickly, the forbidden tell-tale zone, feeling like targets on a shooting gallery. They waited on the far side; another world, out of sight of the Assaad, comrades and safety.

While they waited for the cover group to rejoin them, Rolls crept forward to sit alongside Shanks. The Marine was sat with his feet braced against a small bank. He heard the faint whine of the 'scope as Shanks swept the narrow sided wadi below them. He was pointing the tube along the line of the ridge to his right when he stopped. He lowered the 'scope and flicked his head around to Rolls; his eyes and teeth shone against his blackened face.

'Got 'em!' he hissed. He passed the 'scope to Rolls. 'Where the wadi bends right,' he instructed. Rolls pressed the rubber cup to his eye and the strange, green world of the image intensifier revealed itself. The wadi was bright green against the shadows of the surrounding rocks. Then, where the brightness faded, a light ... then a flicker which left ghostly streaks on the lens. It was a camp fire.

Once the covering groups had rejoined, the patrol moved south along the ridge, just below the skyline. As they neared the bend in the wadi, Shanks halted for another brief scan with the 'scope. He then led them down to a natural ledge about fifteen feet above the wadi floor. He collected each group in turn and placed them in fire positions looking up or down the dry stream bed. After signalling arcs of fire to the machine-gunners he would take a piece of cord from the group leader and pay it out until he was back with his own fire group. Satisfied that the firm base was able to cover the wadi with fire he crept up to where he had left Rolls and Din Mohammed.

'Are you coming for a shooft?' asked Shanks, barely able to conceal the excitement in his whisper.

'Try and stop me,' Rolls glanced round at Din to translate. The Pathan needed no translation. He was primed like a gin trap. The three of them stepped carefully over the prone forms of the right-hand, cut-off group and moved silently along the slope as it curved steeply around the inside of the bend of the wadi. Shanks bent low on the crest of the spur and then lay down. Rolls wormed his way forward to his shoulder. Din remained behind, watching the opposite crests; listening for something other than the cicadas. Rolls felt his heart thudding beneath him as he brought his binoculars up to his brow.

Past the bend, the wadi opened out to about forty metres.

Camp fires glimmered beneath the steep sides. Dark, shadowy figures lay or sat around them. He slowly swept the wadi. Black, square mounds lay at intervals in rough alignment.

'Tubes! Eighty-twos.' Shanks was holding the starlight 'scope over for him. The green, spectral world opened up for him again. One ... three ... four inclined spouts jutted from the sand. He switched left to the fires. The black figures became green men; some wearing darkly chequered wizars, others combat trousers. Bandoliers round their thin shoulders, Kalashnikovs, turbanned headcloths, caps. He stared at the adoo. The first time he had seen them; alive and close up.

'What do you think?' Shank's voice intruded. Rolls lowered the 'scope and made out the wide, luminous pupils glinting with the thought of the savagery and violence in prospect.

'We'd do better with the jets,' whispered Rolls. He sensed disappointment and anti-climax in Shank's face. Now we've got them spotted and combined with the guns ...' Shanks nodded, silently bowing to military prudence. He stared back malevolently at the adoo bivouacs. His head flicked up. Behind him and at some distance they heard the grunting protest of a camel.

They reached the firm base almost at a run. The jundis were already braced with excitement.

'Camel guay!' hissed the wakeel as Shanks plumped down next to him. Shanks set to work. He pulled off the small pack he was wearing and passed out two flat spools of wire to the Sergeant-Major and another soldier. Passing the ends to the remaining jundis of the group they scrambled backwards down towards the wadi, paying off the plastic coated wire with a flickering hand-jive of the wrist. Shanks slithered down the slope in front of them. A foot above the sand he stopped. The spools were run off, the stiffly, snaking wires lay waiting. Shanks set the legs of the Claymore mines and sited them to fire obliquely across the wadi. He jammed them down and clipped in the detonator heads of the wires which would give them a brief but appalling life. With a quick glance down the valley he followed the other two back to the ledge.

Rolls lay braced. The high fore-sight of his AKM just visible against the sand. Din lay to his left, still as a corpse. Then came movement. He felt the communication cord which ran beneath his thighs jerk once ... twice, then a pause. 'Two scouts, maybe?'

'three, four, five ... Men or camels?' He strained his eyes to penetrate the wadi's gloom. Another movement, a shadow or a man? A man! Then two, stealthy but relaxed ... weapons over shoulders held by the muzzle. They moved slowly and silently along the wadi bottom. A rasping snort ... camels ... One, two more behind ... tall swaying. The measured, plodding step contrasting with that of their handlers walking alongside. Rolls finger took up the first pressure on the trigger. Five, six camels passed his sight. 'God! Shanksy. What are you waiting for? Give everyone a target, of course. Seven, eight ... four men in a group.'

Thwam, Thwam. Vision white out. Instant smoke ... the singing wheeze of twelve thousand ball-bearings. Machine-guns yammering. His own weapon tapping out long, raking bursts ... reload. The measured blasts of Din's FN battered his eardrums. Below a bedlam of hoarse, animal shrieks and human screams. Just as he thought it would last forever, a whistle blast. Firing stopped. Silence, no cicadas, just the death throes of the camels below. He listened and waited ... no-one moved. A false signal, a trap set for a wily if desperate enemy. Movement ... running ... long rattling bursts from the MAGs. A groan below, silence again. Two whistle blasts.

Rolls was up on one knee, his thoughts on the four men between the camels. Shanks was moving along his men checking them off. He flashed a grin at Rolls; a Puck incarnate, delighted with his lethal mischief.

'Good kill!' rasped Rolls, his mouth and throat dust dry. 'Get ready to bug out, I've got to check for Int.' Shanks's brow furrowed. Rolls forestalled him.

'No, you get the boys up to the aqabat. I'll take Din. There'll be a follow-up, cover us from there.' Shanks nodded and set about hustling the jundis up the slope. Rolls motioned Din towards him and with the briefest of gestures told him what he was going to do. Abandoning silence for speed, the two men slithered and jumped down to the wadi floor. The air was thick with the cloying smell of cordite. As Din covered with his FAL Rolls stalked quietly in on the scene of carnage. The smell of the camels assailed him first as he approached. He jumped. A camel twitched as it neared death. Then there was the sweet smell of blood; so strong that he could practically taste it. He found three of the four bodies he sought, together. Slinging the AKM so that it rested on his hip, he drew his kukri and moved in. The three lay like torn rag-dolls; lean limbs akimbo. He bent over them. All three glistened in the starlight; dark stains spread over their ragged shirts. He was swift in checking the bodies, foot on neck, kurkri poised, his free•hand searched ... nothing. He looked around for the fourth.

'Hai!' grunted Din. Rolls looked and saw a body face down in a clump of reeds. He ran over, A better dressed specimen, khaki bush-jacket and trousers, leather sandals. A haversack strap crossed his back. Rolls reached out to turn the body. A gasp, a hand flew up. The kukri arced down and bit. Rolls pulled the heavy blade up, the dead head followed before falling back with a thump; retained to the body by skin and sinew. Rolls breathed again. He roughly turned the shoulders; a small automatic pistol fell from lifeless fingers. The kukri sliced through the cotton straps of the haversack. Rolls felt the pouch with satisfaction. He snatched up the pistol and doubled over to Din. A burst of firing came from down the wadi from the enemy mortar lines. They could just make out jabbering commands in the hillmen's dialect.

'Let's go, my Brother!' Rolls tucked the pouch away in his shirt. The Pathan smiled proudly and gave Rolls a hearty clap on the shoulder before leading off up the wadi side.

CHAPTER EIGHTEEN

There was a suppressed air of exhilaration about the jundis, as Rolls and his Pathan bearer rejoined them astride the aqabat. It even showed in Shanks as he ushered them down the track; like a school-teacher on an outing. He cautioned them in a hoarse whisper to 'listen' ... 'watch' ... 'be alert'. For the complacent, the home-run was always the most dangerous. A single report. High over the ridge they were suddenly bathed in the glimmering light of a flare.

'Yallah, Yallah!' Shanks waved the last group down from the skyline. The patrol lurched down the stone-littered slope to the grey expanse of the Great North Road. More flares lit the skyline. This time parachute flares which swayed and drifted along the ridge leaving a wispy spiral of smoke. Once on the silvery gravel the patrol shook out into its open, spear-head formation. Shanks walked swiftly back through the ranks of the kneeling soldiers issuing further cautionary instructions. He dropped down alongside Rolls who was looking back at the pale skyline of the ridge.

'Do you think they'll follow up?' asked Shanks.

'Seems like it. I didn't reckon on them having flares, though.'

'I'm going back on a different bearing, just in case,' Shanks said. 'Then I'll dog-leg back in.' Rolls nodded and watched as Shanks went back to his position at point. The patrol rose and glided off across the wadi. The steep escarpment of Assaad's eastern face reflected the soft, white light of the crescent moon rising behind them.

They were about half-way when the double plop of flare-pots echoed from the dark ridge behind them. The flares burst high over the wadi to their left, making swaying shadows of men and trees alike. The jundis froze and then as the parachutes drifted, sank slowly to the ground. Two shots reverberated along the ridge. Rolls craned his neck upwards to watch for muzzle-flares. There were no more shots.

'They signal. Perhaps they see us?' grunted Din, to his right. Rolls nodded. A stabbing pain of tension arced through his chest.

'Were we being pursued or driven?' He took in a few deep, noisy breaths through his nose. The hyperventilating eased the pain. The flares died on landing; the patrol was up and moving.

The north face of Assaad began to loom higher in their vision. They had now crossed the retreating shadow of the ridge and were bathed in the soft moonlight. Rolls could now see Shanks plainly in the centre of the spearhead. Shanks' left hand came up. They stopped and went down facing out to the flanks or to the rear. Shanks had stopped short of a low, rounded bank. Plainly it was a man-made feature, perhaps the remains of an ancient irrigation bund; the attempts of some long-dead farmer to steal a little moisture from the pitiless sun. The mound was worn on top and had obviously been used as a firm pathway through the yielding gravel. A recognised feature in featureless ground; a likely ambush site. A nagging premonition of danger fought his instinct to run from his pursuers.

'Rashash!' he hissed to the machine-gunners, to men along the line. The jundi a'rashash jerked his head up. 'Naar Saatira!' The gunner and his number two crabbed out to their flank. Shanks waited until the pair were still, their FN machine-gun pointing out over the bund. He waved the second and third groups forward, stood up and mounted the low bank. A flash lit the wadi. The explosion blew them all flat. Dust and sand billowed over their backs. The patter of larger debris rained down. Ears ringing with the shock wave the jundis lay still. A sobbing moan broke the brief silence. Rolls was up. His mind was flashing up the possibilities, mortar ... grenade ... no firing ... mine! A figure lay half across the bund. A sharweesh moved towards it.

'Waqaaf!' Rolls shouted. 'lugm!' Mine! 'Na yattarook.' The jundis froze. Rolls, reasoning and hoping that only the bund that was mined, ran up to the prostrated body on the bank. The jundis lay around, stunned, until their sergeant-major harried them into a hasty defensive perimeter.

Shanks lay on his back, his left arm hanging free over the edge. A crater smoked where his feet should have been. Rolls grasped him by his webbing straps and slowly eased him backwards down the bank. He was conscious. He groaned as the wreckage of his legs were eased down onto the gravel. Rolls reached down and felt the warm, visceral slickness of inner tissue. A jagged shard of bone grazed the back of his hand. He forced himself to look. Below mid-thigh the right leg was reduced to tangled hanks of sinew and muscle. The foot was missing. The left leg shredded below the knee; the boot at an impossible right-angle.

'Tourniquet,' Rolls snapped at the sharweesh who was unclipping Shanks' webbing. Shanks seemed to be in a stupor unaware of his condition.

Rolls had just tightened a rifle sling around Shanks' left leg when a soft plop came from behind him. His shadow fell swiftly across Shanks' blond hair as the flare threw its light across the wadi. Shanks blinked and tried to move.

'Don't move, you're alright,' Rolls lied, poorly. Shanks struggled to push himself upright against the bank. The sharweesh helped him to sit up. Rolls reached inside his own shirt and pulled out his dog-tag neck-cords: two plastic ampoule cases of morphine were taped to the string.

'Don't need that.' Shanks hand gripped his wrist. Rolls stared at him. 'Honest. It just feels numb.' He grimaced as he tried to square his back to the bank.

'We'll get you back, Eddie,' Rolls began earnestly. 'I'll get a chopper into ...' He reached for the transceiver in one of his side pouches, Shanks shook his head.

'No, I've had it, boss. Get going, I'll be fine here.' Rolls stared at him, incredulously. Shanks held him with his eyes. 'The war ends here.' He reached about him for his pack. 'Bundookiya, sharweesh, geebu.' The sergeant looked around and then picked up Shanks' FN and handed it to him.

'You can't,' Rolls started but the Marine officer's strong hand gripped his wrist.

'No wheelchair for me, Matey,' his voice quiet yet hard. 'All or nothing. Now get the boys out of here.' Rolls continued to stare at him, fixed by the determined blue eyes.

'Sah'b, adoo guay!' The wakeel's urgent warning broke the spell.

'I wouldn't make it anyway,' croaked Shanks. 'Now for fuck's sake go!' He pulled his arm away and started easing a waterbottle from his belt.

Rolls straightened up; his eyes swimming. Sharp, hard voices came in snatches on the night breeze. He drew his sleeve across his eyes. 'Wakeel.' The little sergeant-major stiffened in response. 'Prod a way through.' He indicated the bund.

'Na'am Sidi.' The wakeel drew his bayonet and set to work from the edge of the crater in the track. Rolls motioned the others to close in. All the time came the sounds of pursuit.

'Yallah, feesah!' He heard the wakeel on the other side. The jundis started threading their way through sadly, past their company commander. Some reached down to touch his shoulder as they went. Others muttered sad valedictions. Din Mohammed was the last man to the gap.

'You wish me to stay, my Brother?' His eyes glowered in fierce desperation. Shanks looked up and shook his head.

'Thanks Din, no.' Din dipped his head and was gone. Rolls looked down and grasped Shanks' wrist. He squeezed it once and threw himself up and over the bank. He heard a strident shout behind him and a burst of AK fire. He was down and running when Shanks' FN barked off three rounds in reply. At a low crouch he kept going telling the jundis to follow as he passed them. Rounds hissed and cracked into the bushes around them as they charged across the remaining stretch of wadi to the base of the escarpment. The light taps of the Kalashnikovs contrasted with the heavier cracks of the lone FAL.

The FAL clicked on an empty chamber. Eddie cursed himself for not counting his rounds and threw the weapon forward into the gravel. He was feeling dizzy from the effort. He lay back against the bank and listened as the adoo's fire slackened and then stopped. There were two groups, one only fifty yards away behind one of the small rock islands. Reaching down to his pack he pulled out a green cotton bag. Extracting the reel of plastic coated wire he plugged the detonators into the top of the Claymore which still lay in the carrier. He winced as he had to half-roll over to extract the firing switch from his pocket. A guttural voice shouted at him. He smiled at the thought of what he was doing. Predictive thought was an essential tool of the booby-trapper's art. Having made sure of the connections, he pressed the test button. The dull orange light glowed. With the inner satisfaction of a craftsman he finally looped the carrier strap over his head and adjusted the Claymore so that it rested over his heart; its curved front pointing "toward the enemy" in accordance with the instruction embossed in the plastic. He let his head loll back in relief from the effort.

'Yahkeea, mafeesh rashaas!' he called out, quite truthfully. He didn't have any bullets. He waited; crunching in the gravel indicated that someone was moving in for a closer look.

His head felt light, detached. He pulled himself up a bit till the pain in his legs stopped him. Images of gentle, commonplace people came to his mind. Honest, shop-keeping folk who only wanted to give their children a better start in life than they had . He felt a stab of guilt and remorse. Not the self pity of mortal injury but just a sorrow for those who would grieve for him. Ordinary people who could never understand what he did and why. A student nurse in Exeter, wide, vulnerable eyes beneath a dark, page-boy fringe.

A movement brought him back. He clenched his free hand. A shadowy figure stepped into the moonlight, light on his feet, tense.

'Yahkee!' he called. The figure jumped and froze; elbows spread, on aim. 'I found one of your fucking mines.' This time in English. Three more figures appeared, spread across his field of vision. They all held him in their sights. He waited ready, half expecting the lethal impact of their bullets. The shadow in the centre spoke to someone behind him in the rapid-fire speech of the Ridge People. He then advanced to within a few feet of Shanks. He leaned forward holding the AK out in front of him like a prod. 'Lugm,' said Shanks quietly. The tribesman muttered concurrence on the cause of the shattered limbs. The others relaxed and closed in, as did a taller, fuller figure from the rear.

Shanks held the igniter-switch tight in his right hand in his pocket. He studied the adoo fighters. Short, leanly built men. The skin drawn tightly over their faces as though they were shrink-wrapped. Eyes and cheeks hollow, angular brows and jaw-bones. The fourth man joined them. An altogether bigger man, he asked them if Shanks would live: in Arabic. The carefully clipped consonants gave him away as a Palestinian. Shanks recognised the accent as being the same as those of some of his instructors at the Army Language School. Shanks wished them all Allah's protection and squeezed the firing lever.

The flash sent them to ground. Rolls recognised the twanging blast and hiss of the Claymore. He sat up, looking out across the wadi. A dark cloud was drifting through the thorn bushes below. He felt tears coursing their way down his cheeks onto his chin. He felt Din Mohammed's hand on his shoulder and wiped his face with the end of his shemagh.

'Yallah,' he said softly. The jundis rose and plodded their way along the slope to where the standing patrol from One Company would be waiting.

CHAPTER NINETEEN

Shank's death fell heavily on the officers. Cook and Shaw had sat with Rolls on his return. An empty bottle of malt stood before them on one of the packing case tables. Mike Cook could not remember tasting any of it. Dawn's first glimmerings brought shapes out of the grey background of the Headquarters lines. Rolls was leant forward, his forehead propped on his open left palm; elbow on the table. The half tumbler in his right hand dropped from his sleeping grip. It smashed, a light, brittle crash on the shale floor.

'Shit,' said Rolls drowsily. He rubbed his face. Mike Cook leaned forward from across the table and placed his tumbler down.

'Why don't you turn in, boss. I'll take the conference.' He waited for a reaction or protest from Rolls. Nothing came but he went on as if there had been. 'No one, expects you to ...' he stopped. Rolls was absorbed in the process of lighting a cigarette. Harry Shaw guessed that Rolls was preparing himself to say something. He sat up and put a hand out to still any interruption from the Opso.

''S happened to me before, y'know,' Rolls slurred drowsily. He drew long and hard on the Triple 5 feeling the acid aroma assail his nose and mouth. His head cleared as the nicotine filled his system. The listeners waited, tense, perhaps apprehensive.

'The other way round though. I wanted to leave the man behind.' He took another short pull and then leaned across over folded hands. His eyes glistened with dredged up grief and pain. 'One of my lance corporals, Mandahadar Jai, good man, ace tracker and as tough as old boots.' Emotion filled his voice. 'In Borneo, we were across the other side: myself, Jai, three others. We'd gone out as part of a village patrol close to the border and then just stepped over. We were looking for an Indon camp, a big one, battalion base.' He raised his head a fraction and paused as if to fine tune the memory.

'We found the camp about five days march in from the border. The Indon's were relaxed, the recce was easy, almost routine. We were careful though, stayed well off the tracks, no cooking or smoking, just cold rice … fish paste, same as the locals. We were on our way back … not quite half way. Jai was up front when a choki pops up out of nowhere blasts him with a shotgun.' He shook his head and sighed with frustration. 'We were miles from the nearest Kampong, he must have been hunting or something. One of the boys chased him … brought his head back. Jai was in a bad way though. Holy Christ, all the way down his right side, caught the full pattern. He should have been dead, but Christ, he was conscious. I knew he couldn't survive. I mean, the blood he'd lost, Jesus!' Rolls took another draw on the cigarette and impatiently ground it out in the tin cap on the table. He continued the grim saga. His voice now harsh, broken with self-reproach. 'I strapped him up with shell-dressings used nearly everyone we had, he was so bad. I thought no way is he going to make it.

'I said we'd wait, made him comfortable, best we could. He didn't say anything. The pain must have been unbelievable. But he just kept watching me as if he knew what I was thinking: you know, the morphine. It's been done before. SOP in some units: man goes down over the other side, couple of grains, watch them drift away, no pain, no … None of them said anything, they just sat there watching their arcs. Night came and he was still conscious. I thought he can't last the night, but he did.' Rolls stopped and seemed to lapse with some new contemplation of the dilemma. Mike Cook fidgeted in his seat. He longed to ask what happened next but held on. Rolls raised his head again.

'We couldn't stay any longer after it got light. I said, right, let's go. I looked down at Jai and said I'll get you back. Hang on and I'll get you back. In a delirious state one minute, calm, watching, next minute sweaty, restless. We had those Aussie stretcher tops. You remember, Mike. I cut two poles and we carried him. I tell you, it was a bastard off the tracks. Took us another three days to reach the river. Jai was getting weaker all the time. Infection was setting in, for sure, I didn't have the heart to look. He was unconscious for most of it, thank God. But once we got to the border we made for a cleared site where we could get a chopper in. I don't know how but we got through on the set, made a RV. Jai seemed to rally. The boys were shagged but we made it.'

Cook and Shaw leaned forward in anticipation of his triumph. 'Naval Wessex came in, Christ, he was cutting leaves all the way down. I carried Jai forward to the door. He smiled at me and waved as the crewman took him in.' Rolls stopped and sat back, fumbling for another cigarette. His eyes glistened wetly in the brightening light. He sniffed, his hands shakily lit the cigarette. He died before they landed.' Rolls choked back a sob and wiped his eyes with the cuffs of his smock. 'Stupid bastard hung on for my sake,' he whispered. 'Just because I said I'd get him back. Doc said he should have died days before, he was so bad ... he hung on because just because ... I said ...' He rose shakily to his feet. Mike Cook and Harry Shaw rose with him. 'S'aright, fellas, I'll be alright. See the boys are okay, Harry. I'll have a lie down.' He picked up the AKM at his feet and walked stiffly towards his shelter. He stopped before reaching the blast wall entrance. 'Shanksy was right, wasn't he?' He did not wait for a reply but stumbled out onto the rough roadway between the tents.

The dark, turbanned figure of Din Mohammed came out of the shadows of the command post doorway and silently followed.

* * *

It was such a familiar dream that Rolls was able to somehow detach himself from his dream-body and watch the whole performance. The entity, for it was hardly human, was always the same. Big and solid, massively proportioned. He wore some kind of armoured suit, leather or plastic; a deep red or reddish brown. No face to speak of, though he had always thought of it as Oriental. No weapons either, just great, paw-like hands on tree-trunk arms. Nothing could stop the relentless advance, no matter how much of it was shot away or stabbed, it just came closer, growing bigger, enormously so. Just before he awoke, Rolls would be beating helplessly on the hard shell of its head and shoulders as its cold fingers closed around his neck. The smell too; rank sweat, oil and hot rancid breath. He used to wake with a start, hot and sweating, disorientated. Now he just seemed to freeze the action as in a film and simply step back. It had been the same for six nights now.

His watch showed 4.25. It was dark and felt chilly, though the outside temperature was around 65 degrees. He sat up, his shirt felt gritty and rough. Reaching out for his waterbottle, he uncapped it and took a mouthful. It tasted stale; of plastic and chlorine. He spat out the surplus. A shape appeared in the darkness on the dirt floor by the door.

'You wish for tea, my brother?' Rolls heard the Pathan stand up and stretching himself. He thought about sending him back to sleep but relented.

'Thank you, Din, if it is no trouble,' he replied, using the little Pushtu that he knew.

'My duty.' Rolls saw the Pathan tying his headcloth in his mind's eye. The tent flap opened and Din's tall frame ducked out and disappeared. The sound of the generators drifted in from the background. Rolls wrapped his own headcloth, shawl-like around his shoulders and followed Din out to sit on the wall. He bent low to light a cigarette under the wing of the shawl and settled back to await the dawn.

He looked back over the six days since the ill-starred patrol. He found himself still rationalising away the feelings of guilt he held for Eddie Shank's death. He searched every comment, every look from the other officers for hidden reproaches. All his service career had been charted for the promised moment when he would get his command.' Commanding a company was simply not the same. Nor, indeed, were any of the higher, general appointments; too remote, too many bureaucratic screens to get in the way. He had his own command now against all the odds yet the feeling of controlling his own destiny still alluded him.

It had been quiet since the patrol. The request for an air-strike had been turned down on the grounds that the Strikemasters had not yet been sufficiently modified to avoid the heat-seeking SAMs. They had shelled the wadi as best they could with the 75s and the heavy mortars but surprise had been lost with the first adjusting rounds. It must have been close but with such a narrow defile, not close enough. The satchel he had taken contained, disappointingly, only a few old photographs and some newspaper cuttings from Kuwait and Bahrein. As Harry Shaw had suggested, a people who are largely illiterate do not produce much in the way of written orders. He reflected grimly that there had probably been more information in the head that he had so nearly severed. The adoo for their part, had been unnervingly restrained; no more than two bouts of shelling for the week. Rolls felt that the inactivity demonstrated the enemy's ability to hold the initiative and his own relative impotence. He was certain that they would not allow another patrol to sally forth unchallenged. Din arrived with a mug of milky tea. The Headquarters enclave was beginning to stir. Tired and dirty jundis began to stumble about; as in any army it was the cooks who had to break the trail into each new day.

Rolls had appointed Mike Cook as Three Company's new commander and had brought Richard Carpenter in as Ops Officer. Whatever misgivings he may have had about burdening the young Ordnance lieutenant were dispelled during the first week. Callender, it turned out was one of those young men who, disappointed at not being in one of the teeth arms, had more than compensated by his dedication to his stock in trade; supply and replenishment. After keeping up with the logistical caprices of armoured battle groups across the north German plain, the topping up of Assaad was really very small beer, besides Rolls sensed that he was both relieved and happy to be away from the irascible Denby-Smith. There was an air of despondency about the battalion which Rolls could clearly sense as he made his daily rounds of the positions. The combination of monotonous diet, dust and tension was taking its toll amongst the jundis. Sad Panda had done his best by distributing vitamin pills and having his hygiene wallahs spray the sangars and boule areas to keep the flies down. A veteran of long periods of garrison duty in the Punjab and Ladakh, he knew the symptoms well.

Long queues forming outside his medical centre, minor and unspecified ailments which defied precise diagnosis: 'body-ache,' 'tooth-ache,' 'running stomach.' Rolls knew that with the new moon the situation would only get worse. The holy month of Ramadan with its obligation to daylight fasting was always a touchy period even in barracks. He wished the adoo would get on and do whatever it was they were preparing for. They had been warned off for visitors by an early morning signal, so Rolls and Harry Shaw were waiting at the main landing site as the resupply 205s clattered into view. The first two cabs hovered briefly to release their cargo nets before settling down to have their internal loads stripped away. Three figures in British Army jungle-greens stepped out and braced themselves against the whirling dust. They fought a brief but vain battle to stop the porters throwing their collection of bergans and valises all over the landing spot before the down wash of the ascending Huey beat them into submission. The trio staggered to the edges of the landing site; sweat-soaked and choked with dust. A fourth man who had emerged unobserved from the second Huey appeared through the settling maelstrom. A tall Arab in a long, khaki-coloured dishdash, belted at the waist with a bead patterned belt. He wore a curved-bladed khunjah in the centre of his belt and a turbanned headcloth of spotlessly white linen.

Rolls and Shaw walked over to the three Europeans.

'Welcome to Assaad,' Rolls began. Relief surfaced in the faces of all three. 'I'm Colonel Rolls, and this is Major Shaw, my second-in-command.' A round of handshaking took place. The smallest of the three became instantly prominent.

'Squadron Leader Milton,' he chimed in, 'Tony.' He introduced the other two as Flight Sergeant Fenton and Sergeant Askwith. While pleasantries were exchanged Rolls became aware that Harry Shaw had split away to go and greet the fourth arrival. He was deep in animated conversation, in Arabic.

'Harry!' Harry Shaw stopped in mid-sentence and then like a school boy pulled up for his manners guided the smiling Arab towards his Commanding Officer.

'Sorry, Colonel. This is Haji Mansoor, he's our Mullah.'

'Salaam aley'koom, Ya Haji.' Rolls took the Mullah's hand.

'And peace be upon you, Colonel,' the Haji replied in English. He smiled at the surprise in Rolls' face and even more so at the shock in the eyes of the Squadron Leader. 'With the Holy Month only a few days away, I thought I should be of more value here.' He tilted his head and smiled disarmingly. Rolls turned to the others.

'Well, Gentlemen, this has made my day, if not my week. Let's go for a coffee.'

News of the RAF team's arrival had reached the furthest sangar before they had reached the Headquarters. The three company commanders and Mr Thompson arrived within minutes of each other; hungry for news and hope. Squadron Leader Milton seemed on the verge of being over-awed by everything he saw. Perhaps it was for this or some more esoteric reason that he continued to wear his blue, RAF cap. The NCOs looked incongruous yet comfortable in floppy, green bush-hats. As the little officer explained in great detail and with considerable seriousness, they were a Tactical Air Control Party. Their mission was to direct the Royal Air Force's Sepecat Jaquars onto the enemy, when the time came. Milton used the phrase 'when the time comes' a lot. Rolls felt a nagging discomfort in the RAF officer's professed confidence in the technical theory of 'when the time comes.' It was obvious that whatever his expectations about the operation; Assaad and the Third Battalion did not live up to his briefing notes.

Haji Mansoor on the other hand turned out to be the very tonic the jundis and the officers needed. He was a very rare creature in the region; an extrovert Mullah. By the evening of his first day, he had seen or at least been seen by every man on the position.

CHAPTER TWENTY

James Faulkner looked up from his note-book and watched the dust floating through the shaft of sunlight which lanced the entrance of his sangar. The dancing pool of light was advancing across the dusty, blue bed-mats to the far wall. He sat cross-legged without any strain or cramp now. He looked around the nine jundis sat around the walls. He pondered on what his brother Guards' subalterns might think if they could see him now. 'Could it really be the James Faulkner, Doyen of the Knightsbridge and Chelsea Light of Foot who was patiently waiting for a bunch of illiterate, Arab privates to catch up in a dictation exercise'. A year ago James had decided that the prospect of a further two years of London public duties tipped him in favour of a fresh start in the commodity markets or commercial banking. He turned aside any thoughts of an extended Army career. The idea of an eighteen month secondment to the Emir's Forces struck him as a faintly romantic last bash. A good conversation piece for his CV. The colloquial Arabic language qualification would look good as well. Well it certainly was all of that. An 'A' level in French but never considering himself good at languages, he found the Army Language School tedious. He came out top of his class in spite of spending most of his afternoons divided between Wimbledon and the better hostelries of Royal Berkshire. He was quite content to do his regimental bit under the congenial, if fuzzy, leadership of Peter White. He found the jundis as irksome as they found him remote. That state probably have remained unchanged until the end of the tour had not Peter White been wounded.

White's departure had shown James how much he had taken for granted. The raw mechanics of command offered few problems, it was the more subtle aspects of established mutual trust and respect that were missing. The solution came from the last person James would have chosen to approach, Harry Shaw. On his arrival back in the battalion's base camp, James was beset with the most lurid stories of Harry's ferocious drinking bouts and his predilection for young mess boys. Having witnessed the one, in the form of Harry's prostrate body in the flower beds one night, he had no wish to become involved in the other. Consequently he had given the second-in-command the widest possible berth.

In the first few days of James' solo command, Harry had spent much of the day with the company. The jundis were uneasy after the shooting as they regarded the whole affair as a pre-cursor for worse to come. Harry, as the Battalion's father-figure, took it upon himself to purge their collective guilt. It was during this time that Faulkner discovered that beneath the bumbling, avuncular manner lay an intellect every bit as sharp as his own. Harry quickly sensed the young Guards officer's problem and as a remedy introduced him to Arabic writing and culture. James took up the challenge and, with the help of Harry's small but authoritative library and the assistance of those NCOs and soldiers who were literate, found a point of contact with his men. More than that he created a dependency which served them both.

'Eat with us, Sah'b,' the section corporal said entering the sangar with a large tray of boiled rice.

'You are kind, Saleh.' James got up and followed the others outside to wash his hands before eating. He smelt the rice, and the spicy tang of fresh goat stew. The jundis' spirits were lifted in anticipation as they chattered and joked about who would eat the most. Mindful of the approaching dusk and stand-to, James chivvied them along.

The night was still and quiet save for the rasping of the cicadas and the other night creatures in the wadi below. James switched off the transistor radio above his campbed. He had been listening to accounts of Palestinian victories on the Radio Cairo news in the company of his signaller and his sergeant-major.

'Let's go and check the sentries, Wakeel,' he suggested. The CSM, short, stocky hillman from the southern borders, passed James his M2 carbine; a leaving present from Irving Ross. He ducked his head out into the moonless night, when the sky was lit with a blinding flicker of orange flashes. The air pulsed with explosions, six or seven, all at once. The echo rumbled away. Then a fury of cracks and bangs rent the air around him.

'Stand-to!' he bawled. He dropped down and wriggled through the blast walls into the open sangar. The wakeel followed.

'No Guns!' For a second he thought the sentries were dead. Then they started: short, controlled bursts. He stuck his head up, tracer was bouncing through the wire. Two guns were firing, then three, four. Soon the FNs of the rifle-armed jundis joined in. He tried to judge where the enemy fire was coming from. He followed the out-going tracer. Muzzle flashes all along the wire, left flank. 'Christ! They were on the wire!'

'Wakeel illum. Yasaar!' He fumbled for his transceiver switch while the CSM was pulling flares from a tin in the wall. 'One niner, Contact ... Adoo on wire ... left flank.'

'Zero, roger,' Callender's eager voice snapped back.

'Four tubes on your Red One Zero,' Mr Thompson chimed in. James glanced up and out to where the pre-recorded target lay. Nothing, the adoo were too far left. More strobe flashes, more explosions, the blasts were deafeningly close ... just in front of his wall. He ducked as a projectile tore past his right ear; the CSM had set off a flare. They bobbed up together as the flare popped.

'Shoof Adoo!' James looked. There against the silhouette of the Dannert coils, heads. Black shapes weaving about. He pressed his transmit.

'Adoo on position ...' A blinding flash snatched away his vision. The ground heaved. He was thrown off his feet. Ears ringing, he sat up. Men ran past. He was now up with his carbine, more frantic shapes danced before him, guns sparking. Another flash, a blow from no-where. A body flew past his head, its foot caught his shoulder. He reeled backwards, dropping the carbine. The body was up and slashing, spindly thin arms, savage eyes popping. Faulkner backed up tense as a spring. The tribesman advanced, bayonet jabbing the air between them. A spade handle jerked into his sight, low right. He grabbed it in both hands and slashed at the head. Missing, he thumped the back wall. In a frenzy he stepped in on the backswing. The spade stopped dead, an inch deep in ribs. Muscles gripped it tight in spasm. The man coughed wetly and jerked backwards wrenching the handle from Faulkner's shocked grasp. The wakeel was up and firing. The body jumped and was still.

'One niner, Red zero, ready.' Faulkner blessed the anticipation of the Geordie gunner. He reached down and found the rounded handle of the Very pistol sticking out of the sandbag wall. Simultaneously, he fired and shouted 'fire' into his radio. The night was bathed in a ruby red glow. He heard the distinctively hollow thumps of the 81 millimetre mortars from the far side of the hill and pushed the CSM down into the shelter of his command post. Twenty rounds stamped over the position like a berserk giant for a hellish fifteen seconds. On the red Very's light the jundis had dived for the safety of their thick-roofed sangars leaving the hapless adoo exposed to thousands of razor sharp slivers of steel which scythed through the night in the wake of the pounding blasts.

So ended the first assault on the main position.

CHAPTER TWENTY ONE

Few slept on Assaad that night. In every sangar and deep shelter men waited on each hour that went by. Watching the shadows for the slightest change of shape or sign of movement; listening for any telltale sound. Rolls set off up the track to One Company, aiming to arrive just before the sun rose. As Commanding Officer he now had a small retinue, Din Mohammed, the RSM and a signaller. Squadron Leader Milton now also tagged along. Milton had been quite beside himself with excitement during the attack and had spent the rest of the night pumping Rolls and Cook for virtually every known fact about the Hawaafi and the war.

'Do you think they will attack now?' he asked, cradling his Stirling as they left the headquarters.

'No, not with a full day ahead,' Rolls answered. 'And I, for one, would not be going out if there was.' He smiled at Milton's concerned face. The RAF Officer dashed back into his tent and reappeared with a neck loaded with cameras and accessories.

Milton seemed quite disappointed at the apparent normality of the scene when they arrived at Faulkner's command post. The dead adoo had been pushed over the wall. They all sat in silence as the colour returned to the Jebel. As soon as Faulkner signalled 'Stand-down' little knots of jundis started forming at various points on the position. Rolls looked over the sangar wall at the dead man. He was face down. A lump of bone and cranial matter had erupted through the fuzzy, black tangle of curls. A brown stain surrounded two jagged holes on the back of his camouflage jacket. He was bare-foot and bare-legged; his green- and blue-plaid wizzar drawn up to mid thigh.

'I thought you hit him with a shovel?' said Rolls, recalling the breathlessly garbled reports of the evening.

'I did, Wakeel finished him off.' Faulkner leaned over and turned the body over by the shoulder. It flopped stiffly onto its back, one stiff arm, bent at the elbow, pointed up accusingly. 'There.' Faulkner indicated a tear in the man's jacket, a brown stain beneath.

'Jerked the spade clean out of my hands,' he explained to a fascinated Milton.

'What were those double bangs?' asked Rolls, changing to a more professional tack.

'RPG 7s.' Faulkner went over to the CP roof and returned with a piece of olive-green tube. It was finned at one end the other jaggedly curled over like wilting leaves. 'Seven or eight, I suppose. The first two smack on the main sentry post.' He pointed towards the left forward platoon.

'Killed the poor sods outright.' Rolls stood up on the sangar wall. The RSM was walking back towards him with the wakeel.

'Find any more?' he asked. The Baluch shook his head.

'No Sah'b, six adoo only.'

'Not bad, six for two,' Rolls commented.

'How are the wounded?' asked Faulkner.

'Okay, no one worth casevacing. Panda said they'll be back with you tomorrow.' Faulkner and Rolls then walked down towards the wire together. The squadron leader was trotting round from body to body taking photographs: he was still wearing his blue, peaked cap.

The jundis were fascinated by the bodies. The dead Hawaafi were warriors to a man; lean limbed, sharp, thin featured faces. They were a different species from the plumpish, round-faced date farmers who stood around them and stared in awe and not a little fear.

'What shall we do with the bodies?' Rolls stopped.

'Bag them up and take them over to the LS ... Same with the kit.' He caught a look of doubt in Faulkner's eye. 'What do you want to do? Hang them on the wire,' he snapped angrily. The Guardsman flushed around the neck.

'No, I thought ... well ...' Rolls relented. 'The boys don't mind if that's your worry. They don't take it out on the dead.'

Faulkner nodded, feeling more than slightly foolish.

They heard laughter behind the pointing corpse. The scene reminded Rolls of pictures of dead, American gangsters and their self-righteous, G-men, killers that he used to seek out amongst the more lurid weeklies in childhood dentists' waiting rooms. He suppressed an overwhelming urge to march over and give them an impromptu lecture on dignity and respect. He sighed and fought down a wave of mourning and fellow feeling for the Hawaafi.

'Let's go and look at the wire.' He strode off down the hill as Faulkner issued rapid instructions to his wakeel and then caught him up. 'Did you hear those planes last night, James?'

* * *

General Welles noticed for the first time that he could recall that Gilbert Dixon was going bald on top. The colonel, unaware that he was the subject of such scrutiny, was engrossed in the contents of a red, cardboard folder. He finished reading, riffled back through the pages and looked up.

'You know, General,' he began, 'one has to give Henson his due, it's a very attractive plan.'

General Welles wrinkled his face as if sampling a sour fruit. He swung sideways in his chair and played with his cigar.

'The point about the adoo placing their support weapons at maximum range from Assaad and therefore unable to gain crest-clearance to their rear shows remarkable foresight.'

Welles thought about interrupting Gilbert's unreserved praise for the Henson plan but did not wish to appear churlish.

'The Air Staff predict 60 per cent fatalities in the wadis and 30 per cent on the open slopes ...' the Chief of Staff continued.

'Must be true if the Crabs say so,' Welles thought sarcastically to himself. He never exercised his ill-humour on Gilbert because he knew how sensitive he was to criticism. He took a different tack. 'How did the bastard manage to get the okay from Whitehall? That's what I'd like to know.' He continued to stare out of the window at the hazy, blue pinnacles of the Jebel Hassaf in the distance.

Gilbert uncrossed his legs and removed his glasses. 'I understand from the DA that the Crabs are very keen to try out their Jaguars for real now that they have an operational squadron.'

Welles waved his cigar in frustration at Gilbert's inability to mind-read. 'No, I mean the FO. They've never been keen on this place.'

'Ah well, that's where he really shines. Spent half his time in some embassy or High Commission or other.'

'Bloody Mafia!'

'He hasn't fallen over yet, General.' Gilbert replaced his half-frames and peered benignly over the tops.

'Hope to Christ he doesn't fall at this fence,' Welles turned back.

'Not a bad bit of work by young Faulkner last night, eh?'

'No, indeed. Reconnaissance by fire, perhaps?' Welles pushed his bottom lip out.

'Maybe. Seems damn well organised compared with previous outings.'

Gilbert hummed over this one and scribbled a note on his ever-present pad. 'What do you make of the aeroplane report?'

'Hell of a lot of charter stuff about; not all of it logged, either Gilbert.'

Welles shook his head. 'Skyvans from Muscat do booze runs every bloody week.'

Gilbert unclipped a signal from his millboard and passed it over.

'Seventh Fleet send a summary of traffic to all interested parties. I received this from the Air Attache this morning. Picked up by one of their Hawkeyes.' Welles perused the signal.

'Where's this place where they turned inland?' he asked, referring to the longitude-latitude fix in the text.

'Five miles north of Assaad.'

'Transports?' Gilbert nodded. 'Supplies or men?'

'I suppose we'll find out sooner or later.' Welles noticed the date-time group of the radar sighting. In translation it read "ten after midnight, 6 October 1973". He looked up at Gilbert.

'How are the Strikemasters fixed for an eyeball sortie?' His Chief of Staff looked immediately doubtful. He shook his head and removed his glasses again.

'There is no off-the-shelf SAM detector available. The Airserve people are working on a flare dispenser and covers for the exhausts but ...' He shrugged his shoulders as another thought developed. 'I don't think they would see much anyway. Cover's too thick in those wadis.' Welles watched him ponder, not wishing to break Dixon's creative processes. 'Of course there is McNaughton's man, Abu Issa?' Welles leaned back.

'Will McNaughton agree?'

'He'll have seen that signal.'

'Right then, bounce it off him. If he wants any sort of diversion to help with the insertion, that's fine.' Gilbert Dixon scribbled another note on his pad. Welles looked over his head to the wall clock. 'Fancy a set or two this afternoon?'

Gilbert smiled: 'What about bringing the girls in for doubles?'

'Good idea.'

* * *

An air of professional self-satisfaction had permeated the atmosphere of Jebel Assaad. The jundis from One Company took every opportunity to coffee-house around the other positions, embellishing the night's action as they went. The officers too felt that, at last, events were running their way. The RAF team toured the position with their maps and binoculars taking pages full of notes. Speculation ran unchecked. Close air support from half a squadron of Jaguars grew to the proportions of a B52 strike in the minds of the jundis. Although no actual details of the forthcoming operation had been given, they were already speculating on the precise numbers of Inglees Midhalliyeen, English Paratroopers, who would be appearing in the sky bukra, tomorrow. The RAF sergeants were mobbed by admiring jundis where ever they went.

The sun had just begun its steady descent into the western ridges. John Rolls was sitting on the roof of the command post with Harry Shaw. A tin tray with a glass jug of gin and lime and two glasses lay between them. They were watching Mr Thompson explaining some of the finer points of "steam gunnery", as he put it, to the RAF sergeants. Both of the SNCOs were now sporting Geysh-style shemaghs in place of the bush-hats.

'Time for the news,' said Harry, reaching down for a battered, Japanese transistor at his side.

'I sometimes wonder, Harry, if we really exist in the real world or whether we are caught in some kind of time warp.' Rolls smiled and flicked his half-smoked filter tip onto the adjacent roof. The martial thumps of Lillibalero were just dying away when a ragged volley of shots and whooping yells broke out. First from Two Company, then Three, then the gunline. Rolls jerked up to his feet, his right hand dropping to the Browning automatic which he now wore on his hip. More shouting erupted from the HQ Company tents below him. Everywhere jundis were dancing about shouting praises to Allah, hugging each other and loosing shots off into the air.

'What the Hell's … ?'

'Perhaps the war's over?' suggested Harry. The white turban of Haji Mansoor appeared below them. 'Hadji, shoo taqlif?' Harry asked. The Mullah turned and beamed at them, he raised his open palms heavenwards.

'The Egyptians have crossed the canal. They are driving the Jews back across the Sinai.' He laughed, a hint of gentle cynicism in the tilt of his head. 'Allah is indeed generous.'

'May Allah guide them to a just peace, Yaa Haji.' Harry rejoined respectfully. Shots now echoed from all directions.

'Better limit the celebration to ten rounds a piece, Harry, or we'll be firing off our buttons tonight.' Rolls picked up his glass.

'A just peace, Haji.'

'In sha'Allah, Sah'b.'

CHAPTER TWENTY TWO

For the first five days of the October War, every news broadcast English and Arabic was listened to and analysed to varying degrees throughout the Emirate. Less than two percent of the indigenous population knew anything of the political issues involved. More significantly, those who had actually met an Egyptian or a Syrian usually despised the first and loathed the latter. The real point was that Arabs, people like them, were actually winning against the erstwhile invincible Jew. The jundis reserved most of their limited reserves of contempt for all things American. The logic behind this was very simple. As the Inglees pilots flew all of the Emir's aircraft (the advent of an indigenous pilot was not even close) then the Americans flew all of the Jews aircraft. It was a fact of Gulf history that the Americans won the Six Day War for the Jehudyeen. Fortunately, for the officers of the Third Battalion no-one looked even remotely Jewish or sounded at all American.

A few days later Rolls was satisfied that the rush towards world war had stopped on the Golan Heights and in front of the Sinai Passes. Win, lose or draw the Third Battalion would return to normal within a couple of days. What he failed to anticipate was a curtly worded signal demanding that the Starfinder team was to be backloaded with all stores at the first opportunity. An apologetic and dejected squadron leader stood on the edge of the landing site in the still, cool air of dawn the following day. The two sergeants were saying sad farewells to Mr Thompson.

'Thanks for everything, Bill,' one said. Mr Thompson, for once, had lost all of his bouncy good humour and now looked quite desolated. He'd miss being called by his first name for a start. Now he'd be just "Mister Thompson" or "Wakeel Sah'b" again.

'The boss said that he'll write the set off.'

The thought of playing with one of Racal's latest air-to-ground radios lightened his gloom a fraction.

The supply Hueys clattered into view, flying low out of the vermilion sky. Squadron Leader Milton picked up his flight bag and bergan. Richard Callender ran up and passed something to Rolls.

'Oh Tony!' Rolls began, raising his voice above the incoming roar. 'To keep the sun off you, should you ever see it again in UK.' He tucked a freshly tasselled shemagh into the top of Milton's bergan. The RAF officer choked up a thank you and then stumbled towards the open cabin door. Rolls turned to Richard Callender who was watching the Huey begin its long, spiral ascent.

'Thanks, Richard,' he said, concealing his own feelings of desertion, 'Nice touch, that.'

* * *

'The ambassador spent fifteen minutes on the line, himself, last night,' Henson explained. 'I was with him and believe me, they were quite adamant. No direct involvement.' He glared accusingly back at his accusers. General Welles continued his pacing along the seaward wall of his office. Gilbert sat opposite Henson, in front of the desk; dangling his half-rims from his lower lip.

'I thought you had an in with the FO?' Welles lobbed at him, from the window.

'I also have enemies.' He held Welles' eyes until the latter turned away. 'In the normal course of things, there would have been no problem, but now …' He stopped and waved a frustrated hand about above the desk. 'Now … with the Press watching every airbase for American supply planes and whatever, they cannot take the risk.'

'What risk?'

'Questions in the House … It's ideal Tory bashing material.' Henson leaned forward to direct his reasoning through Dixon. 'They were going to keep the whole show under wraps until the end. Then, announce it as a sort of fait accompli, you know, "sorry we couldn't say anything but careless talk … lives at risk" and all that. But now …' He shook his head as if he, himself, considered the whole venture unthinkable.

'Do they know what's at stake?' Dixon asked quietly.

'I don't think they do.'

'Well what the Bloody Hell are you going to do about it?' Henson looked shaken by the General's sudden change of tone.

'I haven't given up.' Henson slowly stood up. He looked at Welles and then at Dixon. 'Look,' he said. 'I know that I'm responsible for this and I'll find a way.' Dixon felt sorry for him. The prim self-assurance was gone. He looked tired, damn tired. 'Give me 48 hours ... Then ...' He halted as if his next thought was unutterable. He recovered his nerve. 'Then plan for withdrawal.' Welles watched him pack away his briefcase. A curious thought entered his tired mind. He felt like a pilot walking back through the passenger cabin with a parachute. He reached the door eventually. He looked back.

'If it's of any help, I've told McNaughton to put Abu Issa at your disposal.' He nodded his goodbye and slipped out into the mid-morning blaze.

'Poor Bastard!' said Welles. Gilbert looked up, surprised at his commander's show of compassion. 'Right, Gilly. Get Laurel and Hardy in and let's see what we can do.' The Chief of Staff put down his glasses and went out to round up his Intelligence Officers.

Henson made his way down to the stifling courtyard. His aide hopped out of the Range Rover to open the door.

'You're confirmed on tonight's Gulf Air, sir,' he said politely.

'Those signals get off okay?' Henson asked. The young man puckered his creaseless brows.

'I think so, sir.' He hovered and then admitted, 'Colonel McNaughton said they would go by Special Means ...' Henson managed a thin smile and relaxed a little in the front passenger seat.

* * *

As fine-tuned as they were to the distant thump and whistling passage of incomers, the first artillery shells caught the jundis by surprise. The flatter trajectory put the first round clean over the top. It was this and the pattern of subsequent adjusting rounds which gave WO2 Thompson a firm indication of the new weapon's identity. Having found their mark the enemy gunners promptly fired for effect. Eighteen to twenty shells whirred across the Great North Road and slammed into the middle of Two Company. The whole jebel shook with each thunderous explosion. It was over inside a minute.

Giles emerged from his thick stone shelter dazed and grey with dust. Some jundis were staggering about holding their ears, others were knelt over retching.

'Ta'al hina! Geebook shaywaal!' His Baluch sergeant-major

was directing every able-bodied soldier up towards the depth platoon. Giles shook his head to try and stop the ringing in his ears and then ran up to see what the problem was. Jundis were scrabbling at loose rocks and torn sandbags with their bare hands to reach those buried inside.

'Don't stand on top, you stupid arses!' he yelled, storming up to them. The offending jundis jumped clear. 'Now lift these beams.' He grasped the end of a splintered main roof support and began to lever it away. The uncomprehending jundis watched for a second and then joined in, resuming their usual babble. Two more beams were lifted clear.

'Al hamdu l'illah!' The thanksgiving echoed round the group as a leathery, dust-coated hand was thrust up from between the twisted sheets of corrugated iron.

* * *

The Gulf Air VC10 touched down just before midnight, London time. Lt Col Henson dozed in the back of the taxi. Usually on home leave or business trips he would indulge himself, like most ex-patriots, in the novelty of English sights and sounds. He had booked into a modest hotel near Marble Arch, rather than into one of the London clubs which he normally patronised. He had stipulated an en suite bathroom and allowed himself a long, thoughtful soak before savouring the chilly luxury of fresh, cotton sheets.

The telephone alarm call brought him out of a deep sleep at 8 o'clock. He ordered a full cooked breakfast and perused The Times till there was a knock on the door. Unlocking it, he found a smartly dressed, young Arab holding a suitcase.

'Sabah al Keyr, yaa Assif.' He brought the Arab into the room long enough only to check the contents of the case and to give Assif a plain, buff envelope. 'Tell his Excellency that I shall call in later this afternoon.' Assif took his envelope and left. Henson looked down at the case. Neatly folded inside was his London winter uniform, grey, chalk-stripe suit, shirts, club ties, Burberry, telescopic umbrella. He felt good, organised, confident again.

Showered, shaved, breakfasted and dressed, Henson stood in the foyer of his hotel and inspected the capital's morning. It was chill with a weak sun hovering in a hazy, grey sky. He checked the time and decided to walk rather than to risk the tailend of the rush-hour with the Great Unwashed. Striding out he went past the more fashionable hotels, through Green Park and Spring Gardens to Whitehall. He stopped outside the monolithic, grey edifice of the Ministry of Defence Main Building. Even as he was being escorted along drab corridors he knew that his forthcoming appointment was going to be a complete waste of time. Civil servants of the ilk that staffed the upper echelons of the Defence Secretariat would never reverse a policy reversal. It was simply unheard-off. He would not even find out who the key decision-maker was. That was one of their Holy Laws, disguise individual responsibility at all costs.

He was ushered into a shabby green and yellow painted room containing a small conference table with chipped varnish and a dozen, assorted chairs. A horn-rimmed, Permanent Under-Secretary, as appropriate to Henson's rank, shook hands and introduced two of his secretariat henchmen. No serving soldiers or airmen to sympathise or give the game away. This was to be short, sharp and pointless. The meeting lasted barely forty-five minutes. The PUS sympathised and understood a great deal. The staffers pointed out the wider political implications and dangers. All three, like a composite Mr McCawber, were sure that something would turn up. Henson was suitably crest-fallen throughout.

As they were leaving, he asked if he might use the telephone to call the Foreign and Commonwealth Office. Following some furtive glances and a considerable delay, a telephone was found. The only officer who could have possible helped was "out of the country, the Middle-East War, don't yer know". Henson handed in his visitor's pass to the uniformed doorman, trotted lightly down the steps and marched briskly up Whitehall. Their expectation fulfilled, he was now free to play the market. He called a cab which dropped him off near Oxford Circus. In one of the anonymous carveries off the side streets, he treated himself to a full lunch with a fine bottle of claret while he waited for his next appointment.

* * *

While Henson was enjoying his lunch, Mr Thompson was displaying his latest finds to Rolls and Callender. A collection of jagged metal pieces were spread out on his headcloth. He fingered a curved fragment and set it on its edge.

'I'd say 'wun twenty-two, Soviets used 'em just post war,' he suggested. 'Three guns by the rate of fire.'

'Air portable?' asked Rolls.

'Very.'

'Well, that may explain the aircraft.' The sergeant-major looked puzzled. Callender reached behind him and lifted the signal file of the Ops desk. He flicked up the sheets before passing the relevant copy to the Geordie gunner.

'Well, the crafty sods!' He looked up. 'I wuz wound'run hows they got them in.'

'They can break them down into small loads, can't they?'

'Aye, they can at a push, Colonel, but its the shells that's the bugger. Don't get many to the camel.' Rolls nodded, thoughtfully, his concurrence.

'Where do you reckon they are?'

'Direction puts them the other side of Cub. They'll use all the range they got.'

'Can we reach them?'

'Ah, no chance, Man!' he said, expressively, 'Even if the seventy-fives had the range with predicted fire I'd be pissin' in the wind.'

'How do they do it?' Thompson grinned.

'They got someone givin' directions and he's good an' all.' Rolls sat down in one of the folding chairs. He blew his cheeks out. The other two recognised the concern on his face.

'This could make Two Company's position untenable: forward slope, observed fire.' He leaned forward and scrutinised the wall map behind the Ops table. 'Everyone keep their eyes open for the OP. We might be lucky.'

* * *

As the midday sun beat down on Assaad, Henson was waiting in a queue of cars at the Sheerness ferryport. He had hired a Granada rather than attract attention with one of the embassy's pool. He would spend a quiet day motoring through the Flemish countryside. A pleasant lunch perhaps in a Bruegel landscape. He hated having to kill time, but it was better than hanging round the London clubrooms with all their amateur spies and gossip-mongers. What he was attempting to do would probably take the speediest joint planning staff weeks to complete. Henson knew that he had a matter of days; a bare fortnight at the outside.

* * *

The first 122 millimetre shell of the day came whizzing through the hot, still air just after 2 pm. The heavy crump came from the eastern slopes below the Headquarters. Callender pushed the on-watch signaller down into the dug-out portion of the CP.

'Get your heads down, lads. He's lookin' out for you.' The unattended transceiver relayed Mr Thompson's voice in metallic tones. Callender squirmed round in the cramped space and listened for the next incomer. The bustle and babble of the Headquarters jundis scrambling into their shelters, died away. The only sound was the buzzing of flies who found themselves alone in the upper world. Then it came; a short ripping buzz followed by an earth-shaking crump. The walls of the dugout shook, rattling down loose pebbles and dirt. It was closer; between the signals sangars and the landing site. There was an agonising wait then came a three round salvo, regular spacing, precise; crump, crump, wham. Callender's ears popped, his teeth snapped painfully together. He jammed his eyes shut, held his breath. The dugout filled with swirling dust. He waited and waited, but nothing else came.

There were shouts outside. He scrambled up and out. The CP was still hazy with dust. He poked his head out through the hessian curtains. There was a small fire amongst the tents, jundis ran around pulling bits of burning canvas down. There was no water to be used, it couldn't be spared. Then he saw Rolls, in amongst the salvagers. Callender went back to the radio desk. He called the signallers out of their shelter. The radio squawked through the dust.

'Hello zero, Shelldrake here.' Mr Thompson's unmistakable voice.

'Zero, okay. No cas,' Callender replied. He stopped himself. No more detail on the air, they might be listening.

'Defi-nately a spotta. I'll see if I can spoil his day,' Callender acknowledged and then on impulse searched around for his transistor. He found it, and then went onto the roof. Rolls was standing amongst the smouldering embers of one of the tents inspecting a crater with a small group of jundis. Callender looked beyond them to the gunline. He could see the broad-shouldered figure of the sergeant-major kneeling alongside one of the American-made heavy mortars. Two gunners were lifting a round up to the shoulder-high lip of the muzzle. They fitted the finned base into the opening and let go; backing away with their hands over their ears. Mr Thompson spun away simultaneously jerking the firing lanyard. The thumping flat boom of the detonation slapped the walls of the sangar.

Callender looked out across the Great North Road towards Cub. He picked up his transistor and flicked to the VHF band. He swept the tuning needle across the display, hearing nothing but the tweeting whine of static. Then he heard what he hardly dared hope for; the tell-tale surge of mush as someone else nearby transmitted. He back tuned but it had gone. A movement caught his eye out on the Cub feature, a fountain of dirt, a thin column of rising dust. The solid thump of the thirty-three pound mortar shell rumbled back. The voice came through the set in clear matter of fact speech; German. His mind struggled to translate, it stumbled over words, he missed several in the effort to recall. The accent was different to what he was used to; High German ... hard, guttural, clipped,' ... close ... behind ... on top.' He jerked up and snatching the field glasses from the bench, searched the shimmering west face of Cub.

'What's up?' He heard the CO's voice behind him.

'The OP, Colonel, I think I've found him,' he answered; his voice tight with excitement. Just then the mortar belched out another round louder than before.

Callender pointed to where the last round had landed. 'I heard a voice on my trannie! He said the shell had landed just behind him.'

'In Arabic?'

'No, German.' Rolls pulled an expression of curiosity which after a moment's analysis turned to sharp interest. He pulled his own binoculars out of his belt-case and focused on the feature. They waited for the round to land but nothing came over the little radio. They lowered their glasses together. There was a brief surge of mush on the set. A distant rumble reached them from an unseen wadi on the far side of Cub. Rolls jumped as the German voice broke through; clear and precise. It sounded light-hearted and relaxed.

'What did he say?' Callender furrowed his brow in concentration. The transmission stopped.

'He said, "it's you he's after", or something like that. The accent's difficult, north or eastern German.'

'You're bloody marvellous,' exclaimed Rolls. He pulled a canvas stool up to the parapet ledge. 'Show me where that first round landed.' Rolls studied the tightly packed contours of the map and then scoured the west face with his glasses.

'I can't understand where the second round went,' said Callender, looking over the gunline.

'Over the top into the next wadi.' Rolls looked up smiling, 'Old Master Gunner there dropped the first one short just to check his line. Second one long to get a bracket ... It's only by chance that the OP felt it necessary to comment. The problem now is how do we get the bastard?'

'How about another shell?'

'Can't guarantee a kill; he might be dug in.' Callender watched as his commander sifted the possibilities around in his mind. Rolls shook his head as if dismissing an unspoken option and leaned back. There was a resounding thump from the mortar followed by seven more over the minute as Andy and Flo, his mate, belched a speculative barrage against the enemy OP on the abandoned positions.

Silently and unbidden, Din Mohammed appeared at Rolls' side. He nodded curtly to Callender and sank down to his haunches next to Rolls' stool. Rolls looked down into the Pathan's dark, still eyes.

'What do you think, Din?' He said in Urdu. 'There is an enemy out there who can tell those gunners how to hit anything on this position any time he chooses.' Din looked out at Cub and then back to Rolls.

'I get him.' His baleful eyes looked for dissent in the CO's face. 'When the sun rises I kill him.' Rolls felt a surge of dread run over him like a cold draught. It would have been unthinkable to suggest it but he had only thought of the possibility and Din had picked it up. To say anymore would be to break the spell. He had his solution.

'When will you leave?' Rolls asked quietly, as if he were in church.

'When the sun is gone.' Din allowed his thin lips to form the faintest of smiles. 'I prepare.' He rose and dropped off the ledge onto one of the blast-walls. Rolls told Callender what Din was going to do.

'You're letting him go alone, sir?' Callender almost whispered. Rolls brought up his hand to pinch his nostrils.

'Why not? It's what he was born and bred for.' He fixed the young subaltern's incredulous gaze. 'Warn Giles off.' Callender nodded recovering his composure a little. 'What gave you the idea of tuning in?' Callender grinned broadly.

'I used to do it to keep awake when I was watchkeeping. That's how I learnt German; listening to their nets.'

'What, just by listening?'

'It's easy really; As conscripts, their radio discipline is awful and they normally repeat everything they say.'

* * *

Din Mohammed squatted in the shadow of a dwarf acacia and searched the dark mass of the Cub feature in front of him. The skyline was clearly outlined against the milky glow of the new moon. Opening his mouth to create a natural echo chamber, he turned his head slowly left and right trying to pick up any sounds from out of the background chorus of night insects. Hearing nothing unusual, he directed his attention back to the dark wall of rock. He had spent the hour before sunset memorising his intended route for he used neither map nor compass. The mulazzim sah'b Callender had pointed out where he thought the adoo artillery spotters might be; a deeply, cleft wadi running down the west face. Din recognised the wadi in front of him. For thirty minutes or so he watched for movement and listened for sounds.

Skirting around the wadi mouth, he started to climb a steep spur line to the left. Keeping the dry river bed to his right, he climbed steadily and silently. He reached the lip of the small plateau just as the thin, crescent moon spilled its weak light down onto the slope of the escarpment. Looking over the top he listened again; able now to see clearly the ruined sangars of Captain Primmer's command post. Certain now that the artillery observation party would descend the wadi each evening to cook and to sleep, he closed in to the edge of the wadi and took a few cautious steps down into it. The abrasive action of a thousand, ancient torrents had left the valley bottom strewn with smooth, rounded boulders and stones. Thorn and succulent cactus bushes stuck up defiantly wherever there was a handful of gravelly sand.

Din moved carefully down the wadi pausing at every twist and turn to listen: his FAL set at automatic, trigger finger tensed. By searching the wadi from top to bottom, and from the friendly side, he was counting on any hidden sentry giving him the benefit of the doubt, even if only for a split second. Then he spotted it, a small, open sangar. It was no more than a rough semi-circle of rocks about three feet high: the enclosed space clear of stones and well trampled. He leaned over the low wall and sniffed the air. A lingering odour of stale, human sweat, the scorched grain smell of khubz, this was the OP. He looked down the twisting valley. Fifty yards ahead the stream-bed wound sharply left and right around a steep-sided spur. The facing slope was bare rock. If caught on the higher side, a man could only run forward; to turn and run back or to stand still would be fatal. Din counted on it being so. He looked behind him, a clear view to the top of the plateau, he would not be surprised. Moving back up a few dozen yards he found a cleft between two boulders. He settled into it, checking his fire position both up and down the wadi for obstructions and comfort. He had no watch but knew that he had three hours to wait before dawn. He settled back and rested, his mind running through the options for the eventualities of the coming day.

The chirping of birds told him of the advent of dawn. The boulders and bushes in the wadi began to take on tentative shapes and colours. Din wriggled carefully up into his chosen firing position. His fingers carried out their checks of the weapon without cerebral instruction; change-lever to single shots, backsight up, two charged magazines in his left-hand pouch. His left hand dropped further back to the pouch on his hip. His fingers found three, cold metal shapes; grenades, two fragmentation ... one phosphorus smoke ... split pins in ... ends closed for easy extractions. He was ready. The sun had risen but the west facing slope was still in shadow. Din looked out across to Assaad, every feature sharp and clear in the early light; the OP was well sited for he could pick out the individual sangars of Two Company and the headquarters. The outlines of the 75s on the gunline.

Movement caught his eye, birds, six or seven small blackbirds with orange wingtips swept around the sangar. They hopped about pecking at the ground behind the stone wall.

'Yesterday's khubz,' thought Din. He leaned into the FAL and sighted down onto his chosen killing ground. The dull clack of rock on rock reached his ear. He took in a breath and held it. One, two then three men, heads down watching their footfall, rounded the spur.

The first was Hawaafi, short but lean, dark-coloured wazzir hitched to his knees, bare feet. He pushed his Kalashnikov out in front of him; an over sized cotton jacket hung from his shoulders, a green cotton magazine carrier bounced across his bony chest. A mass of black curls sprang from his head like a fuzzy bonnet.

The second man was much bigger, well-muscled with a fuller face: Assyrian stock, straight hair trimmed squarely at the sides and neck. He sported a full handlebar moustache and wore sand-coloured fatigues, boots and webbing. An AKS version of the Kalashnikov hung casually from one shoulder. In the rear came a Caucasian, dark hair, fair complexion. He wore a similar uniform to the Assyrian but had better boots. A small, man-pack radio bounced gently on his back, a canvas map case swung from his neck. A pistol holster was at his hip. Din tightened his grip and placed the fore-sight on the Hawaafi's chest.

The man vanished from the back-sight's aperture. Din snapped open his left eye. The ridge-man had stepped sideways off the track. Din saw him nimbly hop across the old water course and up the opposite bank. There he stopped. The other two stopped also. Din stopped breathing … 'Had he been seen?' The Hawaafi was frozen, listening, looking up the wadi. He relaxed a little and half-turned towards the other two. 'No, just jittery or annoyed with his foreign comrades'. But now he was a full quarter left. If Din fired on the Assyrian, the Hawaafi would escape or worse send back a hail of bullets. They moved off again, the Hawaafi still on the opposite side of the wadi. Din held his aim on the Assyrian but focussed his inner voice on the Hawaafi.

'Mountain man, mountain man, Brother … Stop! Danger … go back … go back,' he willed. He concentrated on the dark, close-set eyes. 'Stop … cross over, cross over.' The Hawaafi stopped, his instincts disturbed. A few remaining blackbirds flew up from the sangar, fluttered and wheeled away up and over the lip of the plateau. The Hawaafi's face relaxed, he lifted the rifle and lightly jumped back to the Assyrian's side of the stream-bed. He rudely pushed past them both to assume the lead.

The calloused pad of Din's forefinger took first pressure. He tensed. The Hawaafi walked once more into the rear sight aperture. He squeezed, the rifle bucked. He switched left, squeeze, squeeze. The wadi shuddered with the blasts. All three men were down. Din was up and moving down the valley. The rifle was trained on the sprawling bodies below. Fingers moved, Din dropped to one knee and fired. The bullet entered under the Caucasian's chin and led a vacuum-induced express of bone and tissue out through the top of his skull. Din was over them in an instant. He glanced back at the rim of the plateau; nothing. At his feet the Hawaafi lay in a dark, sticky pool, a discreet hole through the centre of his magazine holder. The Assyrian lay over the Caucasian's legs; Dins's second and third shot had passed through them both. The Pathan reached forward and pulled the wreckage of the Caucasian's head upright by the map-case. He jerked the strap over the head watched it fall back with a grisly thump. Then he was off, rock to rock, down the wadi. At the bottom he stopped; no pursuit. He scoured the flat expanse of the main wadi briefly, then merged into the shadows of the thorn trees and back towards Assaad.

On top of the command post, Rolls heard the three echoing shots, then a fourth. There was no light tapping challenge. He smiled with relief, finished his tea and wearily climbed down to seek an hour or two's sleep before it got too hot.

CHAPTER TWENTY THREE

The pathways in the Vondle Park were already choked with Autumn leaves. Henson always enjoyed Amsterdam. The casual aestheticism of the Dutch appealed to him. He stepped out onto the Vossmis Straat and looked back on the browns and reds of the trees behind him. It was still early and there were comparatively few people about. He adjusted the scarf at his neck against the October chill and stepped out briskly towards the Singel Gracht. The hotel was sited overlooking the waterway. Henson did not hesitate at the door but swept in and crossed the carpeted foyer before the concierge had looked up from his desk. He made straight for the lift not pausing to linger or to appear in any way unsure for to do so would be to invite attention and fix an indelible image in the minds of the hotel staff. He found room 817 at the end of a long cream and brown passage. His watch showed 10 am precisely; he knocked firmly.

The door was opened by a tall, well-built man in a light grey suit. 'Goot Morgen, Meinheer,' Henson said. The man smiled politely and beckoned him, silently, inside. He closed the door quietly but quickly.

'May I take your coat, Colonel?' he asked. His English spontaneous, but accented; the vowels were severely clipped. Henson allowed himself to be helped out of his Burberry. He felt that the man's politeness was part of a well-practised routine for a discrete check on hidden weaponry. He was then shown through to the sitting-room of a two-bedroomed suite. A shorter, broader man with iron-grey hair rose from an armchair.

'Colonel, very pleased to meet you.' Henson shook firm, dry hands as the two men made their formal introductions. 'Please, will you have coffee?' Without waiting for a reply, he motioned his junior partner. A brown earthern-ware coffee set was placed before them; hot and fresh. Coffee served, the Major then took out a note pad and pencil. Henson sipped his coffee and inwardly glowed; for the first time in a week, he felt amongst friends.

The Brigadier and the Major listened intently to Henson's account of Operation Saladin and its ill-fated final phase. Henson opened his thin attaché case and produced a small-scale map of the area. The Brigadier studied the map and its blue and red symbols briefly and then leaned back.

'I see no problem except getting there, Colonel.' He let show an apologetic smile. 'We have no operational requirement for inflight refuelling in the normal course of events. My people are also not too happy about using national carriers for the ordnance, spares and ground crews.' Far from being discouraged, Henson smiled. He had been through the problem in detail with McNaughton. He leaned forward with a happy glint in his eye.

'I trust that you still have the inflight refuelling probes fitted, Brigadier?'

The man with the iron-grey hair nodded gravely. 'Then I shall arrange the refuelling and a neutral cargo carrier; I think that two Canadiars would suffice?' The Brigadier took an affirmative nod from the Major and gave Henson the benefit of a wide reassuring grin.

'I don't suppose you care to tell me who your neutral power is, Colonel?'

Henson shook his head. 'That will be the subject of my next appointment.' He took out a manilla envelope and extracted two printed sheets. 'Major, can I place these in your charge?'

The Major took the sheets which were typed up in the format of commercial telex signals.

'A simple device to ensure privacy,' he explained. 'Just put in the co-ordinates of your refuelling rendezvous points as the last digits of these quantities. The same with your estimated requirements for fuel and cargo.' Henson watched the Major's eyes scan the telex headings. 'The addressee is a genuine shipping firm registered in the Emirate. I'm sure you already have similar arrangements for such traffic of your own.'

'We do indeed,' the Brigadier replied.

Henson rose. 'Well, Gentlemen, thank you for your attention. Will I be seeing either of you at the other end, so to speak?'

'Not me. I just fly desks, Colonel.' The Brigadier laughed as he got up. 'But the Major here will be in command.' The Major rose with the map in his hands.

'One thing, Colonel. What about the marking of the targets?'

'My staff are working on that one,' Henson lied. 'The ground troops also have a talk through facility on their beacon radios.

There will be time for at least one rehearsal and we have ear-marked an area of similar terrain' he added. The Major seemed re-assured and moved purposely ahead to lift Henson's coat down from its peg.

'Have you heard the news this morning?' The Brigadier asked as Henson shrugged on his coat, with the assistance of the Major.

'No?'

'The Israelis have crossed the Suez Canal.'

CHAPTER TWENTY FOUR

As Henson was looking down the Death's column of an early edition of the Times in the departure lounge of Schipol airport, the air on the gunline on Assaad was alive with conspiratorial excitement. The deceased owner of the map case, now in Richard Callender's hands, had been one Oberst-Lieutenant Werner Maas, late of the Artillery Regiment Willie Bredel of the East German Peoples' Army. A precise and assiduous, young officer, he had marked his map with text-book accuracy. Unfortunately for his comrades manning the 122 millimetre guns in the large wadi beyond Cub he had not considered the possibility of his death or the capture of his map.

'What do you think these lines are here?' asked Callender, pointing to a number of dashes in a semi-circle round Two Company's position.

'I'm not sure.' Rolls craned his neck to look from a different angle. 'Too far down to be the wire.' They were standing by the gunline command post. Mr Thompson stopped at Callender's shoulder and squinted at the marks.

'That's 'is check firing mark'ah,' he announced. 'I'd say they were plannin' to bump Two Compan'ee.' He darted away to supervise the stowage of more of his precious mortar rounds from the morning's resupply.

'What do you think, Colonel?'

'I think we'd better go and warn off, Charles.' He turned and looked for the sergeant-major. Mr Thompson emerged from one of the ammunition sangars wiping the sweat from his face. 'I suppose we can expect a double dose of hate once they find out what we've done to their OP?' Mr Thompson pursed his lips in consideration.

'If they had a Gerry out as OP then you can guarantee a few more on that gunline. My guess, sir, is that they'll move it an' as I've said before it's not the guns that's the problem it's the ammunition. I reckon a couple of days at least.'

'I hope you're right, 'major.'

* * *

The Boeing 747 touched down at 4 pm Eastern Standard Time. Henson used his diplomatic status to by-pass the tiresome procedures imposed on arrivals at Dulles Airport Immigration Control and was surprised to be shown straight into a courtesy lounge to await his luggage. His two cases arrived simultaneously with a ruddy-faced man with a silver-grey crewcut.

'Arthur, I thought you travelled light?' He dropped the cases and clasped Henson's hand. 'Good to see you, boy.' Henson felt his fingers crushed and a strong grip snap around his shoulders.

'Nice to see you again, Sam.'

'C'mon the wagon's double parked.' Picking up the cases again, Sam led Henson through a self-locking side door to a Oldsmobile.

Colonel Samuel K Bright was a native of Abeline, Texas. Until 1942 his only first-hand experience of flying had been a five minute joy ride at the age of nine courtesy of some long-forgotten Barnstormer. Joining the fledgling Army Airforce at eighteen he was selected for flying training at the age of twenty, the fourth son of a farming machinery salesman he was escorting Liberators and Fortresses over Germany within a year. Grievously wounded over Mainz he made it back to his East Anglian base just before he passed out from loss of blood. After surgery he was evacuated Stateside to recover only to be told that he was down-graded to transports. The young Shining Bright was shipped out to nurse C47s over the Hump for Vinegar Joe Stilwell in Nationalist-held China.

It was a motto instilled by his irrepressible salesman father that brought a new lease of life to the disappointed ex-fighter pilot; "Bloom where you're planted". Sam Bright's determination to get his bird home brought him recognition from strange quarters. At the end of the war he forsook the great scramble to get home and stayed on to fly for Chiang Kai-shek. Having married a Burmese Christian he was even less inclined to return home even after the warlord's expulsion to the off-shore island of Taiwan. The forty year agony that was drawing to a close in Vietnam kept him busy. So it was that Sam Bright progressed from Air America pilot (he privately called it Close In Airways) to Director of Air Operations at Langley. On this man, Henson had not only pinned the survival of the Third Battalion but ultimately the Emirate itself.

The Oldsmobile sped across the Potomac and out into the clear Fall night of Virginia. Forty minutes drive brought him to an isolated farm house in birch-covered hills. Henson found himself fussed over like a boarder home from his first term. Susy who seemed ageless like most Burmese, applied herself to hospitality as most people would only to the highest form of art. Such treatment made even a confirmed bachelor like Henson envious of Bright's marital status. Eventually, Henson cradled a liqueur bourbon by a roaring log fire. The room was a curiously effective mixture of heavy frontier style furniture with delicate Oriental draperies and ceramics.

'You wanna tell me about it now or do you wanna sleep on it?' Bright started as soon as Susy had closed them in.

'I won't sleep till I've told you,' said Henson.

'Then I might not sleep!' Henson smiled. He was tired. It was 6am, European time. He leaned forward and started to tell the history of the Emir's war against the Hawaafi.

An hour and a half later, Sam Bright got up stiffly and took Henson's warm and empty glass away for a refill of Bourbon and ice. 'Well, you have arrived with con-sum-ate timing, Arthur. That old Jew, Henry's gone, put us on a Stage Two A-lert.' Henson stared blankly at Sam Bright's plaid-shirted back.

'Whatever for?' The Israelis are now back on the offensive, aren't they?'

'That's just it. The Sov-iets are in one Hell of a panic 'case that guy Sharon takes a fancy to sight-seein' the Pyramids.'

'But how long can it last? Both sides must be almost exhausted now.' Bright returned with freshly charged glasses.

'S'alright, fella, I didn't say it was impossible. It's just that I have to pitch for tankers 'gainst a whole mess of folks nowadays.' He leaned back in his armchair. 'Time was when we were the sole guardians of Old Uncle Sams's interests out there, but now there's so many fuck'n agencies it's like a Goddam French farce.' Henson looked as crest-fallen as he felt. 'But don't worry now, Arthur, you'll have your '135s when and where you want 'em. It'll just need a little more than my say so to do it.' He grinned.

'Say, why don't Suzy take you ridin' tomorrow …' he glanced

at his watch. 'Today. I'll be back with the goodies in time for you to catch the Sun-riser out of Dulles?'

'Sam, I can't thank you enough.' Bright drained his glass.

'It's we who should be thanking you, Arthur, last thing we need right now is a Soviet client state on the Persian Gulf.'

Sam Bright had long departed for Langley by the time Henson rose. After a modest breakfast, by Virginian standards, Henson went for a pleasant hack through the birch and willow clad hills with Susy. It was as the horses mooched about in a sparkling stream, that Henson and Susy reminisced about their various foreign postings. Henson had first met them when he was an Assistant Defence Adviser in Kuala Lumpur. He looked up at the golden cascade of leaves which flowed down the hills on either side. He suddenly found himself wondering what he was going to do when the war was over. Even a short stay with a couple like Sam and Susy was apt to conjure up the spectre of isolation and loneliness in old age. Susy broke the spell with an offer of late lunch. Henson tucked in the sleeves of the outsized, borrowed Levi jacket and steered his mount up and out of the stream back towards the house.

Sam Bright's car pulled up outside just as it was getting dark. Henson was already changed for his flight. He stared at the door anxiously as Bright entered the porch. At the sight of Sam's poker-straight face, he felt his heart miss a beat. The old pilot's hands were behind his back, his head hung down. He eyes lifted to meet Henson. The arm rose, a bottle neck in one pudgy fist. Bright's face broke and he performed a loose-kneed shuffle into the room.

'We sold it, Arthur old buddy. We sold it.'

CHAPTER TWENTY FIVE

On the 24th October a Voice of America news broadcast announced the capture of Ras Adubiyeh on the Red Sea Coast and the subsequent plight of the Egyptian 3rd Army. The conference room in the basement of the fort at Eyoon a'Rashid was buzzing with speculation. A full Joint Staffs meeting was winding up. Gilbert Dixon had just finished fielding questions on the co-ordinating instructions for Operation Slingshot. The General took his cigar out from between his teeth and fixed Henson in his mental sights.

'There's a rumour about that the Emir has offered a battalion to the Eygptians. Is there any foundation to this or is it another deception plan we haven't heard about?' Henson felt stung by the whip-end of the question. He sensed ill-concealed smirks from some of the battalion COs and staff officers.

'It is, of course, a token gesture. We are expecting a cease fire to become effective within the next 48 hours and I don't think we'll be called upon to honour our pledge.'

'I hope you're right,' said Welles gruffly. He turned his attention away from Henson and looked down both sides of the table. 'Well, then, anything else before we go?' A thin-faced officer wearing the red shemagh of the Force Military Police put up a nervous hand.

'Yes Gerry?'

'Sir,' the police major began, 'How long do I have to keep the roadblocks on around the airbase?'

'Till Slingshot is done and our visitors have gone.' The major looked unhappy, 'What's the matter Gerry?'

'Well, sir, I'm a bit stretched,' Welles faced him with one of his "Oh my Gawd" stares.

'Not as stretched as they are on Assaad.' He clamped his cigar back between his teeth. The meeting was over.

* * *

'The Sergeant-Major must have been right,' Rolls reflected that same morning. The adoo must have had a considerable struggle getting their stockpiled ammunition moved as the one twenty-twos had not fired for almost a week. There had been some harassing fire from their mortars by night but not enough to keep the jundis awake for long . Rolls had used the lull to strengthen existing shelters and expand the network of communication trenches and walls. Richard Callender had shown the officers how to make improvised cratering charges from tin cans, wire and pieces of cardboard. The jundis needed no extra incentives and in most cases had dug deeply into the flaking rock of jebel. Rolls had been briefed by the Chief of Staff, who had arrived on the dusk resupply and had stayed overnight. Rolls had told the company commanders the outline of the plan but had instructed them not to tell the troops. Instead he visited each section over a two day period and showed them how confident he was.

'Everything is good, In sha' allah, no problems.' At his behest, Stan had flown in extra rations; live goats, fruit and coffee. The jundis looked tired and drawn but he felt sure that they would hold out a little longer; in sha 'Allah.

It had now become the general routine on Assaad for there to be a break during the stifling heat between noon and three. Apart from the sentries everyone else sought the comparative coolness of the old sangers and the new deep shelters. Rolls stepped up from the shallow trench which led from the safety of the dead ground to Giles Denby-Smith's command post. He heard Giles' shrill voice haranguing someone in short bursts of invective; English and Arabic. A small sergeant with mournful eyes and a petulant pout below his moustache emerged in a hurry. The eyes and mouth immediately crinkled into a smile as he wished the Colonel a 'beautiful afternoon.' Rolls gave the credit to Allah and squeezed past him into the dusty gloom of the sangar.

'Taqleef, Giles?' he said, letting his eyes relax from their near perpetual squint. Giles was sat on the farthest end of his makeshift bunk; knees drawn up defensively. A half read paperback lay, cover up, at his feet.

'They bloody well piss me off!' he snapped, 'If it's not the food, it's the water or not enough breaks for prayers.'

'What is it this time?' Rolls pulled his shemagh off and mopped his face with it.

'He doesn't like tuna!' Rolls laughed, Giles scowled not seeing the funny side.

'Yesterday they were complaining because Three Company had dates and we had oranges, I mean … I ask you?'

'Do you talk to them?' Rolls asked recovering himself.

'Well of course I do.'

'No, I mean do you go, round and chat to them?'

'Whatever for?' Rolls smiled while he thought of a diplomatic way of putting forth his meaning.

'Giles, they only come round with these silly, little complaints because they want to involve you.'

'Involve me! In what?'

'In their lives. If you don't go round and talk to them they think you are angry with them.'

'Oh for Christ's Sake.' Giles folded his arms and drew up his knees up tighter to fend off the idea.

'It's true. In the Brigade whenever a new platoon commander took his boys into the ulu for the first time, they'd get the old Gurkha rum out. Get him pissed out of his brains. Then that was it, he'd broken the ice.' Giles was not impressed or inspired.

'I've been OC for six months, y'know,' Giles protested.

'I know but you had Alan Primmer with you then.' Giles said nothing 'Try it yourself. Go round and have shai with them.'

Rolls felt that he had pushed that particular point far enough. He stood up and looked through the open ports out towards the wire.

'How's Darweesh down on the point?' referring to the isolated platoon detached from Three Company.

'Oh, fine,' said Giles, 'Good man, Darweesh. 'Rolls sat down on an ammunition box and started retying his headcloth.

'You know the indications are that this is where their main effort will come next, Giles.'

'Yes, I saw that map,' Giles acknowledged gloomily.

'I've got Mike to organise a counter-attack force; six gun teams.'

'Thanks.' Giles failed to sound either enthusiastic or grateful. An unanswered question hovered between them like a blow-fly. Giles slashed at it. 'I'm not a coward, you know,' Rolls placed his AKM across his knees and leaned forward.

'I know that,' he said quietly.

'That ambush!' Giles stared across the gloom, his eyes showing the hurt. 'I just felt that there was something wrong out there.' His voice wavered. 'It's just that with so many jundis, all over the place … in the dark … I just didn't have control.'

He said too much and knew it. Rolls stood up and casually turned for the steps.

'First night nerves, Giles,' He set his foot on the first step. 'Don't worry. Have tea with Darweesh … you'll be fine.' He thrust his head up into the blinding glare once more. The back of his throat burned as he took in a draught of the still, hot air too quickly.

* * *

Giles Denby-Smith completed his rounds and stood his company down. As he had always refused to share his sanger with anyone other than another European, he sat alone and in the dark. Mike Cook had been over just before stand-to in order to recce his counter-attack tasks; he'd dropped off a brace of lagers. Giles reached down and opened the top of one of them. It was warm and fizzy but under the circumstances, palatable.

An hour passed and he considered tuning in to the World Service but stood by one of the observation ports and watched the clear sky for the frequent showers of shooting stars instead. He was wondering how his mother was coping with his dog: a two-year-old Weimeraner called Jago. He heard a faint rumble but it did not disturb his musing. Then he heard a whispering hiss. A brilliant flash lit up the position from behind. The brain-numbing bang followed by the savage whine of shrapnel. He snatched up his transceiver.

'Two-Nine … Incomers!' His voice was drowned by two more explosions. Jumping away from the port, he dived for the priest-hole he had excavated beneath the rear wall. There on his knees he stopped to think Three more explosions rocked the shelter, from the front this time. Fragments and stones drummed the roof with dull thuds or tinkled lightly over the bare rocks.

'Make or break, you bastard,' Giles sucked in a lungful of air and darted back to the window. Grabbing his belt order and rifle he charged up the steps to the open sangaar.

'Kull, wahed tahkt sitr!' he yelled out at the top of his voice. There were in fact only two jundis still out of cover and they needed no second bidding. Giles grubbed around in the box spaces built into the wall. His hand found the signal pistol and the radio handset.

'79 this is 29,' Mr Thompson answered immediately.

'79, over.'

'X ray zero two, One round illum, at my command fire,' Mr Thompson repeated the fire order for mortar illumination over Two Company's frontage.

Giles ducked as three more incomers whirred overhead to impact on the depth position. He bobbed up, alert, listening and in control.

'29, this is nine, It's your show tonight, Anything you want just give the word,' Rolls' voice came over the set.

'Wish I was in my tank,' Giles chipped back. Three more shells thumped in short, one squarely in the front of a forward sanger. Stones rained down again. Just as he pushed his head over the sandbags a ripple of bangs and flashes came from below the wire. The air jumped with detonations.

'29, fire!' he ducked again as bullets snapped and hissed around him.

'Hajam, hajam ... stand-to,' he screamed. Picking up the Very pistol he sent a green star arcing over the wire. There in the light was a phalanx of black shapes, hunched over, swaying, moving. He grabbed the mike again. '79, zero, zero two fire!' The machine gunners of Three Company opened up as one over the lower slopes. Streams of tracer bullets followed each other out across the wadi; more whipped and ricocheted through the wire from the flank positions. The cacophony of gun fire was suddenly drowned by 81 millimetre rounds erupting in a rapid succession of orange flashes. The light, manic tapping of Kalashnikov fire died away leaving the solid thump of FNs and the yammering bursts of the belt-fed MAGs. Giles passed the order to cease firing to the platoon commanders and the fire slacked to be followed by an eerie silence which fell over the position like a blanket.

' ... I've got about seven who need casivac, they're being brought up now.' Giles was giving details of his casualties to Callender over the field telephone. ' ... Panda's here now, yes ... no ... I think all the tripflares have been blown ... Okay.' He put the handset back and scrambled up to his vantage point between the blast walls of his CP. The heavy-shouldered bulk of Sad Panda appeared breathlessly at the end of the communication's trench.

'Giles, I have to go back to attend these men. My wakeel will treat any minor wounded.' Giles acknowledged with a wave. The Indian Army medic turned and felt his way back along the trench. Giles squatted down between the blast walls and lit himself a cigarette. He stood up and looked around the position. Although it seemed quiet the number of clinks, clicks and the shuffling of boots over the loose rocks indicated that no-one was stood down.

Rolls was someone else who could not rest. Satisfied that the situation had stabilised for the time being, he had gone over to the gunline. There was nothing that he could not have found out simply by lifting the field telephone but he needed to do something other than to sit in the CP. He found Mr, Thompson stockpiling mortar ammunition.

'How's it going?' Rolls asked. Mr, Thompson dumped an armful of green plastic cases onto the waiting arms of two gunners. 'We're okay on ammo, Colonel, but we're down to minimum range on Two Company's wire. I can't drop them any closer.' Rolls nodded.

'What about the guns?'

'Well, we could wheel them over the hill for a shoot over open sights but they're not meant for yer Waterloo stuff; no canister.'

Rolls left him humping mortar bombs. On his way back to the CP, Rolls called in at the medical aid post. Behind light-proof canvasses an equally intense struggle was going on. A jury-rigged set of Landrover headlamps hung from the ceiling lit a makeshift operating table. Panda in shirt sleeves, rubber apron and green surgical mask worked over the thin form of a young soldier. Two kampodas assisted. Panda leaned back and wiped the perspiration from his face with the back of his forearm. One of the kampodas snipped at thread held in his suturing forceps. The soldier moaned, semi-conscious.

'Pulse and BP every fifteen minutes till he stabilises,' he instructed. He walked towards Rolls removing his gloves.

'How are they, Panda?'

'Lost two, I'm afraid.' Panda showed no emotion other than a resigned disappointment. Rolls was relieved. He had always felt that doctors were liable to become emotionally critical of soldiers in the aftermath of action. 'These jundis ...' Panda shook his head, 'They are too small; they cannot lose much blood. It's shock that kills them.' He looked apologetically at Rolls. 'Once their BP falls they fail within minutes; not like our Sikhs, big men, last for days.' He seemed to privately consider the point for a minute … then; 'will they attack again?' Rolls nodded.

'I think so … might be One Company this time.' He shrugged off the threat and patted the Indian on the shoulder. 'Tell Richard the numbers for immediate casevac and we'll get that going.'

He made his way out into the dark. It had been three hours since the last assault. The atmosphere in the Headquarters command post was running down. The jundis protecting its perimeter had stood down to half strength. Rolls recognised the brooding hulk of Ali Akhbar at the entrance.

'Kull she zayn, Ali?'

'Kull she zayn, Muqaddam sa'b.' Ali tilted his sub-machine gun up like a road barrier to allow Rolls to pass. Rolls had just taken possession of a mug of coffee when the now familiar triple explosions of RPG 7s shook the shelter. As commanding officer, Rolls felt totally impotent as he listened to the various elements of his small command move into gear.

'Two-niner, contact, RPGs my position!' Denby-Smith's voice now as controlled and as matter-of-fact as it would be on the squadron net on Sennelaager ranges. Mr Thompson chipped in to confirm his target state. Faulkner and Cook acknowledged to assure everyone that they were awake and listening.

Rolls recalled the rueful comments of a former Commandant at Sandhurst; "the company commander's war". The savage crack of the one twenty-twos was now supplemented by a duller, more hollow-sounding thump; enemy mortars. Rolls pushed his way through the blackout. The eastern flank was again alive with flashes and detonations. He joined Din Mohammed and Ali Akhbar in the roof sangar. He could follow the battle in detail through the terse reports from the platoon commanders over his transceiver.

Darweesh Mohammed, the outpost commander on the extreme right flank of Two Company, was able to look straight along the wire that protected the other two forward platoons. It was the devastating, enfilading fire of his machine-guns which broke the adoo's first assault. Restocked with liners of belted ammunition, he stoically prepared to repeat the performance. He saw only the flash and felt a solid, concussing blow. A triangular chunk of alloy embedded itself in his temporal lobe. It laid him backwards over the wall of sangar. The other jundis reeled away from the torn sandbag parapets, shocked and deafened. The same happened to the other two section positions. The air above them was a cracking, hissing storm of bullets. One or two stood up only to be smashed down like discarded puppets. The rest crouched below the parapets too stunned to move. Giles Denby-Smith jumped round at the ripple of flashes and bangs from the outpost.

Then he saw the flickering stabs of AKs all around it. 'RPG's on Two-five!' he said rapidly into his mike, picking up the company net transceiver, he told the other platoon commanders to fire all weapons onto the flanks of the outpost. There were three more flashes and explosions as another trio of rocket propelled grenades streaked into the outpost. The stabbing flashes closed in. Giles suddenly realised what he was seeing. A series of orange flashes and deep, roaring blasts rent the platoon position; short bursts of AK followed, then nothing. Just the steady tapping of the other platoons MAGs and the howl of ricochets as tracer leapt off into the night sky. The incomers had stopped too. Giles gave the order to cease fire to the platoons. He picked up his other microphone without taking his eyes off the black promontory.

'Two-niner. We've lost Two-five.'

CHAPTER TWENTY SIX

Dawn came quickly. The red ball from out of the eastern ridges, warming away the pre-dawn chill. Rolls and Mike Cook lay in the shallow pit to one side of the depth platoon's sangers. They were watching the outpost, it sat some sixty feet below them and two hundred yards out along its curving spur. It seemed malignant; a once friendly relative who had now turned against them. There was no movement save for would-be scavenging birds hopping about nervously on sanger rooftops. Every now and then a burst of gunfire would thunder out from one of the main positions to thud into its sandbags or whine away off the rocks. Any movement from Two Company attracted a similar response. Rolls wriggled a few feet to his left and studied the broad slopes leading to the wire and beyond. A mass of dark shapes lay like bundles of old clothes in amongst and below the wire.

'How many do you reckon they lost?' asked the Australian.

'Twenty, thirty ... hard to say.'

'Well, they certainly sorted out poor, old Darweesh.'

'Thing is ... What are we going to do about it?' Rolls turned over to look at Cook.

'What would you have done at ... What's the name of that place you were at?'

'Phuoc Tuy.'

'Yes.' Cook pulled his head back from the sandbagged lip of the crater. 'This place reminds me more of a militia post, Xuyen Moc, Any real bad hassle and we'd just call in the Yanks. They'd bomb it or shell it till it was flat; then they'd napalm it. "Never send a man where you can send a bomb." That was their motto.' Rolls found himself nodding agreement.

'No question of trying an assault, especially in daylight,' he said. 'I was thinking of something the Sergeant-Major said last night. Wheeling one of the 75s up to here and blasting it point blank.'

'We might be knee-deep in adoo by then.' A shout from the company headquarters stopped further speculation.

They looked down to their left at the perimeter wire. An Arab in light khaki fatigues and a light green beret stood some twenty yards from one of the forward sangars, a piece of white cloth hung limply from his AK assault rifle.

'Christ! What d'ya think he wants?' asked Cook.

'Hmm, Perhaps he wants to surrender.' Rolls looked back towards the outpost. He dismissed the thought of standing up. He lifted his transceiver.'

'Two-nine, this is nine, tell your boys not to fire or anything, I'll be down there in a sec.' He heard Giles acknowledge as he picked up his rifle and started on his way along the communication trenches and protective walling to the forward section's positions.

Close to, Rolls saw that he was a powerfully built man in his thirties; a strong, full face and black moustaches curling down to his chin.

'He wishes to speak to an Inglees,' the section corporal told him. Rolls searched vainly for something white enough amongst the grimy possessions of the section.

'Sod it!' He took off his webbing and passed his AKM to the corporal. The areef watched him with apprehensive eyes as Rolls climbed slowly up over the sanger wall. He felt a strange sensation as he did so; it was akin to his first steps onto a theatre stage when his aunt had taken him to a pantomime as a child. He walked unreal steps towards the Arab who turned to face him over the coils of Dannert wire. The sweet, cloying smell of putrefaction from the adoo dead already assailing his senses.

'Salaam aleykum.' The Arab performed a brief neck bow. Rolls held out his palms.

'And upon you be peace,' he answered, accepting the blessing of peace however temporary it might be. The Arab the spoke in English. His accents showed American teaching.

'You have dead just as we have dead, yes?' he said and waited Rolls' acknowledgement.

Rolls agreed, 'Yes, we do.'

'We offer truce of two hours. We collect our dead, you collect yours.'

'Including over there?' Rolls pointed to the right, at the outpost. The Arab nodded.

'Yes.' Rolls looked into the man's eyes. They were dark, moist, sincere.

'Alright, two hours.'

'Good, when I come back, you be here. While we stand together no-one shoot, okay?'

'Okay.' The Arab turned on his heel and without another word walked down over the spur and out of sight.

Rolls returned to the sanger, climbed over the wall and picked up his radio. He gave orders for an immediate cease fire but instructed One and Three Companies to be stood to.

'Are they on the level?' queried Mike Cook who had gone back to his own CP. Rolls thought of the Arab's eyes.

'Yes, I think so.' He was going to elaborate but then it occurred to him that they might be overheard. Alan Primmer's radios had never been recovered. Rolls sat back and lit a Triple Five. The areef brought him a mug of tea. The NCO sat with him, describing in exaggerated detail the battle of the previous night and his, not inconsiderable, part in it.

The sentry nearby interrupted, 'Muqaddam sah'b, adoo guay!'

Rolls looked over the wall. The same Arab was walking slowly up the hill; this time his white flag was tied to a stick. Rolls stood up and held his hands out from his sides. He then stepped onto the parapet and then onto the sangar roof. The Arab with the flag reached the wire. He gave Rolls the briefest of nods and then waved his flag at someone further down the slope.

Rolls watched the spur where it fell away into the wadi. Within a minute a line of heads appeared. He looked over to the outpost; small, dark figures were emerging from the sangars. They began to attend to the bodies that lay around them. The blackbirds and crows took off and wheeled away in alarm. Soon some sixty Hawaafi were at the wire. All unarmed, save for their tribal knives tucked in the waist belts over their wazzirs. Unbidden and with the minimum conversation they unfolded coarse canvas mats alongside the bodies of their dead comrades. Slowly the corpses were placed on top of them, their weapons laid by their sides. The Palestinian, for that was what Rolls had guessed that he was, stood impassively by the wire.

'Cigarette?' Rolls took one himself and tossed the pack over the wire. The man caught it. 'Lighter?' Rolls threw that also.

The Palestinian lit the cigarette and tossed both items unerringly back to Rolls, 'Curious,' thought Rolls idly, 'most Arabs can't catch or throw for toffee.'

Just then he saw another khaki-clad figure appear on the spur. A tall Caucasian, the man was muscular, wedge-shaped to the waist. A strong face with a good month's growth of beard. He wore a high-crowned field cap, the peak shading his eyes, Rolls judged his bush jacket and trousers to be civilian. The trousers tucked into high-laced boots; well polished under a thin coating of dust. He walked with an awkward short paced strut, as if he was balancing on a plank. The Palestinian turned to see what had caught Roll's attention and stiffened when he saw the man. He dropped his cigarette.

The Caucasian stopped some thirty yards away. He looked steadily at Rolls for a minute or two and then moved across to intercept some of the adoo bearers. He stopped one pair and made a cursory examination of the body before waving them on.

'Your leader?' Rolls said quietly.

'Aiwa,' the Palestinian confirmed.

'Kassem,' the Caucasian called to the man.

'Sorry.' Kassem made an apologetic eye signal to Rolls and walked quickly over to the Caucasian. All the time the man talked, Kassem stood with his heels together.

Dismissed, he hurried back to the wire. 'Inglees,' he began, 'I am to tell you that if you surrender your position, you will be treated with honour.' Rolls looked into his eyes again and believed him.

'Thank your leader but tell him ... no. We are soldiers of the lawful ruler of this land and we cannot surrender.'

The sorrow at the prospect of more death and injury to come showed in the Palestinian's eyes. He nodded his understanding and looked about him. The last of the Hawaafi dead was being carried away, a slow procession of jundis were making their way back from the outpost behind Sad Panda; a grey plastic, body bag between each pair.

'One more hour then?' said Kassem checking the watch on his wrist.

'One more hour,' Rolls concurred.

Kassem turned and walked back to the Caucasian. They spoke briefly. The Caucasian took one more look at Rolls and then led Kassem over the spur and out of sight.

CHAPTER TWENTY SEVEN

The pilot of the giant Boeing aircraft corrected his heading and throttled back to 300 knots. He was tempted to let the co-pilot take over while they stooged around in a wide, orbiting pattern. There was nothing to see, just the sea below and a layer of alto-cummulus on the western horizon. The second ship of the pair levelled out on the starboard side, 'Jasmine One, 'ah a-ssume you gonna' orbit to the port this time? No variations.' The pilot of Jasmine One grinned at his co-pilot who had just looked up from a paperback. He pressed his TX.

'Roger, Jasmine Two, you have my word as a ge'el man.'

'Las' time I took the wordo' a gen'elman, I ended up dodgin' SAMs over the DMZ.'

'Good ole Reb.' The co-pilot returned to his book.

'Hey, Phil, keep an eye on our fuel 'n time.' The flight engineer rogered from somewhere in the after cabin. The pilot checked his own gauges. It wasn't the secret squirrel nature of mission that bothered him; in this squadron they had seen it all. It was the fact that being so far out over the ocean there was so little margin for error. He would hate to leave the rendezvous and some poor bastard on fumes with no prospect of diverting to an emergency landing. It was made clear at the "pilots only" part of the brief; the "customers" would have no reserve on making the RV.

The two KC135s had been specially prepped for foreign sales; that is they had flexible hose attachments fitted instead of their normal fixed booms, a standard procedure for refuelling NATO aircraft which did not use the USAF in-flight refuelling system. It was a minute to rendezvous and there was no sign of anyone. He was trying to work out a rough chop time when the tankers would have to leave or risk ditching themselves. He had also tried to work out the aircraft types, from the estimated fuel requirement but nothing he knew of would fit. With a word to Jasmine Two he turned into a wide portside turn.

Jasmine One had just gained the home reach of its first orbit when the radar operator's voice cut in on the intercom' loop.

'Four contacts, in formation, bearing Red two-ten, range four zero point six.'

'Kenny, give the man a call.' The pilot then spoke to Jasmine Two. Both tankers banked onto their original heading. The radio operator came back on the loop.

'Miranda One on net, sir. Do you want to be patched through?'

'Thanks, Kenny.' He heard the static tone change in the helmet earphones. Then a clipped voice spoke in English.

'What a pleasure, Jasmine. My sisters and I are quite thirsty do you mind if we dispense with the practice runs.'

'Roger, Miranda, if you feel up to it.'

The tankers diverged and from under the tail unit; hydra-headed hoses protruded and bobbed in the slipstream.

'Have you visual now, Jasmine.' The four blips became four chunky, light bombers. They paired off behind the starboard wings of the Boeings. Whilst one of the pair kept station the other gently nudged its way through the tanker's slipstream to the contact point below and aft of the tail. Then steadying a few feet below the drogues fluttering lips it slowly lifted its nose up and crept onwards until the refuelling probe, jutting out from a point in front of the pilot's cockpit, entered the guide cone. Without further hesitation the probe was pushed home to complete the aerial union.

'What are they, Max?' The pilot asked the boom operator who was controlling the transfer.

'One of those Brit' things they have on their carriers.'

The co-pilot leaned forwards to look at Jasmine Two's customer. He saw the two bombers, their blue-grey paint glinting with a dull sheen in the afternoon sun.

'Buccaneers, and from the size of those ferry tanks they've come the long way round.'

'Whose are they?'

'They got Brit' markings, red and blue.' There was a doubt in the co-pilots's voice. 'What are we doing giving them a feed? They got their own tankers at Gan havn't they?' He turned back to the pilot.

'C'mon, Ace, you know the Company code; 'Fly it and forget it.'

Their fuel tanks replenished the second pair of Buccaneers disengaged and dropped away to merge with the blue sea below.

The tankers retracted their hoses and banked away to return to their island base.

CHAPTER TWENTY EIGHT

Unlike Giles Denby-Smith, James Faulkner was still able to spend his daylight hours above ground. He could walk openly about his position without attracting a hail of automatic fire. For Giles, to visit any of his platoons meant a hectic dash from wall to trench and from trench to wall as Kalashnikov and RPK bursts swept the open ground. Morning stand-to had just ended. Faulkner had stretched out on the sandbag wall of his open sangar to savour the last few moments of cool night air before the deadening heat of the desert sun reached full power.

A shout came from one of the forward sections. He sat up and looked out to where a commotion was now increasing. The tabbaak wallahs had set up their chapatti factories and were now trying to take cover and save their precious Primus stoves. Faulkner stood up as there appeared to be no immediate danger. Over the top of one of the sangars he caught sight of a small, turbanned figure standing patiently on the other side of the triple, concertina wire. The Guards captain dropped down and loped across the slope, his carbine loosely in his hand. He stopped by the sentry's sangar which was full of jundis holding the strange visitor in their weapon sights. The man spoke.

'Good morning. Can you show me the way in?'

Faulkner thought that he was hallucinating for a second then managed a startled, 'Yes of course.' He indicated to the left and the old man, for he certainly looked old, walked along the wire. He stopped at a junction of iron pickets and waited until Faulkner and one of the solders had lifted the Dannert coil aside. He stepped through.

Aside from his massive green turban, the only clothes he wore were a tattered, green plaid, cotton wazzir rolled over at the waist and what looked like an extremely old and faded London bus driver's summer jacket. A thin camel-stick was thrust through his old leather waist-belt. His thin, bandy legs and yellow calloused feet were bare. Faulkner thought he could count every rib of his bony frame. His dark skin clung to him like wet, brown paper. His face was deeply wrinkled and simian with its jutting, whiskered chin and sunken eyes. Over one thin shoulder was slung an ancient Lee Enfield, the stock a greasy brown; in his left hand a small, battered cardboard suitcase.

'May I see Colonel Rolls?'

'Yes,' said Faulkner, whose own speech centre was still numbed by the shaiba's impeccable accent.

'They call me Abu Issa, by the way,' The shaiba shook hands with him as they climbed the hill to the rear of One Company's position.

Faulkner's capacity to be surprised had diminished by the time that he and Abu Issa had descended the track to the Headquarters. He watched Rolls and Issa embrace each other like long, lost school chums and then followed them into the mess tent. The old man became instantly at home as Harry Shaw and Callender joined them at the table. He chatted happily, in English and Arabic, through a wide range of inconsequentialities as breakfast was served. He would flit from reports of mutual acquaintances to the latest news from the Golan and Sinai fronts. Faulkner watched in fascination as the little man talked while the officers ate. The Hawaafi elder himself touched neither food nor drink save for a single cup of coffee.

Breakfast finished with Abu Issa poring over a map of the area and describing what he has seen. Giles and Mr Thompson had now joined them and they all listened in silence as the magnitude of the investing force was revealed. Faulkner marvelled at the shaiba's attention to detail and powers of retention as he confirmed his estimates of the enemy's fighting strength by counting of the numbers of herds of goats and camels grazing in the surrounding wadis. Issa told of the presence of Northerners, by which he meant Palestinians and Syrians and shoyoo'ayeen: communists. Rolls told him of the killing of the artillery OP and the little man smiled, nodding approvingly.

Issa had started to answer the odd question when a signaller came to announce that resupply helicopters were inbound. The company and headquarters officers excused themselves leaving Issa and Rolls alone.

'How do you manage to move so freely among them?' Rolls asked. The Hawaafi's face creased into a non-commital smile.

'I am old, I am one of their own but not so, if you see my meaning,' he replied enigmatically.

'How do you mean?' Rolls lit a cigarette.

'Thirty, forty years ago, life was different. The Hawaafi were little changed from the times of the Prophet. Only one white man had ever been seen on the Great Ridge. The Emir Mansoor, the old one, stayed in his walled city on the coast locked up with his Indian whores.' Issa smiled triumphantly.

'He never ventured here. My people are herdsmen and therefore warriors. The tribes competed for water, for pasture; to survive one had to plunder. Feuding was our way of life.' Issa's eyes appeared to moisten with an inner sadness. He looked up to see if Rolls had grasped any significance in what he had said and might therefore spare him the pain of continuing. Rolls was blank, attentive but blank. He pulled the cotton jacket up to sit more squarely on his fragile shoulders.

'My tribal name is Beni Qassir, you will find no others. I am the last of my tribe.' Rolls looked shocked but Issa now seemed taken up with the story himself.

'My father had sent me away to England. I was fourteen, I did not want to go. I was already a man in Hawaafi eyes but I was an obedient son. My guardian in England was a man called Dalhousie, he worked for your Foreign Office; an advisor.' He thought for a second. 'Political Officer, that's what he was called. My father and he were friends. I stayed in England seven years; very happy years. Dalhousie treated me as one of his own family.

'But there was a feud between my tribe, the Beni Quassir and the Beni Nawaasah. The problem was simple. My father was one of the paramount chiefs of the Hawaafi. He was a progressive man in his own way and wanted to bring the benefits of the West slowly to the Ridge lands. The Nawaasah are an eastern tribe, more Bedu, than Hawaafi. They opposed all contact. The leader of the Nawaasah was a truly dreadful man. Normally feuds were controlled by unwritten laws which went back to before Islam. But to the Nawaasah the score could never be equalled.

'I returned at once. I pleaded with my father to let me negotiate a settlement. At last he agreed and a truce was arranged while I went to mediate.' Issa paused and stared into Roll's eyes.

Rolls shuddered at the depth of pain which lay inside.

'The Nawaasha'syeen used the truce to mass their forces. They fell upon my tribe and killed every man, woman and child. Not even our animals were spared,' Issa said coldly. 'I was taken and nailed to a tree.'

He thrust out his thin leathery palms and then turned them over. Rolls saw, plainly, the weals of old scar tissue in the centre of the palms and on the thin, sinewed backs. He swallowed hard. Issa seemed to relax at that point. He folded his claw-like fingers inward as if to show how they had recovered.

'You may be wondering why I am still alive?' He shrugged.

'I was young, very strong and fit by the standards of the time and, well, the Hawaafi still retain superstitions about killing the last of a family. Not very Islamic but they came to mind when their blood lust had cooled. We learnt the practice of crucifixion from the Turks who even used it as non-capital penalty. They used round-headed nails to limit the damage or prolong the spectacle.'

The sound of thumping rotor blades interrupted.

Issa rose with a pale smile and wished courage and fortitude upon his host. As he walked out of the tent Issa turned. 'The General Secretary of GPLF is a man called Said ibn Nassir. He is Beni Nawaasah.'

* * *

The Force Commander, Gilbert Dixon and Henson left the hanger at the appropriately named "Field of Birds" airfield and were driven back along the coast road towards Ayoon a 'Rashid. They passed through the military police cordon where two areef a'shurtee were arguing with a frustrated fish merchant who was now faced with a seventy mile detour.

'Let's stop here,' the General said. Dixon pulled the Range Rover off the tarmac. They all got out and, led by Welles, walked down to a rocky outcrop. The gentle swell of the Gulf sighed along a short bight of white sand. They sat down.

'They look bloody good, Henson,' said Welles, looking out at the horizon.

'They are all very experienced combat pilots, General.'

The General said nothing for a minute or more, absorbed in his own mental conflicts. He turned back to the other two. 'Rolls' plan for the marking sounds tricky but there's no alternative.'

'Sounds jolly original to me,' said Henson.

'No, Germans used to do it in the Ukraine.' Welles enjoyed the rebuttal; it was petty but satisfying. 'This is a one-shot operation, no regains.' He looked for any dissent. There was none. 'For that reason there can be no recce.'

Gilbert looked horrified, Henson remained poker-faced.

'I know that's heresy to you, Gilbert, but to show them a jet now even a Strikemaster might blow the whole thing. He felt an inner anger at having to not only play Henson's game but play his way as well. He elaborated for Gilbert's sake. 'Look they haven't seen a jet since they shot that one down. Now that they are concentrating their forces for the kill we don't want them to disperse.' Gilbert signalled defeat.

'I can get Mike Clayton to give them a detailed brief,' Dixon said, referring to the Huey squadron commander. 'He's seen more of Assaad from the air than anyone. They also have the practice area. I'll have it marked the same way Rolls is going to do it.'

'Good idea,' Welles felt better now that particular hurdle had been crossed. 'What about D Day?'

'Issa's back, I heard this morning,' Henson chimed in. 'He'll be in tonight on resupply.'

Welles pretended not to hear. 'Well, what do you say we put them under starter's orders for the day after tomorrow.'

Henson frowned, Dixon pursed his lips while the logistics went through his mental checklist. 'I can't see any problem ... time?'

'0800, give them a couple of hours daylight to sort any hiccups out.'

'Where will you be? General,' Henson asked.

'In my Ranger. You coming?'

'Please.' Henson managed a polite smile.

'Good,' said Welles. He stood up and dusted the sand from his Dacron slacks. 'If it goes for a ball of chalk, I'll toss you out, you little prick,' his private voice continued.

* * *

The strain of being in such close proximity to the enemy was beginning to show on Giles Denby-Smith's face. His eyes were bloodshot and dark-rimmed under the grime. Days were now spent either in the safety of the dark sangars or in the stifling heat of the communication trenches and the firing bays. The anticipation of more night assaults ate into the nerves like vinegar into a stomach ulcer. The feeling was shared by everyone on Assaad in the days since the loss of the outpost but it was worse for Giles who faced his inner fears alone.

The prospect of what was felt to be the final orders group resurrected some of his old cantankerous self. The helicopter resupply had been suspended. This was not because of any increased threat of enemy groundfire; the pilots had been quite happy to fly in black onto coloured torch indicators. It was to ensure maximum servicability for the forthcoming operation and to allow an opportunity for very limited practice and rehearsals. Assaad had reserves of food and water for a month but the curtailment of fresh rations and even more stringent water rationing was keenly felt; not the least by Giles. His irascibility had subsided temporarily with the unexpected present of an ice cold gin from the One Company fridge now serving a more honourable purpose in the Medical Centre.

'Sorry there's no tonic,' James said passing out tumblers to whoever wanted one. 'I'll have to change my off-licence if things don't buck-up.' The officers laughed and exchanged facetious toasts.

John Rolls leaned against the trestle table in front of the dusty, sweat-stained assembly and waited for Richard Callender to call them to order and get some of the more prosaic matters of ration and ammunition redistribution out of the way. When Richard had finished he reached out to the packing case lid which served as a map board and flicked the covering headcloth off with his camel stick.

'Gentlemen,' he began, 'Operation Slingshot.' For thirty minutes he spoke without interruption, giving details of the adoo strengths and dispositions as they knew them and as confirmed by Abu Issa. He outlined the plan as given to him by Colonel Dixon including the objectives and tasks of the other battalions and supporting arms. Then he told the unit officers their part in the grand venture.

'Take a minute or two to go through your notes and study the map if you wish. Then I'll take any questions.' Rolls looked from dusty face to dusty face.

'You can't be serious?' suggested Giles, his eyes wide and incredulous. Rolls merely chewed the inside of his lip. 'I mean even if we did get through, as soon as it becomes light …' He shook his head, open mouthed.

'To achieve complete surprise in a single pre-planned strike ... There is no other way,' Rolls answered him calmly, a deliberate, no nonsense edge to his voice. 'The reason I have assigned my bearer to you Giles and the police sergeant to you Mike is to increase your chances of survival and success.' Giles looked at Mike Cook who was sitting alongside. Mike sensed that Giles was tacitly seeking his support.

'Like the boss says, Giles, there is no other way and we are the boys to do it.' Giles thought about suggesting that Faulkner should go instead but dismissed it as it would only confirm what most of them were already thinking. He sighed, sat back and put on his brave face.

'Well then, how about another gin?' Faulkner obliged, letting the officers help themselves from his "Field Sportsman's" ice bucket.

The officers dispersed soon after the supply of gin and ice had dried up. Richard Callender dutifully took down the mapboard and returned to the CP leaving Rolls alone. Since his appointment as CO, John Rolls had found one major difference between his life now as compared with then. Now he felt long, nagging doubts over every decision he made. There was no other way to mark the targets for the air-strike, of that he had no doubt. 'Why had he really picked Giles?' Having arrived at the decision intuitively, he now wanted to go back over the process and match it to some sort of logic; like pieces of a puzzle. 'Mike Cook had to go because he was uncommitted as reserve company commander. Faulkner?, no, The Lion's head separated One Company physically from the rest of the unit and the Guardsman had a good grip on it. Two Company? Harry Shaw could sit in there and if things went awry ... well ... there was Three Company just over the ridge, Mr Thompson, yes, but he was sine qua non of the mortars. Himself, the most preferred option but no ... like the captain of a ship he couldn't just go swimming off when he chose. Yes, Giles it had to be.' He smiled at his pairing Giles with Din Mohammed. Their mutual lack of Arabic would certainly preclude any discussion of the matter.

He picked up his AKM and pushed through the canvas wall into the sharp white blaze of the morning sun. One of the older kampodas was passing, a blacked kettle in his wrinkled hand. He raised the other in half salute as he reached the entrance to the aid post.

'Shai, Muqaddam Sah'b?' Something to do to take away the doubts that grow like a cancerous growth inside him: tea with the medics.

Apart from the brooding, sniping match between the occupiers of the outpost and some of the more malevolent jundis of Two Company, Assaad had had a quiet day. Rolls had spent it going round the companies, sharing tea and danger, seeing and being seen. Everywhere beneath the polite, patient faces Rolls felt the fatigue of men who had been long enough in the line. Three weeks was the norm., according to staff college. They had seen three months.

As the officers on Assaad prepared for their various tasks that afternoon, a new host was being assembled alongside the dusty airstrip at Harrow. The equivalent of three full battalions with field artillery and other supporting arms were crammed into the little tented camp. Jundis in full battle-gear were lying or sitting under every piece of shade that could be found or made. The prefabricated bungalow which served as the officers' mess looked like a departure lounge for evacuees. Stan Meadows, the Quartermaster, had given up any attempt to charge officers for drinks in the tiny bar. He grimly resolved to extract an appropriately large sum from the Force Welfare Fund and instructed his Baluchi barman to 'give it away.' He then poured himself a large tumbler of scotch and went off to see if there was anything else he would give away.

'Why not?' he thought, 'It'll be all over one way or another.' Then he turned his attention to the various items which, that being the case, could conveniently disappear his way.

'Everything set then, Gilly?' Welles was lolling in Stan's revolving office chair, half wondering where he had got it from. Gilbert was reading some of the captions to the Playboy cartoons pinned to the Quartermaster's wall. He came back to the real world.

'Oh yes, General. David Kyle's people start out for their LZ at 1600.' Welles pictured the chunky, shaven-headed ex-para tabbing through the night, thumping stragglers left, right and centre.

'What time is Hughie Maxwell off?'

'Five, sir. Second wave at six. That will have give them two hours to make the east ridge.'

'And Marcus takes the Scouts and the Royal Guard in at eight?' Gilbert nodded. 'Think it'll work?'

'It's all up to the markers.' Welles rubbed his face as he thought of all the permutations of circumstances which could turn decisive victory into unmitigated disaster. He stood up. 'We'll go in with Marcus.'

The sun had lost its power for the day and Rolls had returned to the CP, Harry Shaw was just emerging. He looked unfamiliar, though the only additions to his normal attire were a rifle and belt order of pouches and water bottles. Richard Callender followed him, blinking into the light.

'We're just off, Colonel,' said Harry, slinging his FN from his shoulder.

'Okay, sing out if you have any taqleef,' Rolls watched as Callender strode off towards Three Company and Harry shambled away to the maze of walls and trenches which led to Giles' CP.

'Yaa, Ra'aid, wait for us.' Rolls turned to see the mullah, Haji Mansoor trotting out from between the tents with the RSM at his heels. Haji had forsaken his white turban and dishdash for green fatigues, a geysh shemagh, webbing and rifle. He saw the look of surprise in Rolls face, 'Islam was won by soldiers not priests, Colonel,' he said with a mischievous glint in his dark eyes.

'In sha'Allah, you will protect it, yaa Haji?' Rolls replied. The pair of them caught up with the second-in-command and disappeared round the side of the hill. Rolls went inside the CP and checked the signal's log. Then he went up into the roof sangar and waited for the sun to fall into the blue hills. The eve of any battle always seemed an eternity. Tonight, he felt would prove no exception.

CHAPTER TWENTY NINE

The target marking parties had left via one of the wadis leading down from the west side of One Company's position. It was reckoned that the bulk of the adoo assault force was assembled to the north-east and south-east of Assaad. Rolls had watched them go through the wire near to where Abu Issa had entered. The old man had given precise directions as to how they should reach the "Great North Road".

The night was bright, as the moon was nearly full. The pale cousin of the late afternoon, it had become the cool master of the night. It was possible to read clearly under its silvery radiance. Rolls looked up at the shining face. No wonder the ancient, desert peoples worshipped the moon as the paramount god before the coming of Mohammed. Most of the jundis still refused to believe that a man had walked on its surface.

His radio whistled and then the static broke. Ahmed, the signals officer was checking the ammunition states. Rolls remembered that he had not cautioned Mike or Giles to turn their sets off till contact was made. To have one's radio come alive in close proximity to the enemy could be, at the very least, embarrassing. He was about to go down and tell Ahmed to minimise his transmissions when he heard the now familiar whoosh of one-twenty-twos. He dropped flat. Through squinting eyes he saw the triple flashes reflected back off the hillside behind the CP. The solid, clanging explosions reverberated back out across the wadi. The sangar shook with each successive after-shock. More incomers followed. The squawking sound of mortars could be heard in between the short whirring note of recoiless rifle rounds. The whole east flank of the jebel seemed to assume a hideous life of its own as it flashed, thumped and grumbled under the onslaught. Rolls snatched his AKM and his transceiver and rolled over the sandbags to drop into the entrance bay. He stuck his head through the blackout to listen to the Arabic net. He could hear the platoon commanders reporting, their words drowned by the distorted rattle of gunfire.

He ducked back outside in time to hear Harry ask for mortar

fire on his wire. Glancing over the Headquarters tents and sangars he could see the short stabbing muzzle-flash of the mortars as Thompson's jundis stoked them at the rapid rate. Mr Thompson performing a crouching dance between the middle pair. There was a short whirring almost over his head. Rolls dropped to his knees. The drumming cracks popped in his ears, the hard earth seemed to buck and sway under him. He pushed his head up. The mortar line was a dust cloud, but the dust alone moved. He caught his breath and made to dash over, then there was movement. Mr Thompson scrambling from pit to pit. Then the jundis bobbing up and down; legless halflings feeding their insatiable metal masters. The number one mortar plopped out a round defiantly.

The fighting on Two Company's position had now reached a crescendo. The round shoulder above the position permanently ablaze with the flashes of incomers, grenades and small-arms fire.

'Adoo on position!' Harry's voice came over the transceiver, urgent and thin; the background cracked with gunfire.

Rolls picked up the mike and waited for the Geordie gunner to tell him that it was below the mortars minimum range. But instead he heard a gruff, 'Fire on your position, out.'

Mr Thompson dropped the radio mike and jumped into the nearest pit. Calling out to the other crews to bring all their remaining rounds over, he pushed the startled number one aside. Wrapping his headcloth around the metal-finned barrel, he unclipped the bipod legs and kicked them aside. He realigned the barrel on the flashing skyline and pulled it back almost to the vertical. He gave the order to load. The ammunition numbers fed round after round into the barrel pausing only to let each round hiss down to the firing pin and come hurtling back out with a flat bang.

'Take the bloody rings off!' the gunner yelled. He was half squatting behind the barrel, feet astride, his big hands grasping the middle of the tube. The jundis quickly stripped off the narrow plastic rings that were meant to increase the weapons accuracy. The projectiles now rattled down and came out yawing and swaying to spread out over Two Company's sangars.

'Three-nine, advance to the ridge line.' Rolls waited for Callender to acknowledge. He knew that Two Company must be nearly overrun, Callender acknowledged and Rolls waited for what seemed like an hour for him to get his machine-gunners the hundred or so yards up to the crest overlooking Two Company.

'Three-nine ready!' Callender's voice came up, snatched and breathless.

'Fire when ready, Two-nine acknowledge.' He waited again but no word came in from Harry. The roar of Three Company's gunners became the prevailing sound. The single mortar continued to plop away.

Rolls called out to one of the Headquarters platoon sergeants to get a section stood by. Ducking back into the CP he told Ahmed that he was going over to Two Company. An RPG 7 projectile slammed into the stone breast-work of the CP. Rolls was blown down; blinded and deafened. He struggled to his feet, his lost senses returning in dazzling bursts of light and through the singing in his ears. Two jundis groaned on the other side of the blast wall. The air was suddenly filled with the crackling of bullets. He dived to his right. Coming up around the end of the blast wall, he saw figures, in silhouette, running, dodging. He fired short bursts from his AKM. The figures, only yards away, vanished. Moving right again, he crossed the pathway to the cover of his dugout.

A black shape sprang up, sparks leapt from his weapon. It darted forwards with a guttural bellow, straight for the CP entrance. Rolls hit him with a double tap. He sensed, he turned too late. A flash inked his vision, a punch in the chest threw him down. He could not breath or move his arms. He turned his head to face the man; the old enemy of his dreams ... big ... black. A double flash burst upon him. He couldn't see. Then he was being lifted; a rough hand around his neck. 'So this is how it ends.' He floated higher and higher and higher. He could smell the man. 'Sweat and blood, yes of course, the sweet cloying smell of blood.'

CHAPTER THIRTY

The Landrover headlights shone down with uncompromising brightness. Rolls opened his eyes. He moved his tongue inside his lips. He moved his head, his right hand; The left he could not feel. A surge of panic reached the motive points of his brain. He struggled to sit up.

'Steady, Colonel Sah'b,' a restraining hand pressed him back onto the taut canvas of the stretcher. He focused in on the medical wakeel. Another figure came into soft focus. It shone a thin light beam into his eyes; one at a time. He felt his left arm being lifted, it was fuzzy and distant.

'It's alright Colonel Sah'b.' Panda's dark features came into sharp focus. 'You still have your left arm,' Rolls sighed with relief.

'Panda,' he croaked. His mouth parchment dry, his throat felt gummy and stuck together. A powerful hand cushioned the back of his head and raised him a fraction. A spasm of pain arched across his chest; he gasped in shock and surprise.

'Easy, Colonel,' said Panda. The plastic rim of a beaker was placed to his lips and he felt a sliver of water wash over his tongue and round his lower gums. The moisture unglued his tongue. He passed another drop back to his aching throat. Panda let him down onto his pillow.

'We made it, then?' Rolls asked. The medical captain nodded.

'Yes, we made it.'

'What time is it?'

'Just after six.'

'God, I've got to go!' He lifted his head up but was stopped by the pain across his chest. 'Jesus, what have I done?' he gasped, falling back again.

'You have cheated death by the merest fraction.' Rolls looked intently at the Indian's face, to detect any sign of doctor's flippancy; of over statement.

Panda tilted his chin forward and knitted his brows in what Rolls had come to recognise as his "considered prognosis" expression. 'A bullet entered your chest and simultaneously glanced off your sternum to exit from your left pectoral, enter your left bicep and exit from the same. I suspect some damage to your brachial nerve.

'Will I live?'

'Only if you do what your doctor tells you.' Rolls pretended to look reassured. He tried to struggle up onto his right but the pain in his chest forced him to give up again.

'How come I can hardly breathe?'

'You may have cracked your sternum,' Panda suggested, 'But do not worry, Colonel Sah'b, Mister Callender has everything in hand.' Rolls lay back and tried to pick up a reference point in his memory. Panda busied himself putting Rolls' left wrist in a collar and cuff sling.

'Who dropped the adoo who shot me?' Panda cocked his head.

'That was me,' he confessed, almost coyly. Rolls smiled feeling a little embarrassed.

'I thought you were non-combatant?' The Indian wagged his admonishment aside with a thick finger.

'Technically you were a patient and as such I was allowed to protect you as well as myself.' Voices from outside interrupted any further debate. Fresh morning light flooded in as Richard Callender and Haji Mansoor entered and walked down between the trestle mounted stretchers.

'How's the boss, Panda?' Callender began.

'He is taking notice,' Panda finished tying the collar end of the sling around Rolls' neck.

'Since you are determined to get up, that will immobilise your arm and stop you from breathing too deeply.' Panda moved out from between the stretchers to allow Callender and the Haji bedside space, Rolls saw that both were tired and bedraggled but with the grim cheerfulness of survivors.

'How did it go?' Rolls asked Callender.

'It was close, Colonel, bloody close. Mr Thompson was down to his last half dozen rounds; machine-gunners are on their last belts. Casualties not too bad; ten dead, some wounded.' He paused as if considering carefully his next utterance. 'Harry didn't make it.' Rolls felt an almost physical blow inside him.

'I'm sorry,' he said.

'Haji, was with him.'

Haji Mansoor moved closer to the stretcher. He placed a hand on Rolls' wrist as if Rolls' attention needed any holding.

'We were together in the sangar, Sah'b' he began; he was tense and earnest as if in a confessional. 'A grenade landed at my feet. I shouted "grenade" and we both jumped over the wall.' He stopped momentarily then continued, 'The signals jundis in the dugout started to come up the steps, Raa'id Harry jumped back over the wall and blocked the entrance. There was nothing we could do, he had too many wounds.' His turbanned head bowed in grief.

* * *

Giles Denby-Smith suddenly became aware that he was holding his breath again. He dropped his eyes to the stony soil inches from his nose and tried taking deep breaths. It had been a long nerve-twisting night. The meandering route from Assaad had disorientated him and he was left no option but to doggedly follow the black, wraith-like form of Din Mohammed. Having no mutual language, the Pathan could only communicate in hand-signals and to Giles that was apparently limited to 'stop' 'go' and 'quiet'. After the initial shell explosions on Assaad, Giles took some comfort in the belief that the battle which raged behind him would divert attention from his particular sortie. Instead they were forced on several occasions to lie for heart-stopping minutes while whole columns of men camels trudged past, en route for Assaad. It was past 0400 when they skirted the northern spurs of Cub and struck out across another wadi.

Din had now moved up a gear and Giles was forced into a shambling, creeping run to keep up. They slipped over the edge of a low, flat-topped ridge just as thin clouds on the eastern horizon were changing from purple to lilac. Din flattened the cavalry officer with a descending palm and then motioned him forwards, Giles wormed his way painfully over the sharp stones. At first he saw nothing but a dark grey abyss. Then made out shapes in the wadi bottom; regular spacings, then movement. The impatient Arabian dawn was already throwing out a rosy glow onto the slopes behind him. The shadows of the night steadily rolled back across the wadi. The black shapes assumed depth and form. A fire flared briefly before settling to a steady flickering. Thin grey silhouettes moved between the larger shapes.

Din tapped Giles' belt pouches. Giles jerked up a fraction in surprise but relaxed a little when he caught the Pathan's meaning. He wriggled backwards and, rolling on to his side, unpacked two panels of fluorescent pink, nylon cloth. He crawled backwards a few more yards and laid them side by side. Gathering any stone within reach, he carefully weighted the edges down. It was now light enough to see his watch. A thought had just struck him, 'supposing we are overlooked.' He crawled back alongside the Pathan who was lying motionless, sighting down his rifle at the figures below.

Giles looked over the wadi and was alarmed to find a row of fluted spurs rising up to support a dark flat plateau several hundred feet higher than his present station. He mentally and physically flattened himself into the rock. His large bowel contracted slowly within him. The moment of dread faded, he opened his eyes. Below he could now make out the long barrels of three guns protruding from camouflage netting. He recalled the characteristic jacked-up wheels of the Soviet-made howitzers from dreary sessions of recognition training in Germany. Reaching into his waist pouches, he took out his hand-sized beacon radio. He extended the tin-tape aerial and checked his watch. It was just past six. He rested his chin on the stock of his FAL and wondered if he would live to see this airstrike. In the wadi below khaki-clad gunners chattered happily as they waited for their tabakh to serve their breakfast.

Mike Cook had experienced a less eventful journey than Giles Denby-Smith. His route had been almost due north from Assaad. Akhbar Ali had no pretensions as a guide, so the Australian had dead-reckoned his way by compass and the tedious counting of paces to check his distance. To his relief, as the dawn tinted the acacias and camel-thorns in its pink light. Mike confirmed his position. He was amongst a tangle of low thorn trees on one arm of a horseshoe shaped ridge. The horseshoe ridge lay in the 'Great North Road' wadi where it began to narrow till it blended with the dull-colour mass of the Hawaafa Kabeera, the Great Ridge. It was the heartland and the fastness of the Hawaafi tribes.

He hissed at Akhbar Ali. The Baluch unfolded himself from his squatting position against a dead tree trunk. Mike waved him forward and the pair then stalked cautiously through the bushes. They had covered barely fifty yards when Mike stopped. He was looking through a thin curtain of thorns out onto the wadi floor.

Ahead of him, tucked into the sides of the narrow spurs which spread into the valley like fingers, were clusters of sand-coloured netting. Mike pressed his field-glasses to his eyes and watched with a sense of satisfaction as khaki-uniformed figures mingled with Hawaafi warriors in tribal dress. Beneath the nets he could see tents and piles of boxes. He scanned the other re-entrants; camels, goats. It was just as the old shaiba, Abu Issqa, had described; the adoo headquarters and supply area, all in one spot. He passed his binoculars to the equally fascinated Baluchi sergeant and went back a few yards to a clearing he had spotted on the route in. With a quick glance to make sure that the clearing was indeed visible to the southern sky. He laid out three yellow panels in a figure Tee, the stroke pointing north.

John Rolls felt better under the penetrating heat of the early morning sun. Richard Callender had helped him up onto the command post roof sangar. They sat together, waiting out the final minutes to H hour. Rolls looked about him from the green canvas chair. There was little sense of occasion about it. The stores jundis trotted about with boxes of rations and ammunition. Pairs of them trundled the black, plastic burmails along to the company filling points. Water now had to be decanted into jerrycans for onward distribution as it was next to impossible to manoeuvre the burmails along a comms trench. On the gunline, Mr Thompson was easily discerned helping to shoulder one of his two remaining 75s onto the track leading to Two Company. Airstrike or not, the Geordie gunner had planned a showdown with the adoo-held outpost.

Rolls raised his transceiver mike.

'I'd get your boys under cover, Shelldrake, you know what the Crabs are like.' He threw a sardonic grin at Callender and looked back to watch the distant figure fumbling for his set. 'If they are Crabs?' he added.

'Roger out.' The gun was promptly deserted as the sergeant-major led his heaving party back to the gunline at brisk trot.

'Who's with Two now?' Rolls asked.

'RSM,' Callender replied. Rolls nodded, 'Should we take cover?' Rolls looked at his watch by twisting his left wrist with his right hand.

'No, we should be okay here. Tell the companies to stand-to.'

Callender picked up the Arabic net and gave the order. 'I hope Mike and Giles have done their stuff,' Rolls said.

The first indication was a short, uncurling snarl. Then the air shook with a frenzied roar. Two blue-gray monsters lunged up into the air over Two Company; the ground juddering in their wake. Rolls and Callender instinctively ducked. High above the bombers rolled lazily and then flicked over into a tight turn. Two more roared past unseen to the east. Rolls caught sight of a cloud falling, a shower of specks disappearing behind the humped back of Assaad. Then came a long, echoing crash that seemed to go on and on. The echo applauded from across the wadi. Behind him another long, yammering crash.

'CBUs,' cried Callender looking up from the floor. 'Cluster bombs and Jesus Christ, look at that.' He pointed over to Two Company. A cloud of dust rose like a curtain from the hidden lower slopes.

'Did you see that!' Faulkner's excited voice blasted through the background mush of the command net. A distant rumble came in from behind Cub. Another, like rolling thunder reached them from the north.

Callender reached forward and flicked the switch on his beacon radio. The peculiar twang of a pilot speaking through his throat-mike was in the middle of terse instructions. A second later, two Strikemasters ripped over Assaad and arrowed over Cub. The face of the Cub feature blossomed sand-yellow then grey with rocket explosions. The thick bodied Buccaneers barrelled past again after the Strikemasters, dark cylindrical objects falling away from the hardpoints beneath their stubby wings. They fell with unhurried grace out of sight. The shock waves rent the air over the wadi in a transparent flash. The ground below jumped as the shrapnel from the airburst bombs stabbed down.

'Look! In the wadi,' Callender exclaimed, pointing out across the Great North Road.' Rolls eased himself up from the chair. Far down in the wadi tiny figures streamed out away from the base of the jebel; the general trend of their direction was north.

* * *

The passage of the first Buccaneer took Giles totally by surprise, by the time he had opened his eyes and unclamped his teeth the bomber was rolling out of sight over the high ridge opposite, leaving only a deafening, booming roar to shake the ground. Then the wadi erupted as the CBU's six hundred-odd anti-personnel bomblets came down like a heavy, black rain. They landed in a half mile long exploding carpet down the centre of the wadi. Each bomblet exploding with a piercing crack, its body fragmenting into scores of hissing and singing splinters hurtling out between neck and knee height. Giles pressed himself into the bare rock as spent shards tinkled around him. He looked up. The adoo gunline was shrouded in a thick, yellow dust. He glanced at Pathan next to him. Din turned his great bearded head and uttered one of the few words he found they had in common.

'Mumtaz.' His white teeth sparkled through his beard, Giles felt himself smile back spontaneously.

'Yes, mumtaz, bloody excellent!' As the dust cloud began to lift skywards it revealed a grotesque scene of carnage. The camouflage netting was torn away, shreds hung lifelessly from the skeletal supports. The three guns sat there, stupidly, defiantly, intact. The bloody wreckage of the men that served them lay in the remains of their breakfasts. Giles watched the dazed survivors stagger from body to body; then they scattered. He looked up in time to see the brown and gray camouflage of two Strikemasters blur past him. Fresh dust rose from the wadi. The rattle of their machine-guns bouncing around the rock walls in receding ripples. Din shook his wrist. He looked up to where the Pathan pointed. Hueys were hovering over the edge of the flat topped feature opposite. Strings of green-clad soldiers were sliding down the great, fluted spurs down into the valley. The cavalry had arrived at last.

'Hot shit!' gasped Mike Cook as the Buccaneer flipped over into its rolling climb out of the wadi. He saw the bomb door slide shut in the wide blue belly. Seconds later the left half of the adoo camp disappeared instantly into a swathe of boiling dust. The other half escaped. Mike picked up the Sarbe beacon, wondering what to say when it came to life in his hands. Self-consciously he felt himself do a cartoon double take as the familiar, flyers voice gave rapid commands in thick, unfamiliar English.

'Christ! Fucking Slopes.' Akhbar Ali looked at him, puzzlement in his dark, brooding eyes. 'Africans, South Africans!' Ali shook his head and resumed his watch on the adoo camp as if air-strikes were no-more than routine events.

A bare half mile from where Mike Cook was lying, another Sarbe radio, tuned to the same frequency was being listened to with a different reaction. The man bore the same well-defined characteristics as the other Hawaafi only he was taller and more fully built. The radio had been taken from Alan Primmer's body just after the man had put a pistol shot through each of his dead eyes. Said ibn Nassir had been the de facto leader of the Front since he had liquidated his Uncle, the Front's co-founder and chairman, the previous spring. Now he had discovered fresh treachery. He strode out of his tent. The camp was in chaos; men were running to help the wounded, men were running away. He didn't care one way or another. He made straight for the command post. The camouflage netting was blown away. Ripping a section down he stepped through into the entrance lobby.

Major Rettkowski stood over a trestle table, a radio microphone in his hand. Two Palestinian officers stood attentively behind him. They wore the thunderbolt shoulder flash of the "Shaika" on their shirts. Rettowski straightened up as ibn Nassir entered.

'Said,' he started in flawless Arabic, 'Get every armed ...' the German stopped as Said thrust out a Makarov automatic. In his other hand he held out the Sarbe.

'Traitor?' he barked. Rettowski looked startled. 'The bombers!' Foam flecked his lips, his eyes bulged under the heavy brows. 'They speak like you ...' The pistol shook with each word but never left the German's chest. As if to prove the accusation the Sarbre poured forth a rapid exchange of pilot chatter.

'That is no ...' A double crack from the Makarov sent Rettowski lurching backwards. He rolled off the end of the table and crashed down onto the corner of a camp bed. A dark stain spread across the front of his shirt. The bed tipped, he sank down, his eyelids flickering, his dying mouth opening and closing like a hooked fish. One of the Palestinians knelt beside him and leaned close enough to puzzle over a word in the German's last breath.

'Suidafrikaner.' He shook his head sadly and followed his companions and ibn Nassir out into the spreading dust.

Rolls and Callender were still engrossed in the spectacle of the Buccaneer's rippling salvoes of rockets when the Force Commander's helicopter touched down. It was only when the Agusta-Bell took off that they noticed four figures hurrying down the track towards them. The General, Dixon and Henson were relaxed and confident as they settled around the chair-bound Rolls. An Arab Lieutenant from the Signals Squadron set up his man-packed radio on the sangar wall. They followed the progress of the encircling forces as they closed in on the shattered adoo.

'They're retreating up the Rabw'a,' commented the Chief of Staff giving the Great North Road its correct title. 'Hundreds of them according to Marcus.'

'Where is he?' asked Rolls.

'Either side of the Saidn'iya Pass. They should have it sealed by now.'

The plan in its naked simplicity revealed itself to Rolls in one sparkling, topographical vision.

'If the Hawaafi had been able to see the position from the air they would have stayed at home,' he thought. 'They have been trapped by the scale of their own country. The Rabw'a was a giant bottle, Assaad, a tempting morsel. The right target at just the right time.' Rolls began to wonder who had been the master chess player amongst the three; Welles, Dixon or Henson.

'What's going to happen when they reach the Saidn'iya?' Rolls enquired. Dixon pointed a finger enigmatically towards the sky and then reached into his trouser-leg map pocket. 'You're going to blow away the whole Hawaafi nation?' His voice betrayed an edge that held traces of disgust for massacre, however unavoidable. Gilbert Dixon unfolded a piece of paper that he had drawn from his pocket and passed it over to Rolls.

It consisted of four photographs with a few words of boldly printed Arabic. Two of the pictures showed the Emir shaking hands with Kalashnikov-carrying tribesmen. The other two showed smiling men amongst smiling children with herds of camels and goats. The message was clear, even if you couldn't read: safe conduct, reconciliation. Rolls swallowed hard to hold back the painful swell of emotion in this throat. He couldn't understand why. He just felt that it was all such a waste. The strange thing was that he was thinking solely of the Hawaafi. The efforts and sacrifices of his own men he accepted without question or regret.

Four Hueys clattered overhead; the note of their rotors changing as they tipped back to hover over the landing site. Panda's medics started loading stretcher cases and walking wounded into two of them as soon as they touched down. Mr Thompson appeared at the edge of the roof. He stiffened to a wobbly position of attention on seeing the General.

'Beg pardon, sirs,' he said to the roof-top assembly, 'Sad Panda wants the CO to go on this lift.'

Rolls looked at the General as if to appeal.

'Off you go then, John, it's all over now.' Welles motioned Callender to assist Rolls out of his chair. Rolls exchanged awkward handshakes and farewells with the General, Dixon and Henson and then allowed Callender and the sergeant-major to ease him down onto the ground.

Helicopters tolerate no grand gestures or quiet nursing. Half carried through the stinging dust storm of the down-wash and thrust into a canvas seat, he was airborne before the agony of the jarred chest and arm had subsided. He struggled to the edge of his seat to snatch a last glimpse of Assaad as it spun slowly away below him. He slumped back between the waist-gunner and an old Baluchi corporal with a head wound. He wanted more than anything to stay and go round his unit in its moment of triumph. It was the first time he felt the thrill of possession; his unit, his men. A wave of nausea swept up inside him and he retched dryly. He nearly blacked out. His lungs felt as if they were about to burst. The gunner clumsily lowered him down onto his side. The helicopter levelled out at its operational cruising height and commenced the straight run back to Harrow.

After a swift examination by the Field Surgical Team, Rolls was backloaded to the 'Field of Birds' airbase where he and the other wounded requiring surgery were transferred to a United States Marine Corps Sea Knight helicopter. They were flown out into the Gulf to be treated on board the various support vessels of the American fleet. Rolls was prepped to have his wounds cleaned and repacked but when the first of the Hawaafi wounded came through he was stood down for twelve hours. Rolls watched with a profound sense of compassion as the stretchers were brought down in the lift. Dwarfed by the beefy naval corpsmen, the Hawaafi warriors looked like insect mutants from another world. Priority cases, they were torn and broken by the merciless scything of the cluster bomblets. Away from the jebels of their birthright, they were broken spiritually as well; eyes wide with fear, curled up and shivering from pathological shock and the refrigerator chill of the air-conditioning. Rolls tried to help with a few re-assuring words in Arabic but he knew that, for the Hawaafi the old ways were gone for ever. Henson's victory was complete.

HONOURS AND AWARDS

It was ten weeks before the exit wound in his arm had granulated out to the satisfaction of the Emir's personal, consultant surgeon. Aside from Christmas and New Year, his recuperation in the private clinic just outside Guildford had been very comfortable, if a little boring. He had passed the time taking considerable pains over his various reports and letters. The letter to the parents of Primmer and Shanks had been the most difficult. Rolls was now able to go to a game or two of table tennis with his daughter, Miranda, without stabbing pains in his chest. Caroline had dutifully fussed over him at first but lately had been prone to long silent lapses. Rolls in moments of uncharitable reasoning, deduced that she was daydreaming on how she should have coped with such a rich widowhood. There was no going back though; they were now a comfortably divorced couple.

To some people, London in February has the sort of crisp morning chill that makes a brisk walk both necessary and rewarding. John Rolls just felt cold. He shivered violently as he passed his British Warm to the wrinkled matron in charge of the cloakroom in the Dorchester. It seemed odd that General Welles had chosen the Dorchester in preference to the Cavalry and Guards Club but who was complaining. He was a minute early but the General was there, waiting in the foyer to greet him. Rolls had never seen the General in civilian clothes and was struck by the aging effect that it made on him. The General chatted effusively during the fish course.

Only a handful of the Hawaafi hardliners had escaped through the cordon. The Emir has flown in that evening to accept the surrender of the new moderate leadership and begin the process of reconciliation.

'How's Three Battalion?' Rolls asked to change the tack.

'Fine, they are now back at Midhaak. Giles Denby-Smith is acting CO, y'know. I'm very impressed with the lad, especially when I saw the write-up you gave him. Always thought him a bit wet before.'

John Rolls smiled inwardly. 'It will be nice to get back. I'm just not cut out for English winters anymore.' He was suddenly aware that the General was stilled; loaded fork halfway to his chin. His eyes had lost their smile. Rolls felt a cruel, body blow coming.

'I'm sorry, John, but ...' The General had aged a little more by the time his fork had touched the plate. 'But I'm afraid there's been a change of plan.' Rolls looked at him, not wanting to believe what he knew was coming. 'You see, your contract has been terminated; your visa cancelled.'

The blow fell but Rolls rode it well. He lifted up his glass and sipped with difficulty as a backwash of emotion welled up in his throat. 'May I ask why, sir?'

Welles brought up a hand to help him explain. 'I did my best but it came straight from the palace, John.' He took a pull at his Chablis and continued. 'Henson tried to explain to me ... It's a traditional conflict of interests to the Arabs. To the Emir, someone of your ability and charisma is always a threat when there is no common enemy. British Officers have led a number of palace coups around the Gulf before, you see.'

He looked for signs of understanding or resignation in the younger man's face. 'Kind of an odd compliment, really, I suppose.'

Rolls managed a sad, sad smile, though he felt as if his vitals had been wrenched out of him. 'I suppose it is.' He laid his knife and fork together on his plate.

Welles followed suit. 'Suppose I've spoilt lunch rather, haven't I?' Rolls could only manage the faintest nod. 'You'll receive full compensation, of course. A six figure sum, I understand. This I believe is an interim payment.' Reaching into his inside pocket, the General produced a pale green envelope bearing the Emir's crest. He laid it alongside Roll's plate. 'Look, why don't we go and have a brandy? There is something else and, God knows, I need a snifter as I'm sure you do.'

Rolls picked up his envelope and tucked it away. 'What the hell,' he thought, privately. 'You're acting like some sentimental old buffer. You're a mercenary. Take your money and find another fucking war.'

'Why not?' Rolls assented and followed the General out.

General Welles anecdoted his way through another King Edward cigar and a couple of cognacs. Rolls felt that he was being humoured into staying but could not think why. His attention wandered in and out of his memory, bringing out images of his past life. He felt cruelly marooned from all that he really knew and cared about. He remembered the agonising six months he had spent looking for a job when he had left the Brigade; the isolation, the hostile cynicism of interviews. 'You may have been a big cheese in the Army but you're fuck all out here, lad.' It had been the final straw for Caroline and an awful shock for him.

'Ah, here he is!' The General rose.

Rolls was jerked from his reminiscing. He levered himself out of the deep armchair. A small dark figure made his way in bouncy, over-striding steps towards them. He looked uncomfortable in a light grey suit that seemed to fit his diminutive frame only where it touched. His grey-white beard was trimmed into a neat Van Dyke.

'Salaam Aleykum, Yaa Muqaddam.' Abu Issa dipped his gaze and then warmly shook hands with Rolls in the Islamic hand and elbow grip. 'I am pleased to see that you have made a full recovery.'

'His Excellency has only taken up his post this week,' Welles pointed out.

Rolls opened his palms in the colloquial gesture of surprise and congratulation.

Abu Issa waved aside the gesture in a modest show of refusal. 'What reward is this?' The shoulder-padding of his suit rose at right angles. 'I am made to wear trousers like a woman and live in a city of lunatics.'

Fresh coffee was served and Abu Issa continued in light vein about the rehabilitation of the Hawaafi.

'I have a duty to perform,' he announced at last. 'My first and probably most pleasant.' He reached into one of his pockets and withdrew a small, green leather case. 'Regrettably, the peculiar manners of my country do not allow for any degree of formality and for that I must apologise.' He opened the case and handed it to Rolls, 'Mubarak?'

Rolls looked at the 'Medal for Valour', Rolls thanked the ambassador with a cracked voice. Together they drank a discreetly seated toast to the Emir; the General and Rolls in brandy, Abu Issa, to the consternation of the waiter, with Dr Pepper's.

It was a quarter past three when Rolls emerged from the Dorchester. He tried to clear his head and his emotions with a few deep breaths in the face of a weak, afternoon sun as it settled lamely over Hyde Park. He was still thinking with some bitterness of his severance from his loyal comrade in arms, Din Mohammed. How would the Pathan with his simple concepts of right and wrong understand why he was not coming back? Would anybody take the trouble to explain? He was half-way between Piccadilly and Pall Mall when he saw a gunsmith's discrete facade. Angry with the world, he strode in. Explaining only that the weapon was for export through the Emirate's diplomatic bag. Rolls brushed aside the pandering obsequiousness of the sales assistant and selected a hand-tooled SIG automatic rifle. He had thought of one of the sleek, mahogany-finished Weatherbys but opted instead for the Swiss self-loader on the practical grounds of ammunition. NATO 7.62 was far more readily available then .377 magnum. Making a mental note to phone Abu Issa and to write to Mike Cook, he paid cash and left. He continued down St. James' Street with the savage satisfaction of the image of Din opening the leather-bound case.

Reaching Pall Mall, he stopped and realised that he was running blind. He needed a plan, for now, for this evening, for the rest of his life. Remembering his last encounter in this void, he walked back until he found the building. Checking with the receptionist that the agency was still in operation, he went up to the top floor in the lift. The reception hall had altered a little in seven years, discreet, utilitarian; potted plants and water-colours of London parks the only decoration. A thin balding man in regimental tie and shirt-sleeves came smartly up to the glass partition.

'May I be of assistance, sir?'

'I would like to register, please.' Rolls felt a warm breath of hope as the man smiled politely and drew a blank card from a box on his desk.

'May I have your name, sir?'

Rolls hesitated on the first syllable of 'Lieutenant' and then said 'Major Rolls'. He watched his name appear on the top of the card in the rapid copper-plate of an ex-superintendant clerk.

'If you would be so kind as to complete parts A and B, sir, I will see if we can arrange an interview this afternoon,' He peered at Rolls through the glass to see if that was convenient.

'Thank-you, that will be fine.' Rolls turned away and looked for a seat. He passed a stand of cork-faced boards plastered with white job notification cards. Each board was labelled according to employment classification; Technical Sales, Administration and Secretarial, Rolls stopped at board G; Overseas, Military and Quasi-Governmental.

* * *

Giles Denby-Smith served the remainder of his tour as Commanding Officer. He returned to his regiment from leave expecting to spend a pleasant, sporting summer in Tidworth before throwing himself into the Army Staff College for a year and a bit. Instead, some over-enthusiastic staffer in the Adjutant-General's office had thought him ideal material for an exchange year at the Pakistan Army Staff College. Giles was inwardly appalled at the prospect but accepted with grace. Mike Cook served Giles, and the seconded colonel who followed as the unit second-in-command. When the day arrived some two years later when there seemed no-one left who could remember the Jebel Assaad, he left. He was killed in action just north of Inyanga, Southern Rhodesia, on a bright May morning in 1979.

James Falkner left the Guards on completion of his commission and with a little inside assistance to his modest A level grades in the sciences, obtained entrance to a respected medical college in the north of England. Captain Arvin Sadrapandi of the Indian Army Medical Corps received his long awaited majority in recognition of his services. He was promptly posted to command a field ambulance in the mountainous province of Ladakh.

The dead with the exception of Edward Shanks, whose body was never found, remained buried at the cemetery at Harrow. At the request of Haji Mansoor, Harry Shaw was buried amongst the soldiers. His grave like theirs was decorated with the characteristic wall and miniature tower of stones. As the Emir's Forces became more Arabised, Harrow was renamed Al Maidan a'-Shadeed; The Hero's Field.

The Pathan, Din Mohammed, received a medal for distinguished services from the hands of the Emir himself. He remained in the battalion for a further two years till the time came for his long leave. It was a leave from which he would never return. Landing at Guadar, he journeyed through Pakistan, up towards his village in the Panmir foothills of Afghanistan. He sold his medals for a good price to an Iranian trader with only the minimum of intimidation from his blade. The SIG automatic was the treasured possession of his family. Din became the bodyguard to his tribal chief and fathered children at the rate of nearly one a year from the teenage girl who became his wife.

Din Mohammed would have been content to play out his role on the terraced slopes of his mountainous domain had not the 'Godless ones' deposed the Afghan king. Din saw in them a familiar pattern of deceit and subversion. His warnings were heeded by his chief and all his council. So he took the SIG and set out into the hills to join up with the embryonic Mujaheddeen to resist the Afghan Communist Party and its agents. To kill or to be killed in accordance with the implacable will of the One God.